VENGEFUL JUSTICE

MO FLAMES

FLAMES
ENTERTAINMENT

Copyright © 2025 by Mo Flames

Flames Entertainment, LLC

All rights reserved.

No part of this book may be used or reproduced in any form or by any electronic or mechanical means, including information storage and retrieval systems without the prior written permission from the author except for the use of brief quotations embodied in critical articles or reviews.

This book is a work of fiction. Names, characters, businesses, organizations, places, events, and incidents are the product of the author's imagination or are used fictitiously. Any similarity to persons, living or dead, events, locales is entirely coincidental.

Contact info: info@flamesentertain.com

Cover design: Designs by Charly

Editor: Krystal Clarke

ISBN-13: 979-8-9892058-6-8

DEDICATION

To Crystal Luckey, one of my fave book influencers and good friend. Thank you for seeing Angela's story before I could. Hopefully you love this as much as I enjoyed penning it.

AUTHOR'S NOTE

Dear Beloved Readers,

Thank you for purchasing and/or downloading this book.

While this story can be enjoyed as a standalone, for a richer experience and better understanding of the interconnected characters and plotlines, it's highly recommended to read *The Enough Series*. The events of this story unfold and run parallel to the timeline in those books.

The spotlight now falls on Jamal Edwards and Angela Washington, once supporting characters, now locked in a deadly game of love and betrayal.

Jamal, living a dangerous double life, hides the dark secret of orchestrating Angela's brother's death—while keeping her close with lies. Angela, broken by grief and caught in a destructive cycle of alcohol and prescription drug use, clings to a love already lost, unaware Jamal's heart belongs to someone else—Christian Hilcrest.

When tragedy strikes, every secret comes to light. In this raw tale of identity, deception, and revenge, only one of them will survive the fallout.

Keep in mind that this is a fictional story, so things you might find unrealistic or unrelatable, may be real and relatable to someone else.

TRIGGER WARNINGS

This novel contains strong language, detailed sexually explicit scenes, physical and emotional abuse, drugging, poisoning, rape, sexual assault, torture and certain topics that might be sensitive to some readers.

Please be mindful of these and other possible triggers.

This novel is for mature audiences only.

TABLE OF CONTENTS

Dedication	1
Author's Note	3
Trigger Warnings	4
Playlist	7
1. There Is No Turning Back Now	9
2. I'm Finally Getting Out Of Here	21
3. Make Me Wanna Marry You	37
4. You Need A Big Boy	45
5. No New Fucking Friends	57
6. Training Starts Today	79
7. I'm Finally Living In My Truth	99
8. We Can't Change The Past	111
9. Love Takes Center Stage	125
10. This Tea Is Piping Hot Too	135
11. That Man Was No Good For You	139
12. No Regrets	149
13. I Need To Give You Some Celebratory Head	167
14. Work In Progress	177
15. Not Gon' Make It	187
16. A Long Road Ahead	191
17. It's Really Me, Boo	201
18. Aww, Babe Don't Cry	213
19. This Will Be His Day Of Reckoning	221
20. A New Beginning	233
Epilogue	239
Thank You	245
Afterword	246
Also by Mo Flames	248
Connect with Mo	249
About the Author	250

PLAYLIST

While in the writing lab, there's always music playing. There are some dope tracks that kept me inspired throughout penning this story. You can check out the vibe for this book on Apple Music and/or Spotify, under the same title, *Vengeful Justice*.

Apple
https://apple.co/44Fh0n5

Spotify
https://spoti.fi/3EGm7Ja

1

THERE IS NO TURNING BACK NOW

Four months ago...

"I'm only going to say this one more time. Get your ass out of there and come home to me. Or I'm going to snitch you out to Desiree and Angela."

The line went dead. Jamal quickly flushed the toilet, then took a shower and dressed in record time. He rushed through the kitchen and into the living room, where his girlfriend, Angela, greeted him with a hug.

Jamal tensed up and let out a frustrated curse, "Fuck!"

Angela froze.

He reached out and placed a comforting hand on her arm, gently rubbing it. "I'm sorry, sweetheart. I have to go."

"Where are you going?"

"To the hospital." He fumbled through his words. "There's a patient and umm . . . the other surgeon he, uh, can't . . . well he could, but look, it's complicated and they need me in the OR. You know I'm on call. I have to go, sweetheart. I'll try to give you a call later."

"Okay, baby. Are you coming back?"

"I'll call you later, Angela. I have to go. I love you." He kissed her on the lips before running out the door.

As Jamal sped toward Rico's house, he thought about his dilemma. He was tired of the gay stuff. He'd had a feeling that one day Rico was going to push him too far. There was no reason he should've ever let things reach the point where he was at Rico's mercy. Deep down, Jamal knew his worst fear was staring him in the face, but he wasn't about to let Rico make the decision for him.

Jamal arrived forty-five minutes later and parked his car in front of Rico's apartment building, but he didn't get out. He wasn't ready to face his friend. Rico had already made up his mind, and nothing Jamal could say would change it. Despite Jamal's efforts to keep his relationship with Angela under wraps, Rico had uncovered the truth. Rico must've thought by threatening him, he could somehow make things go his way. Jamal weighed his options and considered what was about to unfold between them. Deep down, he knew that being together as a couple was simply not in the cards for them, and there was no way he would let himself be forced into something he didn't want. After finally exiting the vehicle, he made his way toward the front entrance. He raised his hand to knock, but before he could make contact, Rico pulled the door open. Jamal tried to brush past him, but Rico stood firm in the doorway.

Jamal glanced heavenward and silently prayed for strength. Then he looked back at him and spoke in frustration, "The fuck, Rico! You wanted me here. Are you going to let me in?" Rico stepped aside and allowed him to enter. Once he closed the door, Jamal began pleading his case. "It doesn't have to be like this. Why are you doing this?"

"You violated what we've established. I could deal with Desiree because it was only a matter of time before she was out of the picture, but that other girl." He paused and held his hand up. Suddenly, his expression changed. Then he clenched his jaw, balling up his fists. Rico began shaking his head, mumbling incoherently, and pacing back and forth.

Jamal tilted his head in confusion and asked, "What?"

Rico turned red and a vein popped out of his neck as he shouted, "No! Your ass fucked up! I don't believe this shit!" He got in Jamal's face

Chapter 1

pointing his finger, "You chose the wrong fucking girl! Why her of all people, hmm?" Rico walked away and threw his hands up.

Jamal frowned. "What do you mean, 'why her?' She's somebody I met and—"

"No, you're going to return that car, tell her that you have to sell that fucking condo, and then you will cut her off!" Rico was back in his face and speaking through gritted teeth. "I don't give a fuck how you do it, but you will. She's off limits. You hear me? Off limits! You're going to end it with that one today or there will be consequences. You're mine, Jamal. And we're in this together, forever."

"Do you hear yourself, Rico? Do you even know how this shit sounds? You have lost your mind. I told you I'm not gay."

Rico let out a sarcastic laugh. "No, I haven't. And your ass is in denial if you think you can keep away from this ass. The sooner you accept everything the way it's going to be from now on, the better." Then he walked to the bar and grabbed a glass filling it with cognac. "Here, I know this will help loosen you up a little bit."

"No, thank you. I don't want it."

"Take it. We both need to calm our nerves, especially me because I really feel like fucking you up right now."

With hesitation, Jamal accepted the glass from Rico's outstretched hand. He held onto it while he stared at Rico, his brow furrowed as the liquid slid down his throat. Jamal handed the empty glass to Rico, who immediately refilled it without pause. Jamal tilted his head back and downed the second drink. Despite his reluctance to consume any alcohol in case the hospital called, Jamal knew it would help him relax. He'd never seen Rico lose his composure before. It was unsettling to see his friend so upset over a woman. Jamal handed back the tumbler while giving Rico a questioning look.

Rico spoke in a more relaxed tone while pouring the cognac into Jamal's glass for the third time. "I'm doing this for us, Jamal. You wanted to have your cake and . . ." he paused, his face splitting into a devious grin. "Well, you won't be eating that kind of cake anymore, that's for sure. Now drink up. You're going to need the stamina to keep up with me. It's going to be a long night of celebrating."

Jamal avoided Rico's eyes as he peered up at the ceiling. He needed to figure a way out of this situation and fast.

Rico refilled Jamal's glass again. "Do me a favor. There's some fruit and other stuff on the kitchen table that we'll need. They had a farewell party for one of my co-workers today, and you wouldn't believe it, but all the stuff that nobody wanted is perfect for us. Can you go grab it and meet me in the bedroom?"

Jamal sucked his teeth when he looked at the table. There was a basket of fruit along with a can of whipped cream and chocolate syrup sitting in the middle. He walked over, hesitating for a split second. Jamal leaned against the counter, needing a moment to regroup. Even though the alcohol was creeping up on him, Jamal was trying to think of a way to get out of the whole situation. He was not about to let Rico drag him into his gay delusions. Out the corner of his eye he noticed there was a pack of salted nuts. He opened it and popped a handful into his mouth. As he chewed, a smile formed across his face. Jamal grabbed some more, threw the whipped cream and syrup in the bowl, and went to the bedroom. He stopped in the doorway.

Damn! He wasn't playing when he said it would be a long night. Rico had handcuffs, a blindfold, a leather whip, lube, and other toys.

"Come on in," he said seductively as Jamal put the bowl on the bed. Rico handed him the glass he'd filled in the living room. "Let's make a toast. What do you think we should toast to?"

"I guess to . . . umm . . . to new beginnings."

Rico nodded. "Yeah, I like how that sounds. To new beginnings."

They both took sips from their glasses before Rico collected Jamal's and set them on the nightstand. Rico then returned to kneel in front of Jamal. "You know I've missed you, right?"

Jamal didn't respond. Rico unbuttoned Jamal's slacks, and for a second, Jamal let himself get lost in the sensation of Rico's touch. But then he regained his focus. He took hold of Rico's hands and steadied himself.

Chapter 1

"No. This time we're going to do things differently. New beginnings, right? You've always been in control of setting the mood. If this is what we're going to be from now on, I want to give it a try."

Jamal was never the one to take control of their sessions, and with the alcohol running its course, Rico didn't put up a fight. It was obvious he loved that Jamal was displaying spontaneity for a change.

"Show me what you got," Rico said excitedly.

Jamal grabbed the chair from the desk on the other side of the room and placed it next to Rico. "Sit down," he commanded.

Rico obeyed and allowed Jamal to handcuff him to the chair's lower rails. Jamal then grabbed the bowl of fruit and placed it in Rico's lap. He took the blindfold from the bed.

"You ready?"

"Hell yeah!"

Jamal stood behind the chair and placed the silk material over Rico's eyes. Just to keep him from getting suspicious, he purposely kissed Rico's neck and pinched his nipples.

"Awww shit! I knew you had some freak in you!" Rico cheered him on.

Jamal moved back in front of him and grabbed the whipped cream from the bowl. "Open your mouth."

Once again, Rico obeyed Jamal's orders without question. Jamal popped a finger into his mouth and when Rico eagerly sucked on it, he couldn't help but notice Rico's growing arousal. *I knew you'd love it. Enjoy it while it lasts.* This was exactly what he needed—for Rico to be fully committed in the moment.

"You like that, huh?"

"Mmhmm . . . it tastes good," Rico moaned around his digit.

"You want more?"

"Uh-huh. Give it to me."

"Open up."

Jamal grabbed a strawberry and covered it with cream and chocolate. He allowed Rico to bite into the berry but pulled it from his mouth before he could get a good taste. Some of the juice trickled down his chin.

"What are you doing?" Rico writhed a little, shrieking, "I want more!"

"That's called teasing."

"And you're doing too good of a job! Hurry up so we can get to the dick part!"

Jamal relished seeing that Rico was caught up in his foreplay act. *You haven't seen anything yet. Hang on for the big finale, lover.*

"I want some more please," Rico politely requested after swallowing the strawberry.

Jamal dipped his hand into his pocket and retrieved the crushed nuts. He then emptied them onto his palm, revealing their finely ground form.

"Open your mouth and keep it open until I tell you to close it," he instructed. Jamal took a ripe strawberry and rolled it in the nuts and gooey chocolate, before tossing it into Rico's eager, awaiting mouth. As a finishing touch, Jamal topped it off with a generous dollop of whipped cream and commanded, "Close it."

Jamal waited for Rico to finish chewing before offering him another strawberry, along with a medallion of banana coated in the fine nuts, chocolate and topped with cream. He made sure to repeat this two more times, ensuring that Rico had enough of the decadent treat. Once Rico swallowed that last bite, Jamal placed the gag ball in his mouth. Jamal removed the blindfold and stared at him for a moment. Rico moaned.

"Hmm, aren't you in an interesting position? You see, the chocolate, whipped cream-covered strawberries and bananas I fed you had some nuts in them," Jamal finally announced.

Rico's eyes bulged as he struggled to stand, only to realize that his wrists were handcuffed to the chair. In a desperate attempt to break free, he lunged toward him, but Jamal shoved Rico backward. Rico stumbled, toppling over onto the floor.

Grunting, Jamal righted the chair into its original position. "If you don't relax, you'll only make this worse."

Within a few short minutes, tears started to spill from Rico's eyes. He let out a low groan when he looked down at his chest and legs. Perched on top of the desk, Jamal observed the hives beginning to form and Rico's

Chapter 1

face swelling. It was only a matter of time before his airway would become constricted. Jamal removed the gag from his mouth.

"Give me my EpiPen, Jamal. Please," Rico begged, his voice strained and hoarse.

"Now why would I want to do that?"

"You . . . know, I-I-I can't . . . take this. I'll die, Jamal."

Jamal ignored him and began walking around the room. The alcohol coursing through his body had impaired his judgment. He knew he wasn't thinking clearly, but he couldn't stop at this point. Rico had sealed his own fate. "When they find you, they'll rule your death as an accident."

"Please don't do this," Rico pleaded desperately.

Jamal waved him off and taunted, "Don't go begging now. It's too late. I told you I wasn't a fucking fag, but when you didn't get your way, you just had to go digging around. You don't have to worry about anything anymore. It'll be over real soon."

Rico kept attempting to free himself. He writhed back and forth. When he fell over with the chair again, Jamal left him and began clearing the room of any evidence that Rico had a visitor that night. It wasn't until he'd cleaned up the dishes and wiped everything down that he returned to the bedroom.

Jamal flinched a little because he had never seen a severe case of someone dying from anaphylactic shock. Rico's swollen face was hideous. He carefully unlocked the cuffs. Then he took his time wiping the chair down before he did a final sweep of the room.

As Jamal headed out of the bedroom, he stopped for a moment and thought about what he'd done. *There is no turning back now.*

He felt strongly that he did what he had to do.

Present day . . .

"*You're mine, Jamal. We're in this together . . . forever.*"

"Shit!" With a loud cry, Jamal jolted up in the bed. He gasped for air, his chest slick with sweat. In the darkness, his eyes darted around the room, unable to focus on anything specific. A hand grabbed his arm, and Jamal jerked away.

"Jamie, sweetheart. Babe? It's me, Christian."

The soothing voice, filled with concern, helped ease Jamal's frayed nerves, and he began to relax. He heard the bed covers shifting, followed by a clicking noise of the lamp being turned on. A low ambient light illuminated the room. Jamal shifted his gaze and glanced at his partner, Christian Hilcrest, as he stretched and got out of their king size bed. Christian walked out of the room stark naked. He returned a short time later with a bottle of water in hand.

"Here. Drink some," Christian instructed, twisting off the cap.

Jamal's throat was parched. He didn't hesitate to take it, chugging half of its contents. After quenching his thirst, he handed the bottle back to Christian. Jamal then fluffed up the pillows and reclined against the plush headboard, letting his head sink into the tufted cushions. Despite his efforts to relax, sleep seemed out of reach for the time being. Christian set the water on the end table next to Jamal's side of the bed. Without a word, he disappeared into the ensuite bathroom. A minute later, he emerged with a washcloth in hand. As Christian climbed onto the mattress, it dipped under his weight. He settled onto his haunches and used the cool, damp cloth to wipe away any lingering traces of sweat from Jamal's skin. When he finished, Christian finally spoke.

"Another nightmare, huh? You've been having a lot of them lately, Jamie. Are you nervous about the new position?"

I wish it were that. But Jamal couldn't tell Christian about the recurring nightmare that had been tormenting him almost every night for the past few weeks. How could he? As a candidate for chief of surgery, Jamal would be in charge of the entire surgical staff at Northside Regional Hospital. With this promotion came increased responsibilities and added duties concerning patient wellbeing. His moral compass was spinning out of control. As a doctor, he pledged to save lives. Yet, he'd taken one. Rather than tell Christian the truth, he told a lie. "Yeah, I think deep down, it's hitting me. I'll be taking on a lot if I do this. I don't know if I can." Jamal dragged a hand across his waves, releasing a heavy sigh.

Chapter 1

"Oh, Jamie." Christian tossed the cloth aside and reached out, interlocking their fingers. "You know you're the best Northside has. You don't have anything to worry about."

"Yes I do. There are some people who want to see me fail. Look at me, Chris. They don't think my face fits the image of someone qualified for this job." Jamal gestured with his fingers to show air quotes. He shook his head and added, "And they definitely don't want me, a Black man, heading up their department. I can think of at least three or four of them that'll give me their asses to kiss."

Christian sidled up closer to him and dropped a kiss on his shoulder. "First of all, there ain't nobody but me giving you their ass to kiss. Secondly, don't worry about the naysayers. Fuck 'em. They can't do nothing about it, right? You were the one the board chose. If they don't like it, they can move around."

"You think it's that simple?"

"I do. Unless there's something I'm missing here. Didn't you say you had the backing of your mentor and a few of the board members? And who reminded me of their credentials when we first met? Right! My man is about to be the H-N-I-C up at Northside. So yeah, it is that simple, Jamie. They can get their asses in line or, like I said: Move. Around. Seriously, stop worrying. You've got this. Those other candidates ain't got nothing on you."

Jamal grinned from ear to ear hearing the conviction in Christian's voice. Christian meant every word he'd said too. When Jamal first shared the news that he was up for the position, Christian assured him it was already his. But although he had the experience, the support of his mentor, Dr. Mitchell, and the backing from a few members on the board, Jamal didn't want to jinx his chances by getting too confident. "You're just saying that to make me feel better."

"Is it working?" Christian asked coyly, peering up at him and batting his lashes.

Nodding in response, Jamal smiled back. "It is. I really appreciate your support."

"But I wish there was something more I could do to help you relax.

Something that could really help to calm your nerves." Christian slipped a hand under the covers, giving Jamal's limp member a tug while whispering against his lips, "'Cause, I know stressing over this can't be good for the doctor."

"Mmm, it's not. But what you're doing for damn sure is good and just what the doctor ordered. Don't stop. Ssss, fuck!"

Right as Christian's head dipped past his waist, Jamal's phone rang. Despite wanting to ignore it, Jamal was not able to. Not with him being on call at the hospital. He reluctantly eased Christian from his lap.

"Hold up, Chris. You know I'm on call. Let me grab this."

Jamal moved to the side of the bed and grabbed his device on the fourth ring, answering without looking at the caller ID. "Hello, this is Dr. Edwards."

"Hi, babe. Sorry to call without texting first. It's just . . . I-I couldn't sleep again. I was thinking about you and, well I, I just wanted to hear your voice."

Fuck! Jamal's body went taut. His heart raced, pounding against his ribcage. "Uhh, could you give me a minute? Let me get to my office." Jamal removed the phone from his face and turned to glance at Christian behind him. With a quick and sneaky gesture, Jamal swiped across the screen to put the call on mute. "Chris, I need to take this call in the office. I'll be right back."

"Of course, babe. I'll be right here," Christian gave him a quick, chaste kiss.

Jamal put on the joggers he'd taken from the bench at the foot of the bed and left quickly. He headed toward the home office that he'd been using ever since he started spending more time at Christian's house. After shutting the door, he moved behind the desk and unmuted the call.

"Hey, sweetheart. I only have a few minutes. I'm meeting with the surgical team soon for an OR prep." The lie slid off Jamal's tongue with practiced ease.

"I didn't mean to bother you."

"It's no problem. Was there something you wanted?"

"Well, no. Yes. I'm . . . It's I-I just miss you, Jamal."

Chapter 1

Didn't you see me yesterday? He had to hold back from letting the snide remark slip past his lips. "Yeah, I . . . miss you too, sweetheart."

That wasn't true. Jamal didn't miss her. He hadn't even been thinking about her. Angela Washington had been his mistress while he was married to Desiree. They carried on their affair until everything unraveled after one life altering phone call from Rico. Somehow Rico had figured out he was having an affair with Angela too and threatened to tell Desiree everything unless he left Angela to be with him. Instead, Jamal had taken Rico's life but not before Rico had gotten to his wife, Desiree. Rico told Desiree that Jamal was not only living on the down low, but he had also purchased a home and a car for his mistress, Angela. As a result, Desiree kicked him out and filed for an immediate divorce.

Jamal had no choice but to find refuge in the home he'd helped Angela purchase. But a few days later, police appeared at her door to inform Angela that her brother Tré had been involved in a homicide. Jamal received the biggest shock when he realized Tré was, in fact, his lover Rico that he'd killed. Shortly after, Angela fell into depression, leaving Jamal to his own vices. Lonely and seeking attention, Jamal had met Christian on a dating site. While Angela suffered through the grief of losing her brother, Jamal focused on building a relationship with his new lover. Jamal shook his head, reasoning if it weren't for Rico pressuring him to come out of the closet, he wouldn't have taken his life. Maybe he would still be alive today, and Angela wouldn't have suffered a mental breakdown. Perhaps his marriage would have stayed intact as well.

"Jamal?"

Angela's soft voice yanked him out of his thoughts. "Yes, sweetheart."

"Do you think we can get away this weekend?"

Clingy. Exactly the reason I got rid of your brother's gay ass. Jamal reclined in the executive office chair and released an audible sigh. "You know that I can't when I'm on call. Tell you what. I'll check my calendar and see where I can squeeze it in. Where would you like to go?"

"I can pick wherever?"

"Absolutely. Wherever. You tell me, and I'll take care of it."

"Okay! I'll start looking right now."

"Alright, let me know what you come up with. I've got to go. I'll call you in the morning. Get yourself some rest."

"I love you."

It was as if his tongue weighed a ton. Just six months ago, he was easily able to declare his love for Angela. But since Christian came into his life and turned it upside down, Jamal's feelings for her had changed. He was no longer in love with her. Jamal cleared his throat. "Love you too."

Jamal didn't bother waiting for Angela's goodbye before ending the call and releasing a long breath of oxygen. Leading a double life was no easy feat. Jamal wouldn't be able to keep it up forever. Eventually he would have to let Angela go. She deserved that much. But for now, he lacked the ability to do it. He didn't want to cause any more damage to her already fragile mental state. The guilt of hurting her was the last thing he wanted weighing on his conscience. Jamal didn't want to be the cause of another breakdown for Angela. He didn't know how long he could continue juggling his two lovers without them discovering the truth about each other.

2

I'M FINALLY GETTING OUT OF HERE

Four months ago . . .

"Jamal?" Angela croaked as she regained consciousness in an unfamiliar room. She tried to sit up, but she was in restraints. Why? She scanned the confined space, trying to make sense of her surroundings. A high ceiling. The sterile walls with rounded corners. And the all too familiar scent of antiseptic permeated the air. It was clear: she was in a psychiatric ward. Her inquisitive gaze landed on steady dark brown eyes that were not Jamal's.

"Angela, you're safe now." The mystery man loomed above her, his voice calm and reassuring. But his measured tone did little to quell the panic clawing at her insides. Where was Jamal? Why wasn't he here with her?

"Wh-who are you? And, and where's Jamal?"

"He needed to take care of his patients. I'm Dr. Mitchell, a colleague and a close friend of his. He brought you to Northside because you weren't well. He felt it was best to be under my care for a little while."

Angela balled her hands into tight fists, her fingernails digging into her palms as she struggled to control her breathing. Confusion clouded her thoughts, making it hard to decipher how she ended up in this situation. Had she accidentally taken too many anxiety pills? She vaguely remembered finishing off a bottle of wine. But did she do it on purpose? Angela furrowed her brow and shook her head, trying to piece together the events flashing through her mind like a movie on fast-forward.

"Angela, sweetheart, can you hear me? Open your eyes for me. Angela?"

"What's going on Dr. Edwards? Who do we have here?"

"Her name is Angela Washington. She's uhh, a friend and she's taken an extra dose of her anxiety meds. She's also been drinking."

"Is this for an overdose then?"

"She lost her brother recently and has been self-medicating to cope with the depression."

"I see."

"I already put a call into Mitchell. She's going to be under his care. If she wakes asking for me, please call me. Here's what she's been taking."

Angela wasn't sure how long she'd been unconscious, but she woke up in a strange room and started banging on the door for help. She retreated to the corner of the room when a nurse entered. Dr. Mitchell, with his salt-and-pepper hair, strode in confidently behind her. His posture exuded authority and wisdom. The tailored blazer, crisp dress shirt, and slacks he wore only added to his air of sophistication. However, Angela couldn't shake the fear that consumed her standing in his presence. He wasn't alone either. Trailing him were two more nurses. She was no fool. They were coming to sedate her.

"Where's Jamal? Let me out of here!"

"Angela, you've been through a lot. We're here to help you."

"No, you're not! Stay away from me!" She screamed, lashing out when the nurses tried to restrain her. Her eyes darted from one unfamiliar face to another, searching for a way to escape the nightmare she found herself in.

Dr. Mitchell turned to the nursing staff with explicit instructions. "Keep her as still as possible. We don't want to break the needle."

"No! Please! You don't have to do this. Ow!" Angela shrieked as the pointed end pierced her skin.

She tried to yank away from the nurse restraining her, but his hold on her was too tight. Angela wasn't giving up without a fight. There had to be a

Chapter 2

way out of here. But how? She whipped her head around, looking, but it was pointless. Dr. Mitchell and his nurses were blocking the exit. Out of nowhere, her limbs felt heavy. No! Angela fought against it. But despite her efforts to resist, the darkness crept in, blanketing her vision, dragging her into an endless black hole.

Angela awoke to cold sweats, shaking. Her heart was beating wildly, relentless in its torment, thumping against her rib cage. Her body shook uncontrollably on the rough sheets, betraying her with involuntary muscle spasms and tremors. Each breath was a struggle.

"Is, is anybody . . . here? Please, help . . . me."

"Angela, you need to relax."

"Jamal?"

"No. It's Dr. Mitchell."

"Make it stop. Please," she begged, feeling her tears mixing with sweat as they streamed down her face.

"Unfortunately, I can't do that. But you're almost through this part of it. Hang on. Let me give you something to rest."

"But I don't want it. Please, Dr. Mitchell. Where is Jamal? I need . . ."

Once more, the darkness came. And the haunting dream began again. Tré was dead. But how could it be? There was no way she was imagining things. Every time he visited, he hugged, kissed, and held her. They spent hours talking, and Tré promised they would be together again after he took care of some unfinished business. Shadows flickered across the room, dancing with the memories of her brother. Each one pierced through her, leaving a hollow space where laughter and warmth used to live. Angela cried out as she tossed and turned.

"I know what I saw. Why doesn't anybody believe me?"

"Angela?"

At the sound of Dr. Mitchell's voice, Angela jolted awake from her nightmare. However, this time when she awoke, Angela realized she was alone and no longer restrained. She hopped up, surveying her surroundings. A platform bed, one chair, and an open wardrobe with no doors were the only pieces of furniture in her small room. That was to be expected. She was in the hospital's section reserved for those who might harm themselves or others. Anything sharp could become a weapon in the wrong hands. Angela crossed the space to stand by the window, noting that the sun was low in the sky. It was still morning. How long had they confined her to this room? Where was Jamal?

The door suddenly swung open without warning. Of course, privacy wasn't a luxury she could expect in here, unlike in a regular patient's room. It was two Black nurses dressed in green scrubs; while the one held the door open, the other with waist-length braids strolled into the room, balancing a tray with several cups. Angela realized it was time for her daily dose of medication.

"Hello, Ms. Washington. How are you feeling today?" the younger nurse greeted her in a sing-song tone.

Confused. And I want my man. Not betraying her true feelings, Angela shrugged, "I don't know. I just want to talk to Jamal Edwards. He's a doctor here. Do you know if he's coming today?"

The nurse's lips curved into a small smile as she handed Angela the paper cup filled with pills. She took them with a sense of defeat. It would be pointless to ask her for anything. The nurse then offered Angela the water to wash down the medication and motioned for her to open her mouth and lift her tongue. It was protocol to ensure that she had taken the pills and not stored them away to dispose of later once the nurse left.

Angela proudly stated, "See. All gone. I know the drill. I happen to be a nurse at Piedmont Medical Center."

"Umm, okay. Well, Dr. Mitchell is doing rounds and should be here to see you shortly. You may want to freshen up in case you happen to have a visitor come by today," she suggested before pivoting on her heel and walking out, not giving Angela a chance to ask any further questions.

With a sigh, Angela trudged to the bathroom, which was just as barren as her room except for the basic necessities. Staring into the shatter-resistant mirror, she took in the woman staring back—her once-luminous chestnut brown skin dulled by exhaustion, dark bags pooling beneath her eyes. Her thick curly mane, normally full of bounce and pride, now clung in matted clumps to her scalp, deflated by neglect. She let out another breath and reached up, trying to tame a few strands into something that

Chapter 2

resembled order. Smoothing out her Caribbean blue scrubs, she ensured they were free of any creases or lint. It wasn't about looking stylish. These were the standard hospital attire—but at least she could look clean, composed. Like she hadn't completely come undone.

However, no matter how much she primped and preened, Angela couldn't shake the anxious feeling bubbling in her gut. She longed to see her man and know what was in store for her next. By the time she finished taking care of her hygiene, she was doing her best to tame her unruly curls, when Dr. Mitchell arrived.

He entered the room with a cheerful greeting. "Angela, hello. How are you feeling today?"

"I'm okay. I guess." She hugged herself tight, almost as if preparing for a negative response, and then she asked the question that weighed heavy on her mind: "Have you heard anything from Jamal?"

"I think you'll be excited to know Jamal is here."

"Where?" Angela squealed, leaning to the side, in hopes of catching a glimpse of him walking in, but the door was closed.

Dr. Mitchell spun around and typed in the code to unlock the barrier between them and her man. "Follow me, I'll take you there. He's waiting for us in a conference room down the hall."

Angela could barely contain her excitement as they made the short trek down the seemingly endless corridor, leading them to the conference room. When they passed by the recreation area, she observed the other psychiatric patients, each engrossed in different activities—reading, watching TV, and playing board games. A tremor rippled through her at the thought of ending up like these people. *Dear God, please don't let me be stuck in this place much longer. I'm not crazy.*

Dr. Mitchell led her into a small room with a round table and a few chairs. Angela's heart raced with anticipation. And when she spotted him, Angela rushed to embrace him, throwing herself into his arms.

"Jamal!"

He pressed his face against hers and caressed her hair. "Hey, sweetheart," Jamal whispered in her ear and kissed her cheek.

Angela turned her head toward him, and his mouth met hers with a more welcoming kiss. She didn't want it to end and felt an immediate loss when Jamal withdrew from her lips and began caressing her cheek.

Her voice was barely audible as she admitted, "I've missed you so much, Jamal."

"I've missed you too, sweetheart."

"Can we go home now?"

Jamal avoided looking directly at her. "I'm sorry sweetheart, I wish I were coming to take you home, but Dr. Mitchell doesn't think it's best right now. Come here. Let's sit down. There are some things we need to talk about."

He guided her to the two-seater couch in the center of the room. When they sat down, he pulled her into his arms and held on tight for a moment. He kissed her forehead before loosening his hold. He took his time explaining Dr. Mitchell's suggestion for the path forward in her recovery. Dr. Mitchell wanted to keep her there for a few more days for further evaluation. He then mentioned sending her to a rehabilitation facility to continue her recovery.

Angela slammed her fists on her knees. "No, Jamal! I can't stay here any longer or go anywhere else. I wanna go home!"

"Shhh. I know, sweetheart. I know, but this is how it has to be. Your mom and I can't be home with you and, well, under the circumstances with the medications and alcohol, we have to do this. It's only for a little while. At least until you get better."

Tears flowed like a river streaming down her cheeks. Jamal tried to wipe them away while explaining the benefits of the program.

Angela shouted, "I'm not mental! I wouldn't be here if you listened to me. And you knew him?"

"Wha-what?"

"My brother, Tré, you knew him?"

Angela narrowed her eyes to thin slits noticing his Adam's apple bobbing as he swallowed hard. The day before, a couple of detectives had stopped by asking questions, including whether she was aware of Jamal's friendship with Tré.

Jamal rubbed a hand across his waves and released a long sigh. "I

Chapter 2

didn't know your brother as Tré. Rico never shared much about his family. I had no idea y'all were siblings until, well umm, when I saw that picture."

"Why didn't you say anything then?"

"I was stuck, Angela. I didn't know what to say. Hell, he'd never even said your name, let alone discussed anything about you."

"Of course, he wouldn't," she mumbled.

Jamal grabbed her hands. "Sweetheart, I didn't mean to keep this from you. I didn't think anything of it. Besides, it wouldn't have changed what I'm feeling for you."

"Did . . . did you know he was gay?"

"Well, uh yeah. He made it clear he was ready to come out of the closet."

"And he couldn't even come out to me. I'm his family," Angela sniffled. Jamal pulled her into his arms as the tears fell. Between sobs she shouted, "I don't get it! Why was he so hard on me about my relationships? Why? He was out here fucking them all! Now he's dead, and it could've been one of them that did this!"

"Angela, shhh, please calm down."

"No! He did this to our family! He was out here lying to everybody!" She jumped up from the chair and began screaming, "Why, Tré? You get in here now and tell me why. Why, dammit! Why?"

Jamal got to his feet and embraced her as she collapsed into uncontrollable sobs. The door burst open. Dr. Mitchell and two of his female nurses hurried into the room. Angela noticed the quick glances exchanged between Jamal and Dr. Mitchell, and she realized they were planning something.

She screamed, attempting to wriggle free from Jamal's arms. "No! I'm not staying here!"

"Sweetheart, please calm—"

"No! Let me go!" She snatched away from his grasp.

Both nurses grabbed an arm to restrain Angela. In her anger she spit in Jamal's face. While he went to the table for some tissues, Angela yanked loose from one nurse and swung, hitting her right across the cheek. In her stunned state, she left Angela's other hand free. Angela attacked the other nurse, landing several slaps and punches to her face. In an instant, Jamal seized and restrained Angela by pinning her arms behind her. Her chest heaved up and down. She thrashed her head back and kicked her legs out.

"Angela, stop this right now! You're only making things worse!" Jamal shouted, his voice echoing throughout the room.

Dr. Mitchell exited hastily, only to return a few moments later with a syringe in hand.

Jamal questioned, "What's that for?"

"Edwards, I have to give her a sedative to calm her down. She can't go back out there like that."

"Understood."

Angela began kicking some more. "No! Stop it! I wanna go home! Please, Jamal! Please!"

A couple of nurses joined them in the room, moved into position, and assisted Jamal in holding Angela as still as possible. Dr. Mitchell inserted the needle into her deltoid muscle and emptied the syringe. It took several minutes, but Jamal and the nurses didn't loosen their hold until her body relaxed. Jamal nodded for them to let go as Angela leaned against him.

"Jamal, why did you let them do that?" she whimpered.

He pressed his lips against her forehead. "Shhh, sweetheart, everything is going to be okay. This is for the best, trust me. It's time for you to get some rest."

Jamal ushered her into the waiting hands of the nurses who took over. Dr. Mitchell instructed them to take Angela back to her room. They strolled down the hallway side by side. Halfway through, Angela halted and turned to Jamal with an expression of concern.

He silently mouthed the words: "I love you."

Present day . . .

A sliver of sunlight peeked through the blinds, casting a spotlight on the swirling and twirling dust particles in the air. Entranced by their move-

Chapter 2

ments, Angela found a momentary distraction from the heavy silence of her therapy session. After her discharge from the psychiatric ward, they'd admitted her to the Berean Wellness Center for Women, a residential facility specializing in treating substance and alcohol abuse. The goal was to recover, improve, and maintain the skills needed to cope with everyday life after loss. Days blended into weeks, and weeks into months, all devoted to the relentless quest for healing. Amidst her emotional turmoil, Angela found comfort in adhering to her daily routine.

Her mornings started with group therapy, where she shared her struggles and received support from others who were also working toward regaining control and returning to a healthy, productive lifestyle. In the afternoons, she had a one-on-one session with her therapist, Dr. Peterson, taking small but significant steps toward recovery. Her evenings were dedicated to journaling, diligently jotting down her thoughts and experiences. She also committed to yoga sessions, which helped her regain control over her physical and mental well-being. A sudden throat clearing snatched her back to the present.

"Angela?"

She blinked, her attention shifting from the window to the middle-aged man sitting across from her. Dr. Peterson always dressed in fall-colored mock turtlenecks and khaki slacks. Angela often wondered if his wardrobe comprised anything else. An inaudible sigh escaped her lips. "Yes, Dr. Peterson?"

"We've made progress, but I feel you're still holding back. Is there anything else you'd like to share?" Dr. Peterson's inquisitive eyes searched her face.

Angela took a deep breath, acknowledging the truth in his words. For weeks, she had been grappling with the source of her guilt, trying to uncover the root and break free from its suffocating grasp. It was finally time to get to the bottom of it. After releasing a long breath, Angela spoke.

"I told you about my dad leaving my mom, and how Tré stepped up as the man of the house, right?"

"Yes. You did."

"Well, he took his role too seriously. Tré was always up in my business. He claimed nobody was good enough for me. Don't get me wrong. I know he was looking out for me like any big brother would. But sometimes he went too far. It went to his head. He really thought he was my daddy." Angela let out a small laugh, pausing for a minute to collect herself before continuing. "And that's exactly why I kept my relationship with Jamal a secret for so long. I didn't want Tré bullying him into breaking up with me like he did with my exes. But deep down, I knew he couldn't do that with Jamal. He loves me and would never let Tré punk him. Anyway, we met for dinner to catch up and Tré saw that I had a new car. He kept asking who my sugar daddy was. I tried to get him to drop it. Of course, he couldn't let it go. Without giving up his name, I told him Jamal was a doctor. Tré pretty much threatened to use his connections to find out more. He said he would beat Jamal up if he found out I was being played. But you wanna know something funny?"

"What's that?" Dr. Peterson asked, raising his eyebrows.

"Tré and Jamal already knew each other."

"Really."

"Well, Jamal knew him by the name his friends outside of our family called him—Rico. They even worked out at the same gym and hung out at the golf club together. Jamal swore Tré never said anything about me. Of course he wouldn't. But if I knew that would've been the last time that I was going to see Tré . . ." Angela's voice faded away as she reflected on her regrets.

Dr. Peterson leaned in, his tone understanding and supportive. "That's a difficult burden to bear, Angela, but it's important to remember we can't change what's already happened. What we can control is how we move forward from here. Are you ready to take that step?"

A persistent sting behind Angela's eyes preceded a torrent of words. "I-I don't know if I can. I know he only wanted the best for me. I wish he knew how much he meant to me before he died. I just miss him terribly."

"I want to help you loosen the hold guilt has on your heart—so you can finally breathe again and move toward real healing," Dr. Peterson reas-

Chapter 2

sured, reaching out to offer comfort. "Angela, Tré knew you loved him. It's okay that you didn't get to say goodbye."

She nodded in agreement with Dr. Peterson's words. It was as if a dam had burst, and all the emotions she had been holding in for the past couple of months came pouring out. Tears rolled down her cheeks. Angela's body shook with sobs, experiencing the unmitigated pain of her loss. In doing so, she also had a sense of relief and closure that she hadn't experienced since Tré's death.

"Okay. I understand. I forgive myself. It's okay I didn't get to say it. And, and I know this isn't goodbye. No. This is just so long for now," Angela declared once she calmed down.

Dr. Peterson gave a comforting squeeze as he spoke in a kind and motivating tone. "That's it, Angela. Let your emotions flow freely. Your dedication to getting better is truly admirable. Every day you've made incredible strides towards your recovery. Just remember the process of rebuilding takes time. I believe in your strength and perseverance."

"I have you to thank for helping me to get this far."

"Keep up the good work, and you will go further. As much as I enjoy having you with us, I'm happy to share that your time here is nearing an end."

Angela sniffled, her face splitting into a huge smile. She used the back of her hands to wipe her cheeks and asked excitedly, "Are you serious, Dr. Peterson?"

Smiling, he extended a few Kleenex from the box on his desk to her. "Yes, I am. You're almost there. We will need to have a couple of follow up sessions after you've been discharged. But you have three weeks left, give or take. Are you ready to start your new chapter?"

As she grabbed the tissues from Dr. Peterson, Angela rose to her feet with enthusiasm. "Yes! Of course, I am! And I couldn't have made it this far without your help. Thank you again. But umm, Dr. Peterson, would it be okay if I called Jamal? I need to make sure I have a ride home."

"Absolutely. Go. Have a good evening, Angela. I'll see you tomorrow."

Without wasting another minute, Angela rose from her chair and exited Dr. Peterson's office in a hurry. She made it to the front of the center in less than a minute where there was a designated area for the patients to make personal calls to their family and friends. Angela checked in with the nurse on duty and found an open pod where she held her breath and quickly dialed Jamal's number. It wasn't until after the third ring and he answered Angela released the oxygen from her lungs. "Babe, I'm so glad you picked up."

"Is everything okay?"

"Yes. As a matter of fact, it is. I just finished another session with Dr. Peterson. He told me I'll be coming home soon."

"Oh yeah? When?"

Angela beamed "Less than three weeks."

She could hear muffled voices and shuffling in the background when Jamal spoke again. "Just a minute, sweetheart. Let me get to one of the co-op rooms where it's not as noisy." After a short pause, Jamal returned to the line. "Okay, exactly when are you coming home?"

"Dr. Peterson said in less than three weeks."

Jamal released a deep sigh in her ear. "Hmm, looks like I have to talk to your mom. We need to iron some things out. I'm scheduled to be in D.C. with Mitchell for this research project. He claims it's supposed to be groundbreaking and worth getting us some grant monies. Then I have a medical conference to attend in Florida. With all of this happening, I've got some other news to share with you."

Concerned by his tone and everything he'd shared so far, Angela settled on the chair closest to her. "Okay. What is it?"

"This might not seem like the best timing, but our head surgeon is retiring and I'm one of the candidates they're considering to take his place. Of course, there are two other doctors that'll be up for it too, but yeah. If all goes well, I'll be the chief of surgery."

Thankful it wasn't anything else, Angela exclaimed, "Wow, babe! That's wonderful!"

"Well, it's not mine yet."

"It will be," Angela quickly reassured her man. He could do anything he wanted.

Chapter 2

Jamal chuckled before thanking her. "I appreciate your confidence in me, sweetheart. It means a lot to me."

"Of course. You know I've got your back, babe."

"Again, thank you. But back to your discharge. I can talk to your mom and see if she can come—"

"No. Don't bother her. I'll check and see if Mia can come get me."

"Are you sure, sweetheart?"

"Yes. We can go see Mamá after she picks me up."

"Okay then. I'll be there tomorrow. I'll talk to Peterson and find out the exact date of your discharge. Let me get back out on the floor."

"Okay, love you."

"Love you too."

Once Angela hung up, the disappointment of knowing Jamal wouldn't be coming to pick her up festered in her spirit. She should've been happy for his announcement of possibly being promoted, but Angela wanted Jamal to be there when she was discharged. Angela silently prayed that when Dr. Peterson gave the exact date, Jamal would be in town. She wouldn't get her hopes up too high. And as she dialed Mia's number, Angela's mind settled on her best friend being the alternative in her man's place. After a few rings Mia answered.

"Hey, Ang. How're you, girl?"

"A lot better than I have in the past couple of months."

"Oh yeah. Why is that?"

Angela boasted proudly. "I'm finally getting out of here."

"Really? When?"

"In about three weeks."

"That's great, Ang. Are you ready?"

"Yes! I am. I'm feeling like myself again. As a matter of fact, that's what we talked about in my session a little while ago. I've been guilt tripping myself over not saying goodbye to Tré. But Dr. Peterson said Tré knew I loved him. I could finally release this guilt. I understand and accept that Tré is gone. And there are better ways of coping with my loss or any setbacks for that matter without wanting pills or wine. That's when he said our time was nearing an end. Which is why I was calling you. Jamal might be out of town. Think you could be my standby and pick me up?"

There was silence from the other end of the line. Angela pulled the device from her face to check if the call had ended. It was still active. She spoke up to get her best friend's attention.

"Mia, did you hear me?"

"I'm sorry, Ang. No, I didn't. What did you say?"

"I was asking if you could be on standby. One of Jamal's colleagues asked him to come help out on this groundbreaking research. That means he'll be in D.C. for a few weeks. Then he has this medical conference in Florida. I'm not sure if he'll be able to come pick me up. Would you be able to come and get me? I'd have to be back no later than Sunday evening. I would only have to come back for outpatient sessions for another week or two and then that's it. I'll be done with this place."

Once more it was quiet. Angela didn't get an answer.

"Mia!"

"I'm sorry, Ang. My mind is elsewhere." Mia's voice cracked.

"Hey, are you okay?"

"No, I'm not okay."

"What's wrong? Did Troy hurt you?"

"No. But Troy's been hurt, and I don't know where he is," Mia cried.

"Goodness, I hate that I'm here, and I can't come to you. Please, calm down. Can you tell me what happened?"

It took a few minutes for Mia to pull herself together. When she could stop sobbing, she took her time to explain everything. "I don't know where they took him, Ang. MJ brought me back here, but he still wouldn't tell me anything. He said they were doing what's best for me. I should've known. They've been plotting against us for weeks. I don't know what to do."

"What can you do? Max thinks this is best, and maybe he's right. Mia, you and Troy—"

"No! Don't you dare agree with him, Ang."

"I'm not taking Max's side. That's not what I meant. What I'm saying

Chapter 2

is that after everything you've been through with Troy, you have to believe Max is looking out for you."

"Looking out for me, how? By beating my husband up, huh? I can't believe you think my daddy was right in this. I don't care what I did or what anybody thinks! Troy's *my* husband! This is *our* marriage! Everyone needs to just mind their own fucking business and leave us alone!"

"Look, I'm sorry. I don't mean to upset you."

"Uh, Ang, I gotta go. I'm not feeling so hot."

Mia didn't give her a chance to respond. She ended the call. Angela stared at the phone for a moment before placing it back on the receiver. Her best friend had a mess to deal with—trouble with her NFL husband, headlines she didn't need, and now her powerful father, a Georgia senator, along with her brother, a sports attorney, were stepping in. The last thing Mia wanted was their interference, but it looked like she no longer had a choice. Angela rocked her head back and forth, pushing aside Mia's problems. She needed to focus on her own. Angela returned to the young girl behind the desk.

"Do you mind if I come back a little later to try my friend again? She wasn't feeling well and had to hang up."

"Sure. I'll be here."

Making her way back to her room, Angela found herself happier than she'd been in weeks. She paused at the door, fingers resting lightly on the knob. A deep breath steadied her before she pushed it open. The familiar space greeted her like a quiet witness to all she'd endured. When she first arrived at Berean, she'd been drowning in grief, caught in a dangerous cycle of alcohol and prescription drug use—numbing the pain until it nearly consumed her. But now, after months of hard work, she was a transformed woman—stronger, wiser, and determined to rebuild her life from the ground up.

The pain hasn't vanished... but it doesn't own me anymore. What comes next? That's mine to write—and I'll do it with clarity, power, and grace.

3

MAKE ME WANNA MARRY YOU

Where is he? Jamal's fingertips tapped against the slick surface of his desk. The fluorescent lights above hummed a dissonant tune to his mounting impatience. His gaze flicked to the door, ensuring it was locked. The screen of his personal laptop flickered. Jamal's heart quickened when Christian's face materialized. That smile. It cut through the tension that had knotted Jamal's shoulders.

"Good afternoon, Dr. Edwards."

"Good afternoon, Mr. Hilcrest. Running a little late, aren't we?" Jamal peeked down at his wrist, watching the seconds tick by before looking back up at the display.

"I know it's not like me. But a regional director popped up. Now he has everybody in panic mode."

Jamal nodded in understanding.

Christian threw out a question. "So, how's your day been?"

"Busy. I won't complain."

"Do we have enough time?"

Jamal leaned back, a smirk curving his lips. "No. Punctuality is key in this office. You know the rules, Mr. Hilcrest."

"Aww, but what if I'm worth making an exception?"

"Conceited much aren't we?"

"Confident, Dr. Edwards. There's a difference."

"You're lucky you're so charming."

"Charming enough to steal a top surgeon's precious time?" Christian's brown eyes sparkled with mischief.

He always knew what to say to inflate his ego. Christian had been calling him the top surgeon or hinting at him being the best since Jamal shared he was being considered for the head of surgery position. Jamal couldn't hide the smile splitting his face.

"Steal implies I didn't offer it willingly. On a serious note, I wish I could, but my next few appointments include full exams. With the rest coming in, I'll have to keep the schedule tight. We won't be able to. So, what else have you got going on today?"

"Not too much. Just thinking about what else I can do to keep my sexy head surgeon from stressing over this position. This weekend, we're already set for our spa day. But I need to do something else, I know. What're you doing this evening? Working late?"

"No. Not tonight." Jamal sat up straight, placed his elbows on the desk, and leaned in closer to the screen. Hiking up his brows, he asked, "What're you plotting, Chris?"

"Well, you're always doing it for us. How about I cook for you?"

Jamal's rumbling laughter echoed throughout his office. He heard Christian kissing his teeth, but he couldn't stop. He'd never seen him so much as boil a pot of water since they'd started dating. With Christian it was breakfast in bed, an upscale dinner, or takeout. When he calmed himself down, Jamal wiped his eyes and held up a hand. "I'm sorry, Chris but how about you what? Do you even know how?"

"I'll have you know I can cook, Jamie. My mama taught me to make more than just breakfast. Now I might not know how to throw down the way you do, but I can whip something together." With a sharp neck rotation, an exaggerated lip-pop, and a dramatic eyeroll, Christian delivered a sassy retort. "Don't play. I'mma fuck around and make this 'marry me' chicken, and then whatchu gon' do?"

Jamal snorted, rocking his head from side to side. But looked right

Chapter 3

into the screen when he responded. "I guess I better get your ring size then."

"Oop." Christian placed a palm against his chest, sputtering through his words. "Uhh, err, oh okay. Well then, umm I guess the only thing I need to ask is, are there any foods that you're allergic to?"

"No. Nothing. So, this should be easy, right?"

"Right." Christian pushed out a nervous laugh.

He'd thrown Christian off with that ring comment. Jamal knew marriage wasn't on the horizon. Not yet. But being with Christian for a long time sounded good. He reclined in his chair, grinning. *Yes, it better be good enough to make me wanna marry your ass.* As if he heard his thoughts, Christian's lips twisted like he was ready to read him. Before any saucy words could leave his mouth, the shrill ring of Jamal's cell phone sliced through the room. Jamal's body went rigid. Angela's name glared up at him from the screen, demanding his attention.

What does she want now? The professional mask he'd momentarily shed snapped back into place. "Hey, I need to take this."

"Of course, duty calls. See you when you get home."

"Have my chicken ready, Chris."

"Uh huh. And Jamie, my ring size is an eight. Byeeee!"

Christian ended the call, flashing him a dazzling smile that sent an electric shot straight to Jamal's dick. He shook his head and adjusted himself. *Back to reality.* Jamal straightened his spine against the leather chair as he reached for the phone.

"Hello, Dr. Edwards?" His voice slid into the practiced ease of professionalism.

"Hey babe, are you busy?"

"You've got about ten minutes. I'm in between patients. What's going on?"

"I've got a break too. And ten minutes is all I need. I was thinking, since we didn't get a chance to do anything last week, maybe we could use this weekend to get away. What do you say?"

Angela had been home for almost a month now, constantly pressing to spend more time with him. She was just like her brother—always needing him close, always pulling, always wanting more. Across the room, the framed medical diplomas seemed to watch him, silent witnesses to the charade he was about to perform. Jamal swiveled slightly, allowing the motion to mask his disquiet.

"I'd say that sounds wonderful . . ." he lied, the words smooth as the scotch he'd pour himself later, ". . . except there's a neurology summit this weekend. It's in Savannah."

"I see."

The disappointment in Angela's voice tugged at the corners of his conscience, but he pushed it aside.

"Sweetheart, you know it's critical for this position," Jamal assured her, the lie cresting with ease over the line. "Mitch will be there. And so will those other two candidates. I can't miss this."

"Of course, you can't."

"I wish it were different."

"Me too."

"Tell you what, as soon as I get back, I'll have them block off my calendar. We can go next weekend. How does that sound?"

"Really? You promise, Jamal?"

"Promise."

"Okay, sounds like a plan. So, what are we having for dinner? Should I take something out? Do you need me to pick up anything on my way home and get it prepped?"

"No, sweetheart. I won't be home until late if at all tonight. You know when I cover shifts, I'm on until the morning. By the time it's the last round and I make it home, you'll be heading out."

"Right. Well then, I guess I'll go check on Mia, then swing by Mamá's when I get off. I'll still make dinner and leave it for you to take for lunch tomorrow."

"Okay. Thanks, sweetheart. Be safe. Call you later. Love you."

"Love you too," she replied before the line went dead.

The silence that followed was deafening. Jamal reclined, eyes closed, the aftertaste of deceit bitter on his tongue. How did he get here? When did things become so complicated and out of his control? The struggle to

Chapter 3

balance two relationships was getting to him. His conscience wouldn't let him push aside the lingering guilt. He wasn't sure how to let Angela down without hurting her. Until he figured it out, Jamal would do whatever it took. Even if it meant leading her on for a little while longer.

Jamal spent the rest of his afternoon conducting annual physicals, consulting three new patients, and treating two sick patients. His day concluded with an emergency surgery that he was called to perform. As he pulled into the second parking spot in front of Christian's condo, a home-cooked meal sounded more appealing than cooking himself. Jamal unlocked the door with the key Christian had given him a couple of weeks earlier. As soon as he stepped inside, the delicious aroma of rosemary, thyme, cumin, basil, and garlic filled his nose, causing his mouth to water and his stomach to growl. Even though Jamal wasn't feeling hungry before, he was now. He casually dropped his bookbag in a corner of the foyer and toed off his sneakers, careful not to track dirt onto Christian's plush carpeting.

"Hey, what're you cooking in here?" Jamal called out after he began heading toward the kitchen.

Christian spun around from the hot range oven wielding the tongs in one hand and the other clenched into a fist, ready for action. His eyes widened in surprise after he recognized Jamal standing there. Jabbing the silicone tips in his direction, Christian shrieked, "Jamie! What the hell! You can't be sneaking up on me like that."

"I wasn't." Jamal chuckled, pointing at the tongs. "But that isn't going to do shit for you if somebody was trying to sneak up on you."

Christian rotated his neck and retorted. "While the focus is on these tongs, my fist would be tagging their fucking face. Please do not let my size fool you, Jamie. I will fuck somebody up."

"I believe you. But for a moment you looked shook." Jamal grabbed Christian's wrist and pulled him close. He inhaled, letting out a deep grunt and whispered against his ear, "Tell me, Chris, what're you cooking for your man? Is it so good it'll make me wanna slap my mama? Or as you said earlier, make me wanna put a ring on it?"

Steam hissed and billowed into the open area, mingling with the sound of Christian's labored breaths. They were standing inches apart, their chests rising and falling in unison. Jamal watched Christian nervously chewing on his bottom lip. When Jamal reached out and slipped a hand at the nape of Christian's neck, his breath hitched. He stumbled over his words.

"Uh uh ... umm, err chicken."

"Tell me, Chris." Jamal inclined his head, nibbling on Christian's earlobe. "How'd you make it? Baked, roasted, or grilled?"

A soft pant escaped his lips. "It-it's baked."

"What sides?"

"R-r-roasted potatoes ... and-and some steamy, no I mean—"

"You meant what, Chris?"

"Umm steamed, I meant steamed broccolini."

"Mmm," Jamal replied, planting a few wet kisses along the side of Christian's neck until he reached his lips. He gave him a quick peck before pulling back and flirting, "You taste as delicious as that sounds. But first, I need to take a shower and get the stench of this hospital off me. Is everything done?"

Christian simply returned a wordless nod.

"Do you want to join me, and help wash my back?"

Without breaking eye contact, Christian tossed the tongs onto the counter. He reached out, turning off all the ranges. Grabbing Jamal's hand, Christian tugged him and nodded toward the other side of the condo.

"Let's get you cleaned up."

Christian guided Jamal to the master bedroom and into the bathroom. They had previously taken showers together, so the water was already at a comfortable temperature. Christian took care of Jamal, washing him thoroughly from head to toe. Jamal appreciated the attention. He needed it. What Jamal didn't expect was Christian to drop to his knees. He gripped Jamal's pipe and peered up at him with the sexiest brown eyes Jamal had ever seen.

"Wanna watch me as I swallow you whole?"

Chapter 3

"Yes!" Jamal hissed, grabbing Christian's shoulders and jutting his hips forward.

The moment Christian's jaw slacked, and he encased his lips around the leaking tip, Jamal shuddered. Christian held onto Jamal's thighs working his engorged shaft in and out of his mouth. On a couple of the thrusts, Jamal tapped the fleshy flap of tissue dangling at the back of his throat. With his hand wrapped around Jamal's throbbing erection, Christian tugged hard, eliciting a strained grunt. The way he worked his palm in perfect synchronization with suctioning, it was some of the best head Jamal had ever experienced. He caressed the underside of Christian's jawline, watching his cheeks expand and sink in with each bob. His lips were the softest. His mouth the wettest. And his tongue, by far the most lethal he'd ever come in contact with. Jamal marveled at how Christian appeared to be swallowing his dick as if he was getting ready to eat it whole.

"Fuck, Chris! You trying to make me bust?"

"Mmhmm . . . yeah, please give it to me Jamie. Fuck my face until you come in my mouth," Christian moaned around his swollen mushroom tip.

Jamal held onto the back of Christian's head, increasing the speed of his pumps. The thought of coming in his ass was more appealing, but the build-up of pleasure in his groin had progressed from a steady pulse to a more intense throbbing. His muscles began contracting in his mid-section and at the base of his member. As Christian continued sucking and jerking, Jamal's rigid flesh swelled in size. A wave of heat surged through him, causing his back to arch. Soon, a stream of his hot semen spurted down Christian's eager and waiting throat.

"Arrgh!" Jamal cried out, quivering through his climax.

Christian gulped greedily, not stopping until Jamal had to pull him off. Orgasms continued to ripple through his body. Shuddering once more, Jamal leaned against the wall for support. He outstretched out his hand and Christian placed his palm in it, standing up to his full height with a satisfied grin. Drawing him nearer, Jamal angled his head and simply stared.

Christian laughed nervously, "What?"

"You, is what."

"What about me?"

"You're the best thing that's happened to me in a long time. I know this is all still new, but I'm here. I'm all in."

"That's all I want, Jamie. 'Cause I'm all in too."

Jamal would never deny his hesitancy at first when Christian wanted him to accept his sexuality. He was a coward. Society's traditional disapproving views on gay men had Jamal hiding in the shadows. Now with Christian he could live in his truth. Jamal lowered his face. Christian met him the rest of the way for a passionate kiss that left no questions of what either wanted. Their tongues tangled and swirled sloppily together in a frenzy, moving around the other as if they were snakes engaged in a seductive dance. The continuous splashing water served as a backdrop to their intimate moment.

A minute later Christian withdrew from their smooching, resting his forehead against Jamal's and teasingly inquired, "Are you gonna let me finish relieving this stress so I can get that ring?"

4

YOU NEED A BIG BOY

"When I told him I wanted to get away this weekend, he shut it down saying he had some summit in Savannah. But if it's not a summit, it's a conference. And if it's not a conference, he has to do an extra shift. And even if there's no shift to cover, there's always some emergency surgery that comes up. It never ends. There's never enough time for us anymore. I just don't get it, Mia. It didn't used to be like this," Angela complained, waving her hand animatedly.

"Yes, it was. You were practically floating on cloud nine, happy that he could sneak away to fuck you. Hmph. You probably thought Jamal's shit smelt like them funky ass flowers he brought up to Berean. But couldn't nobody tell you nothing."

"Really Mia?"

Angela diverted her attention from the road to her phone, meeting Mia's intense, slanted obsidian eyes staring back at her. Her best friend raised a perfectly arched brow and pursed her full, glossed lips, before flipping her long, jet-black hair over her shoulders. She was now pregnant and glowing. Bearing a striking resemblance to her mother, Mia had Asian features that were beautifully complemented by her father's African American roots. Seated in the private section of her stylist's salon, Mia was waiting for her turn. Angela shook her head and focused on the cars ahead of her, navigating through traffic.

"Yep, and I've told you this before. There's something about him that just don't sit right with me. Okay, so he bought you a condo and then the car. All those were green flags 'cause you love gifts. And when he left his wife, you finally got what you wanted, right? You were overjoyed. But no one could have prepared you for the devastating loss of your brother and the way you handled the grief. That man is always too busy when you need him. Before you argue with me, I'm talking about the way you *really* need him. How is it, he's a doctor and can take care of everybody else except his woman? Does that make any sense, Ang?"

Mia's statement proved difficult to dispute. She had a point. It had been a couple of months since Angela had returned from the rehab center, and Jamal's recent actions had become increasingly perplexing to her. Lately, she noticed that she wasn't high on his list of priorities. He always appeared available for everything else, yet whenever she needed him, he was suddenly nowhere to be found. It seemed she needed to schedule an appointment just to spend some one-on-one time with him. Angela finally answered with a sigh.

"No. It doesn't. I've been trying to find time with his busy schedule. But I can't even get him alone long enough for us to talk about what's going on and how things have changed."

"And that in itself is a problem, Ang. You're trying to talk, and where is he? I get it that he's up for this new job, but seriously he needs to learn how to manage his calendar better. 'Cause this is about to be history repeating itself."

"What do you mean?"

"Didn't he have a problem with his ex-wife being out of town and not giving him quality time? Isn't that how you got him? Sounds to me like y'all are headed down the same road. And y'all ain't even married. Big red flag, Ang."

Angela found herself speechless. She hadn't considered this, but it was undeniably true. The same problems that Jamal had complained about with his ex-wife had now surfaced in Angela's relationship with him. The

Chapter 4

realization was harsh, and it hit her like a punch to the gut. Angela needed to address these problems before they spiraled out of control. But she and Jamal still had time. She refused to let their relationship fall apart without trying to fix it first.

"You're right, Mia. And I'll talk to Jamal. He said after he gets back from Savannah, he's going to have them block off his calendar. Then we're going to Curaçao for a weekend away."

"I hope so. 'Cause you're finally in the right headspace. This should be the last thing you're stressing over."

"That's why I'm not. Everything will be fine soon enough. Now, I've been going on and on about Jamal. I haven't even asked how things are going with you."

Mia casually waved her hand in a dismissive gesture. "You were already coming with me to my doctor's appointment, so I was planning on telling you about it then. Long story short, MJ came by with Tanya the other day. MJ's tired of seeing me upset. He's gonna talk to Daddy. I don't wanna get my hopes up but maybe I'll get to see Troy soon."

"Well, that's good. Hopefully Max will have a change of heart."

"We'll see. Okay Ang, I gotta go. She's ready for me. Call you later."

The timing could not have been better. Their call ended right as Angela pulled into her mother's driveway. A large black truck, unfamiliar to her, sat parked on one side. It must've been someone visiting with her mother. Shrugging it off, Angela killed the engine of her Mercedes coupe and got out, taking a moment to look around the neighborhood where she had grown up with her brothers.

Nestled in the cul-de-sac at the end of the street, the cozy, ranch-style house sat in a peaceful and secluded area with minimal traffic. Bianca Washington had chosen this neighborhood because of its proximity to her job and for the location of the house, which allowed her children to freely play outside. Not much had changed in the community of Misty Waters.

Cars were parked bumper-to-bumper, and overhead, a lattice of power lines crisscrossed the sky. The streets buzzed with energy. In the distance, sirens wailed, their sound absorbed into the background noise of a street full of life. A group of children played basketball on a nearby court, while a street vendor pushed a colorful cart filled with snacks for passersby. The air carried a unique combination of scents: the smoky aroma of grilled food mixing with the acrid smell of exhaust fumes. Occasionally, there would be a pungent odor from overflowing trash bins or stagnant rainwater in the gutter. And underneath it all, there was always a subtle metallic scent, reminding her of the urban infrastructure nearby—train tracks and industrial zones.

No house in the row exceeded three bedrooms, two baths, and a two-car garage. They were all quite modest. The area between the homes lay barren, with no sign of lush greenery. Although Angela's mother and her neighbors had tried their best over the years to keep their lawns looking nice, neglect by some residents, leaving cars and trash on the streets and in front of their homes, detracted from the area's appearance. Growing up in this Decatur neighborhood, Angela and her brothers were surrounded by inner-city life. Though not necessarily dangerous, Misty Waters certainly lacked the wealth and curb appeal of the Buckhead neighborhood where Angela currently lived.

She turned the key and pushed against the weathered door. It swung inward, the squeak of its hinges announcing her entry into the living room where family portraits and a mishmash of furniture filled the space. Soft murmurs of conversation floated in from the kitchen, one voice belonging to her mother and another unfamiliar one. She tried to figure out who the unknown speaker was. Could it be the owner of the truck parked outside? Did her mother have a male friend? His deep and melodic tone spoke in fluent Spanish, piquing her curiosity.

Rounding the corner, she spotted her mother, Bianca. She was a stunning woman with long, brown hair streaked with blonde highlights. Angela, whose appearance reflected her African American father's traits, shared only her mother's complexion. Her brother Tré, on the other hand, had inherited their mother's facial features entirely, including her striking green eyes and light golden-brown skin. However, it was the unknown man sitting across from her mother that captivated Angela's attention, as she witnessed their animated conversation in Spanish.

Chapter 4

Bianca raised her voice, leaning in to ask the man what he'd said to his coworker. "¿Y entonces qué le dijiste?"

"Consigue que alguien más lo haga," the man responded, stating he had told him to get somebody else to do it.

Bianca cackled as if he'd shared the funniest joke, and they exchanged a high-five. Angela blinked. It dawned on her who the stranger was. What was *he* doing here?

"Mamá?" She called out, cutting through the conversation.

He turned his head, sunlight catching the espresso brown color of his eyes. A smile lit up his devastatingly handsome face, softening the sharp angles of his chiseled jawline. Pits formed on each side of his cheeks, framing a set of perfect teeth. *Damn! When did he glow up?*

"¡Qué sorpresa! Mamá, esto es inesperado," his voice mirroring the cadence of his light chuckle.

Her mother nodded enthusiastically. "Sí, this is unexpected. She didn't call to tell me she was coming by. Menuda sorpresa, mija."

"Me coming to visit you is a surprise now, Mamá?" Angela asked, arching an eyebrow.

Instead of her mother, the unexpected stranger responded, flashing her again with his Colgate grin. "Indeed. I'm pleasantly surprised to see you here, especially since we were just discussing you. Hello, Angela."

Talking about me? Why? And had his voice always been this deep? Her heart knocked against her ribcage, upbeat and erratic. She steadied herself by the kitchen doorway as she watched him rise from the chair. He crossed the room and reached her in less than three strides. Angela was of average height, neither short nor tall. Yet, with his towering stature being well over six-feet-five and broad shoulders, he seemed to dominate the entire space. Angela shook her head a little and waved with a friendly smile. "Uh, hey, Simeon."

Returning a head shake of his own, Simeon opened his arms wide and moved closer. "No mi amiga, necesito un abrazo."

Friend? A hug? To Angela, they were acquaintances at best, having played together as kids, but that was ages ago. Although her brother Tré was older than both of them, Simeon Ingram was only a few years her senior. Simeon had grown up to be an incredibly attractive man. He was tall and muscular, his smooth skin an umber dark brown. But the manly scent engulfing her senses made it hard to think straight. She stepped into the massive, inked sleeves belonging to her childhood playmate. Angela tried to maintain some distance by giving him a quick "church hug" and moving away, but Simeon drew her closer to his ripped physique. He let go after a second and she quickly took a step back, clearing her throat.

"Wow, umm all these years, I had no clue you spoke Spanish."

Angela's mother unfolded from her seat. She crossed the room with outstretched arms, enveloping Angela in an embrace that smelled of jasmine and home-cooked meals. "Mija, he's been speaking Spanish since Junior brought him and his brother Lijah over. Really, you didn't know?"

Angela pulled away some, narrowing her eyes at Simeon's self-assured grin. "No, Mamá. I had no idea."

"Well, your friend—ahem, *our* friend, Simeon here is *very* talented."

Angela's gaze danced from her mother, who was beaming with joy, to Simeon, who appeared completely at ease. But Angela was skeptical. What was his real motive for being here?

"Uh huh, well the Simeon I know was just like the rest of the boys out here in the Mist: lame, nappy headed, annoying, pimple faced, dusty, musty—"

"Angela!"

"I'm serious, Mamá. Those boys were unbathed."

"Ay, I'm not that musty lil' boy who used to run in these streets. I know how to wash my balls among other things. Like Mamá said, I'm *very* talented. You gotta get to know the man I've become."

Her mother snapped her fingers and quipped, "You better tell her, Simeon. You ain't no lil' boy no more. What them girls on the clock app say? They want a big boy. Or is it a big dog? Either way, here ya' go. He's right here, mija. Thank me later."

"Mamá, please. No. And why're you still on there? Didn't I tell Junior to delete your page?" Angela gave herself the facepalm.

"She says you need a big boy in your life. What's up?" He extended a closed fist, which her mother eagerly met with her own while snickering.

Chapter 4

Simeon threw his head back, and his boisterous laughter echoed throughout the room.

Why did that gravelly, yet jovial sound find its way to her pussy? Then he locked his eyes directly on her. His intense, dark chocolate stare had Angela feeling somewhat lightheaded and giddy inside. No other man had ever affected her like this. Not even Jamal, whom she'd been exclusively focused on since the beginning of their relationship. Yet, here was her childhood friend causing her horny twat to act like she didn't have any home training, leaking out in excitement. *Heffa! We have a man!* Angela silently chastised. She tried to be as inconspicuous as possible when she clenched her thighs, reprimanding her body for its sudden betrayal and lack of control.

"Ahem, well, nothing is up, Simeon. Sorry, but I got a *big* man."

With an exaggerated roll of her eyes, Bianca scoffed. "Jamal? Por favor, he's not *this* big," she remarked sarcastically while pointing at Simeon. Her expression then turned serious as she warned with a stern finger gesture, "I know Jamal's not the one for you."

Angela had to eat that. Her mother made no efforts to hide her dislike for Jamal, but she hadn't really had the chance to get acquainted with him. Out of nowhere Tré's words crept into Angela's psyche: *"If he's such a good man, I would think you'd want Mamá to meet him by now."*

Angela hadn't introduced Jamal to her mother or anyone close to her before Tré passed away. Although Jamal offered emotional support during their loss, it didn't sit well with Bianca that her son never approved of the relationship while he was still alive. Bianca's distrust and dislike for Jamal began when Angela nearly overdosed. He'd called Bianca to inform her that Angela had been hospitalized. Overcome with panic at the thought of losing another child, Bianca allowed Jamal to make all decisions regarding Angela's care, as she was unable to think clearly without her eldest son, who had always taken charge. Looking back, Bianca regretted giving him that authority. Jamal's solution was to have Angela admitted to the rehabilitation facility after the hospitalization, which Bianca wasn't fully on board with. But with her demanding work schedule and no option to stay home and care for Angela herself, she reluctantly agreed. And now,

Jamal's frequent absences weren't helping to improve his reputation with her. Bianca's sharp emerald stare cut through Angela, the warmth of their embrace fading into a distant memory.

Simeon cleared his throat, breaking up the tense moment between mother and daughter. "Mamá, could I get a refill on this sweet tea?"

"Sure thing, mijo." Bianca grabbed his glass, replying in a saccharin-laced tone. She then instructed, "Angela, why don't you take Simeon to the living room? You two have a lot of catching up to do."

Son? And what do we have to catch up on? Angela grumbled inwardly. She knew her mother had good intentions, but like always Bianca was trying to control her life. Again. Typical. Angela should've been used to it. Her brother Tré had picked up the same tendency to meddle in her affairs, most likely because of their mother's influence. She had to push back and stand up for herself. Respectfully.

"Mamá, this is hardly necessary. I'm sure Simeon has better stuff to be doing with his time. Like spending it with his girlfriend. I came to see how you were doing. And check up on Junior."

"Angela, that's why I'm here. To check up on Mamá and Junior. After Tré passed, I heard what happened to you. I've been stopping by to make sure things were good with them."

"Oh. I see," Angela mumbled, while looking away, shuffling her feet.

"Yeah, and I wouldn't worry about where my time is spent. I don't have a girlfriend right now. So, how are you doing now that you're back home?"

I'm horny as fuck! What? No! Her twat oozed her brazen reply before Angela could open her mouth. When did it get so hot in this kitchen? Was her mother cooking something? More importantly, why was Simeon having this effect on her?

Angela drew in a deep breath, pushed the loose strands of hair from her face and let the air out slow. She still could not look this gorgeous, dark specimen directly in the eye. Her gaze wandered around the kitchen, until it settled on the old, rusty paella pan that her mother used to cook everything in.

Chapter 4

"I'm much better, thank you for asking. And that's kind of you, Simeon. I'm grateful that you were able to do that while I couldn't."

"Just looking out for my people."

He sent a dimpled smile her way that her lusty pussy thanked him for. *Good grief, could this man get any finer?*

Bianca spoke over her shoulder. "Simeon was just telling me how he's this director up at—ay dios mío, I done forgot. What's the name of your company again?"

"Alder Media Group."

"Right. Why don't y'all go ahead to the living room? I'll bring your tea to you. And I know you need some water, Angela, sí? Ahora todas adelante. Go!"

Ignoring her mother's shade calling her thirsty, Angela sighed quietly and did as she was told, gesturing for Simeon to follow her. The kitchen and living room were only a few feet apart, but Angela fought to keep her balance with every step. She knew Simeon was right on her heels. The jeans she had on fit snug and had her derriere sitting up nicely. Was he enjoying the view? When they made it into the cozy space, Angela reached out for the sofa, and sank onto it, scooting to one end. Simeon lowered his enormous frame onto the cushions, sidling right next to her. She struggled to remain composed. Angela needed to put some space between them. With a subtle move, she angled her body away from him, creating a small gap. But it was pointless. His intoxicating cologne had enveloped her. He smelled unbelievably good. Too good. It was time to find another distraction from this handsome, deliciously scented man. Angela decided to ask him a question to strike up a conversation.

"Spanish, huh? Who taught you?"

Simeon grinned, revealing his dimples before speaking. He leaned back, sinking into the plush cushions of the sofa.

"Junior did at first, but I also took classes in high school and then college."

"Why?"

"So I could talk to you and your family. Coming around as much as I did, I picked up quick that Mamá preferred we speak Spanish in this house."

Her childhood friend-now-grown-man sounded so good. Speaking Spanish definitely added a certain sex appeal to him. Angela tilted her head, gazing into his deep chocolate-brown eyes. In that moment, something unexpected happened. It was as if the rest of the world faded away and sparks flew between them. They hadn't touched, but Angela sensed the strong magnetic pull toward him. She brushed her hair out of her face and pushed out a small, uneasy chuckle.

"Oh okay. Well, what else is going on with you, director at Alder Media Group?"

"I'm doing great. Better than ever. But I need you to keep it real with me, Angela. How are you really doing?"

"I'm maintaining, I guess."

"Hmm. Is there any—"

"You two won't guess what I found."

Bianca sauntered into the room, balancing Simeon's tea and Angela's bottled water in her hands. She passed the drinks to them before revealing the two books she had tucked under one arm. Angela wanted the floor to open up and swallow her whole in that moment. Leave it to her mother to go digging in some boxes for the most embarrassing thing in her child's life —their high school yearbook.

"Mamá no, por favor. Absolutely not. We are not looking at those."

"Oh, we most certainly are. Hand 'em over to me, Mamá," Simeon teased, reaching for a coaster before setting his glass down with a grin. He then took both hardcover albums from a snickering Bianca, who was more than eager to give them to him.

Once again, Angela was in shock as she watched this man who seemed to have a close relationship with her mother. The journal of memories he now held in his hands was from Angela's freshman year, meaning that Simeon had been a senior. It was time for the earth to split apart if it was going to do it and not a moment too soon. Angela reached out for the book, but Simeon smoothly shifted away from her grasp.

Chapter 4

"Nah uhn, you gotta be quicker than that. You wanna call folks pimple face. Let's see who had pepperoni all over theirs, huh?"

"¡Jajaja! 'Cause she shol' had some on that pie face of hers," Bianca cackled, pointing at her.

Angela kissed her teeth. "Mamá, you're not funny."

"Oh, but wasn't it you a little while ago trying to clown Simeon about him being musty and having pimples. But I don't think he ever had one breakout on that handsome skin."

Simeon shook his head in agreement. "Nope, Mamá. Not one."

"That's 'cause it's in his Haitian blood. His daddy, mama, sisters, and brothers got that—"

"Okay, bye, Mamá." Angela threw a hand up, waving her away.

"Alright. I'mma leave y'all alone. I have to get this food started anyway. Oh, and Simeon was staying over for dinner. Lijah and Junior will be here later. Are you going to be able to join us?"

Angela's thoughts drifted to Jamal. He wouldn't be coming home tonight anyway. Her mother always cooked enough to feed a small army. There would be plenty of food for Angela to take for her and Jamal's lunch. She stole a peek at Simeon, who had a hopeful look in his never-ending Hershey's dark chocolate pools. He was trouble. Yet, something about Simeon intrigued Angela, and she wanted to know more. After all, he had suggested she get to know him better. But with Jamal already in her life, was it appropriate for her to pursue a friendship with Simeon? What harm could come from spending time with an old friend? Surely it was innocent enough, right?

"Mija, will you?" Her mother asked once more, breaking Angela from her internal struggle.

Angela kept her eyes fixed on Simeon. She nodded and answered with a playful grin, "Sì, I'll stay and hang out here with the *big* boy."

5

NO NEW FUCKING FRIENDS

"Enjoy your flight, Mr. Edwards."

"Yeah. Thanks." Jamal muttered, slipping his iPhone into the pocket of his joggers. He began wheeling his luggage toward the jet bridge, where Angela was waiting for him up ahead. They were boarding a flight to Curaçao. He'd spent all month dodging her, but he couldn't avoid it anymore. He had promised her a weekend getaway, and it was time to make good on it. Jamal had agreed to let her pick the destination, but he was caught off guard when she said they were leaving the States. Over the past few weeks, he'd been fabricating excuses and telling lies to distance himself from her. His original plan for this weekend had been to say he was needed for an emergency surgery and had to return home. Now, that escape route was no longer an option. This also meant he wouldn't get to see Christian, which he hadn't anticipated.

Although he had grown accustomed to deceiving Angela, Jamal hated lying to Christian. He used the same lie that he would be at a conference for why he wouldn't be able to talk to Christian for the next couple of days. But as soon as he could, Jamal would call. Being away from Christian like this was going to be hard. Jamal was already missing him.

"Are you excited, babe?"

Ugh. Jamal ground his teeth together. Her voice never annoyed him before. Now it grated on his nerves. How could he possibly survive three days in a foreign country, on an island, with her? Jamal realized then that he and Angela had never spent that much time together in a single week. What in the hell was he thinking? This was a bad idea.

Angela plucked the earbud from his ear. "Babe? Please, can you not play your podcast right now? I'm trying to talk to you."

"I'm sorry." Jamal held out his hand, nodding his head toward it. He asked in a polite tone, "What were you saying?"

"I asked if you were excited about this trip," Angela answered, practically shoving the tiny earphone into his palm.

She didn't wait for his response, stalking off. The people in front of her had moved forward. Jamal trailed behind her, stuffing the bud back into his ear. It was definitely going to be a long weekend. They settled into their seats toward the front of the plane, just behind first class. Choosing not to make a long flight even longer, Jamal leaned in and planted a gentle kiss on her cheek.

"I didn't mean to be rude. Yes. I'm very excited to spend this weekend away with you, sweetheart."

Angela turned to face him, her hand reaching up to caress his chin. Pressing her lips against his, she whispered, "I really appreciate you making this happen for us. It means a lot to me. I just want this weekend to be perfect."

"And it will be."

Angela threw her arms around him, and Jamal reciprocated with a tight squeeze. His conscience nagged at him, but he pushed aside the guilt. It was all a formality now, a means to get what he wanted in the end. In due time, she would grow weary of his frequent absences and break up with him on her own terms. As he ran his fingers through her thick, curly hair, Jamal gazed out the window at the busy workers preparing their plane for takeoff. Just like they were ensuring everything was in order for a smooth flight, Jamal wanted to make sure this weekend went according to plan as well—for the sake of his sanity.

They had been in the air for less than four hours. To make the most of

Chapter 5

their first day on the island, they left early in the morning. It took them less than two hours to disembark, go through customs, and get picked up by their private transfer, a much faster process than Jamal had expected. He had experienced long lines and delays on previous trips out of the country when going through the entry procedures. But today, the heat only added to his discomfort. It was still summer, and the sweltering island sun was almost unbearable, even with the mild breeze in the air. He was grateful to finally arrive at their luxurious hotel where they would stay for the next few days.

"This place is beautiful!" Angela praised once their driver opened her door, and she stepped out.

Jamal admitted, upon observation, the all-inclusive, adults-only 3,000-acre property was impressive. With sixteen different restaurants serving international cuisine, eleven bars offering unlimited drinks, various water sports, live entertainment shows, golfing, and a spa, there was no shortage of things to do at Royal Suites Curaçao. While they waited for their check-in process to be completed, a hostess offered them a beverage. Jamal politely declined and requested for their room to be "dry" during their stay. He wanted to remove any temptation for Angela by keeping alcohol out of the room. However, if he needed a drink—and he was certain he would—he planned to visit one of the bars on-site. A few minutes later, they were being escorted to where they would stay for the next three days.

Angela's eyes lit up when she heard about their bungalow on the coast at the far end of the property. "Really?"

Jamal nodded his head toward the concierge. Beaming proudly, the young man in a white shirt and navy shorts motioned for them to get into the golf cart, their luggage already inside.

Angela gave her praises again. "I'm loving everything about this place."

"Just wait until you see where you'll be staying for the next few nights, Mrs. Edwards."

"We're not married." Jamal promptly corrected him.

As soon as the words left his mouth, he saw Angela's uneasy expression. Her voice dropped low, but Jamal was certain the young man heard when she snapped back.

"You didn't have to say it like that."

"No use in pretending, sweetheart," Jamal replied bluntly with a seriousness that he did not waver from.

Angela's lips pressed into a straight line, like a taut rope. It wasn't a lie. The last thing Jamal wanted was for anyone at the resort to assume Angela was his wife. The concierge cleared his throat and pointed out various amenities as they continued on their way to the room.

"Over there is where you can go to grab a bite to eat without the worry of getting dressed up or making a reservation."

In the distance, the young man gestured to a row of vibrant food trucks parked in a courtyard with scattered tables around them.

Angela nudged Jamal, pointing out, "There's a lot to choose from."

"Yes ma'am, the food trucks offer a variety of options. They're open from noon until 5. If you miss it, there's a café nearby. And don't forget about the butler service available to you. Here at Royal Suites, you won't run out of food to eat or activities to keep yourselves busy."

Less than five minutes later, they arrived in front of their room. Jamal opened the door to their bungalow while the young man removed their luggage from the cart. Once the concierge provided him with the extension to reach their butler service, Jamal gave him a generous tip and joined Angela in the expansive space. He was awestruck by the bungalow's luxurious features: elegant grey hardwood floors, high vaulted ceilings, and a custom-made king-size bed that begged for them to sink into it. The bathroom's spa-like atmosphere featured his-and-hers sinks, a spacious walk-in rain shower, and a stunning backlit mirror accented by mosaic tiles.

Jamal stepped outside to a secluded private patio complete with a sprawling sun deck, a soaking tub draped with privacy curtains, and plush loungers that were perfect for basking in the island sun. Nestled on the edge of the coast, the bungalow offered breathtaking views of the Caribbean Sea, with a private infinity pool providing the perfect vantage point to soak in the majestic beauty of the azure waters. Beyond them, the ocean stretched into the horizon, its constant crashing waves providing a peaceful soundtrack. A light sea breeze and subtle scent of salt filled Jamal's nostrils when he breathed in the fresh air.

Chapter 5

Angela twirled around and exclaimed, "Jamal, this is absolutely amazing!"

"Yeah. It is pretty amazing. What do you want to get into first?"

"I wanna get out of these travel clothes and into my bathing suit."

"Sounds like a plan. Let's go."

Without wasting another minute, they changed into clothing more appropriate for the balmy weather on the island of Curaçao. While Angela opted for a hot pink bikini with an off white, flowy cover-up dress, Jamal sported a shorts set adorned with prints of coconut trees and tropical plants. After getting dressed, they decided to have a meal at the beachside café they'd spotted earlier. By the time they arrived, most of the lunch crowd had dispersed. This meant that there were tables available on the outside patio, overlooking the ocean—just as Angela had requested.

"Do you think we'll have a chance to do any excursions?" she asked after they sat down at their table with water and coffee.

Without looking up from his menu, Jamal answered in a flippant tone, "I don't know, sweetheart. There's a lot to do. Did you look at the app like they told you?"

"No. But I figured we could do something simple but fun and romantic. Is there anything you wanna do?"

"We can do whatever you want. I got us here," he shrugged, his eyes remaining on the vibrant page filled with images of delicious-looking dishes.

It didn't matter to him. His focus was deciding between the enticing eggs Florentine with fresh spinach and creamy hollandaise sauce or opting for the classic eggs Benedict with Canadian ham.

Angela kissed her teeth and complained. "I want you to have a say in what we do, too. I don't wanna choose something and then you're not having fun."

Sighing, Jamal lowered the menu. "Sweetheart, I just asked if you checked the app. We only have two more days here. It's not a lot we can do. But I'm good with whatever you decide. Just pick something."

His tone may have come off harsher than he intended, but Jamal was over it. She was really irking his nerves. He needed something to eat before he snapped at Angela again. With the foldable plastic card before his face, he rolled his eyes and regretted agreeing to come on this trip. All Jamal wanted was to be back at home with Christian. He wondered what his lover was up to. Was Christian missing him? Instead of going on an excursion with Angela, Jamal would much rather spend some time talking to Christian over a video call. He needed to ditch Angela so he could make that happen.

"Are you ready to order?"

The sound of their server's voice yanked Jamal out of his thoughts. He set the menu down and met Angela's intense stare. *Great. Now she had an attitude.* Unfazed, Jamal casually nodded in her direction. "I'm ready, if you are, sweetheart."

Without answering him, Angela rattled off her order to the young lady in the white blouse and beige slacks, who scribbled away on her notepad. When she finished, Jamal gave his request for the eggs Florentine, a side of crispy red potatoes, and a bowl of fresh fruit. The minute their server walked away, Angela didn't hesitate to start up again about the excursions. This time she had her device in hand pointing.

"Okay. Since you want me to choose, how about we do this jet ski tour that goes all around Caracas Bay to the Spanish Water. Says here that it's about an hour. They'll pick us up from the lobby at nine."

"Let's do it."

"Cool! Let me see if it's available." Angela returned to her phone, eagerly scrolling through options and squealing with excitement. "And maybe we can try to fit in an ATV ride, explore the city on electric scooters, or go on a tour. Oh wait, how about a couples' massage! We could definitely fit at least one of these in."

"Whatever you decide, sweetheart."

For the rest of their meal, they engaged in idle chatter about insignificant topics. Jamal played his role as the doting boyfriend, pretending to care about whatever Angela said. She seemed content now that they had a jet ski tour scheduled. As much as he dreaded taking part in this activity with her, there was no way out without causing a fight. Jamal had to go along with it.

Chapter 5

After leaving the café, they strolled down the path that led them to the highlight of the resort: a two-tier infinity pool on spacious upper and lower decks with breathtaking, endless views of the Spanish Water. There, he and Angela spotted an unoccupied oversized lounger. Jamal plopped down on it, admiring the crystal-clear, blue water in front of them. In the tiki hut's shade, the DJ spun a Soca mix which included "Turn Me On" by Kevin Lyttle, keeping the mood lively and the guests in high spirits. The aroma of barbecue blended with the salty tang of the ocean. Jamal relaxed deeper into the plush cushions of the chaise lounge, savoring the momentary peace and calm.

Angela set her beach bag down on the open space next to him. "Be right back. I'm gonna look around."

Jamal gave a distracted nod, swiping open his phone to queue up the next segment of the podcast he'd started during the flight. Once Angela had wandered a few feet away, he switched to a different app: LetzChat—the one he used to talk to Christian.

He glanced up and spotted Angela chatting with a woman who easily commanded attention—rich mahogany skin, legs that stretched for miles, and long braids swinging down to her lower back. The lime green bikini she wore didn't leave much to the imagination. A year ago, Jamal would've taken notice, maybe even stolen a second glance.

Back then, Angela had taken up space in every corner of his thoughts. She was sexy, undeniably beautiful, and the one woman he had wanted just as badly as his ex-wife, Desiree—maybe more. At five-foot-six with a slim, yet curvy, chestnut-brown frame, Angela filled out her scrubs in all the right ways. Her skin glowed under any light, and that long, jet-black, curly hair spilling past her shoulders always smelled of fresh mangoes and coconuts. Her exotic look— those sharp eyes and full lips—had once been absolutely breathtaking to him.

But things were different now. Everything had shifted.

His thoughts didn't linger on Angela or the woman in green. They were on someone else entirely—someone leaner. Less curvy. Someone with a sharper tongue, and a firmer touch. A man who had crept into his life and taken hold of his heart in ways he hadn't expected.

His fingers moved swiftly over the device, a smile tugging at the corner of his mouth.

> Hey lover, what're you up to? Miss me yet? ~Jamie

After a few seconds, the bouncing bubbles appeared on the screen. Jamal smiled, releasing a sigh of relief. Since Curaçao was an hour ahead, he'd been hoping that Christian would be online and able to talk.

> Hey! Hanging out with a couple of friends. Of course I miss you. Frfr I'd rather be having you for brunch. How's everything going? ~Chris

> It's boring. Like you said I'd rather be what you're having for brunch. As soon as I get a free moment I'll call ~Jamie

> Food just got here. Don't wanna be rude. Call me later ~Chris

> Send me some pics ~Jamie

> When you send me yours ~Chris

Jamal's boldness in sending that last message surprised even him. He'd never solicited nude photos from anyone. But it was Christian. With him, Jamal let his inhibitions go. He'd already had sex in public. *Why not?*

Jamal rose from his seat and headed for the men's restroom they had passed on their way to the pool area. He stepped inside and made a beeline for the last stall, not hesitating to pull out his dick. The memory of their last night together replayed in his mind as he stroked himself to full length. Once satisfied with the photos he took, Jamal couldn't calm down. He needed to release the built-up tension.

"Ssss." Jamal's low grunt filled the air, thrusting his hips back and forth into his fisted palm and imagining Christian's mouth wrapped around his rigid organ.

Chapter 5

He leaned forward, using the back of the stall for support and pressing his left hand against the cold plaster wall. Memories of Christian's skilled technique flooded Jamal's thoughts, bringing him to the edge of ecstasy. Christian was so good at giving him oral pleasure. From flicking his tongue around his swollen helmet to gently sucking on his balls, Christian drove Jamal wild with desire every time.

So fucking good. Jamal started tugging harder and jerking faster, chasing after the nut building in his loins. Disappointed that it wasn't Christian's throat, Jamal begrudgingly settled for the toilet bowl as his target. The first rope of his lusty release splashed in the water below. He quickly grabbed his phone and took a few more pictures, sending them off to Christian as a reminder of what they were missing out on together.

> Here you go. Make sure you're spread wide. And it's winking at me. ~Jamie

Jamal cleaned himself up in haste. He stepped out of the restroom, almost colliding with Angela.

"Oops. I'm sorr—oh hey, sweetheart. Are you okay?"

"Hey! Yeah, yeah. I'm fine. How about you? I saw when you went in. And you were in there for a while."

Dragging a hand across his waves, the lie slid off Jamal's tongue as slippery as a snake. "Yeah. It must've been something in those eggs or that hollandaise sauce. But I got it out, I feel a lot better now."

∼

Unlike Angela, Jamal placed a lot of importance on being punctual. He glanced down at his watch, grumbling under his breath at her disregard for timeliness. He raised a finger to signal to the guy waiting for them in the cart. As he closed the door to their bungalow, he called out to her.

"Angela, come on! We need to go. The guy is here to take us up to the lobby."

"Okay! Okay! Here I come," she shouted back, racing from the bedroom with two pairs of sneakers in her hands. Angela held them up and asked, slightly out of breath, "Which one do you think matches my outfit better?"

Are you fucking kidding me? Jamal removed his designer sunglasses and didn't hide the eyeroll when he huffed. "Does it matter? They both match. Just pick a pair and let's go. We're late as it is."

Without waiting for her to respond, Jamal slipped the shades back on and headed for the door to their bungalow. He opened it, expecting Angela to walk out before him. When he turned his head to look back, Jamal found she was standing where he'd left her. Angela shot him the dirtiest of looks.

The nerve of this fucking woman to have an attitude. "What's the problem now, Angela?"

"You are, Jamal!" Angela tossed aside the black pair. She slid her foot into the white sneaker while griping, "Ever since last night you've been in a funky-ass mood."

"Ask yourself why."

"Oh my god! Are you really mad at me about that, Jamal?"

What do you think? Behind his dark sunglasses, he hid an eye roll. He had meticulously picked out an ideal beachside restaurant with a sundeck view for a delightful five-course dinner, but Angela invited the scantily clad woman she had met by the pool and her husband to join them. The upscale, sophisticated experience was spoiled by this couple from Alabama with their uncouth, hillbilly manners. Naturally, he was pissed off about the previous night, and Jamal didn't hesitate to voice his annoyance to Angela.

"Mad? No. Was I irritated? Hell yeah! Because you were nagging me and complaining about wanting us to spend more time together. What was the point of coming on this trip, huh? Why would you invite two complete strangers to have dinner with us? They were acting like loud, country-ass idiots!" Jamal yelled while he shook his head in frustration.

Angela winced, her lower lip quivering. "First of all, can you lower your voice when you talk to me? And, I didn't realize I was complaining or nagging you, Jamal. I just wanted to spend time with my man who is all of a sudden too busy for me."

Chapter 5

"Don't go there. You know I'm—"

"No, Jamal. Don't *you* go there. I know you're up for this big promotion, but you haven't made time for us. And you're right. That is what this trip is about. I should've made sure you were cool with me inviting them to eat with us." Angela finished tying her sneakers and stood up straight, facing him directly. "I apologize, okay? But you didn't have to give me the cold shoulder and be this rude about it."

Although every fiber of his being wanted to argue, he looked back out at the young man who'd been sitting in the cart, waiting patiently, engrossed in his device. Jamal let out a heavy breath and conceded. "You're right, sweetheart. I didn't. I apologize. Now, come on. We have to go."

They reached the lobby to find several groups of people waiting by several parked buses. Individuals with uniforms and clipboards directed everyone where to go. They climbed out of the cart and walked over to the bus that had a mural of various recreational activities including water skiing, parasailing, and jet skiing painted along its side. A young man wearing a red cap, yellow shirt, and khaki shorts smiled and extended a warm greeting.

"Good morning! Would you happen to be Jamal Edwards and Angela Washington?"

"Yes. We are." Jamal answered, ushering them closer to the bus.

"Great! We've been waiting for you. Climb on in and we'll be on our way!"

Jamal assisted Angela up the short set of stairs into the cabin of their chartered bus. They weren't a few feet past the first row when a voice had Jamal clenching his teeth.

"Look, babe it's our peeps! Our favorite ATLiens in da hi-zouse! Ay, whaddup yo?"

This cornball. Jamal forced a smile and dipped his head in their direction. He placed a hand on the small of Angela's back, guiding her to the only available seats that were several rows up from the couple. This was exactly where Jamal wanted to be—as far away from them as possible. The moment they settled in and were on their way to the destination, Jamal leaned in with a question.

"Did they tell you they were coming too?"

"No. I had no idea."

"Hmm."

"What's that's supposed to mean?"

"It's funny that they're on this bus and didn't mention anything about it," Jamal retorted, his voice echoing through the semi-quiet cabin.

Angela looked around before answering in a hushed tone. "Why would they? It never came up."

Unconvinced, Jamal replied, "They talked about everything else they did on this island before we got here and all of their plans for the rest of the weekend. You did too. So, I find it odd."

"Why does it matter?" Angela shrugged and whispered back, "We won't even be around them."

"Good. And if they do try and talk to us, I'm counting on you to handle it. Because I don't have the energy for them," Jamal muttered, turning his body to face the window.

Without another word, he jammed his earbuds into his ears. Inside he seethed. Not only were they the last ones to arrive at the lobby. To make matters worse, that couple he didn't care for were also there, on their excursion. Angela had to have known about it, he thought bitterly. Now they were heading to do an activity that Jamal had absolutely no interest participating in. His regret for agreeing to this trip only intensified. All he wanted was to be back home, away from this mess and with Christian. Jamal swiped through his podcasts until he found his favorite one and cranked up the volume, shutting out the rest of the world. Determined not to speak to Angela for the rest of the ride, he closed his eyes.

"Babe, wake up. We're here."

Jamal didn't realize he'd dozed off. Stretching his arms above his head, Jamal peered out the window. They were now parked in front of a white commercial building with black trim. Other passengers had begun unloading from the bus. Jamal reached under the seat to grab his stowed backpack and joined Angela in the aisle. Everyone trailed behind the man who had called out their names in the lobby, following him through the double glass doors.

Chapter 5

"Good morning, everyone and welcome to Curaçao Coast Tours!" A tall, brown-skinned man wearing sunglasses with the same red cap, yellow shirt and khaki shorts waved to them. "I'm happy you all could join us here at CCT! My name is Daniel, and you already know my friend here, Gilbert, who drove you to our beautiful beach. We will be your guides today while you're touring our lovely waters."

Daniel excitedly informed the group they would spend the next hour riding Seadoo GTX jet skis and promised breathtaking views of the ocean and a quick trip to a nearby lagoon. First, he showed how to operate the touring personal watercraft and its various components. Then, Gilbert took over to explain the safety rules for being out on the water as a group and what was expected of each person.

"If you are the passenger on the back, we ask that you do not lean too much. Otherwise, you will cause the jet ski to flip over. And before you ask, yes. All of you will have life vests on. But we're letting you know this is what will happen. It's not fun when you're going too fast. Also, no standing up or doing tricks. If we catch you out there breaking any of the rules, we will ask you to stop, and you will come back. No refunds. Any other questions before we head out?"

A few arms shot up. Daniel and Gilbert took turns answering them. Meanwhile, other staff members helped Jamal, Angela, and the rest of the group complete their consent forms. Next, they proceeded to the bathrooms and lockers to use the facilities, change, and store their personal items. Everyone received and fastened their life jackets before departure. Finally, they gathered at the dock where a line of jet skis awaited them. Every rider took their time climbing onto the watercrafts. Jamal got on their jet ski first, then outstretched his hand to help Angela get on behind him. She wrapped her arms tightly around his waist and pressed her thighs against his.

"Ay! Whaddup peeps? Y'all ready to brave some waves?"

Jamal thought Angela said they wouldn't be anywhere near them. Yet, the boisterous man and his wife from Alabama had found their way to the side of the dock where they were. He tapped Angela on the upper thigh.

"There go *your* peeps."

Angela waved. "Hey! You know we are! Make sure you keep up!"

"Now why would you say that to him?" Jamal angled his head, throwing her a dirty look and scoffed, "You know damn well we don't need him playing around with us in this ocean."

"And you heard what those guys said in there. I highly doubt he'd risk blowing their money and being told they have to come back for breaking the rules."

"You better hope so."

"What is your problem with them, Jamal? You didn't even try to get to know them. They were really nice to us last night."

"Why are you ready to hang out with other people? This weekend was supposed to be about us, right?"

"Jamal, I—"

"No, Angela. You wanted a weekend away from my job, interruptions, and everybody else. You got that. So why are you so ready to be up in other people's faces? How about you be in mine. Unless you're trying to swing."

Right as Angela opened her mouth, Gilbert blew a whistle, waving from his position on a jet ski several feet away from the group.

"My friends! Are we ready?"

A chorus of 'yeah' resounded from the other riders. Jamal heard Angela let out a frustrated sigh when she leaned against him once more, but not in the loving way she had earlier. He knew she wasn't feeling how he spoke to her just now. But it was hard for him not to be annoyed with her for being too friendly with that guy moments ago. Jamal didn't want him or his wife riding alongside them for even a minute, let alone the next hour. Absolutely not. In fact, in that second, he didn't even want Angela riding behind him anymore.

Another whistle blew.

"Riders, start your engines and let's go!"

Jamal followed Daniel's instructions: turning the ignition switch and pushing the throttle, he steered them forward using the handlebars. The group cruised about five to ten miles per hour until they were away from the shoreline. They picked up speed, jumping a wave and causing Jamal's

Chapter 5

adrenaline to surge. He was happy they'd gotten goggles, which shielded his eyes from the spray of ocean water. The experience was actually thrilling. Angela's squeals were being drowned out by the constant revving of the engine, but he could tell she was enjoying herself. Peering up ahead, he saw Gilbert waving to the group to veer to the left. Jamal tapped Angela's thigh and showed his intended direction.

The landscape was unlike anything he'd seen previously. He marveled at the pristine sands, swaying palm trees, and rugged limestone cliffs they passed. The natural rock formations jutted out from the glistening turquoise waters. The salty mist continued to kiss his skin as they sped over the sea, which shone like a precious gem. After cruising for a little while, everyone dispersed with the separate guides. Out of nowhere, the Alabama couple appeared on Jamal's right. He pretended not to see them and maneuvered the watercraft away, heading to another open area. However, the guy kept up, waving them down.

"Ay, whaddup my peeps!"

Ugh. This guy, again. Jamal wished he would take a hint and leave him the fuck alone. He turned the jet ski around and ditched them. Angela's grip on him tightened.

She pressed her thighs closer to his and shouted, "Jamal! You're going too fast. Slow down!"

He wasn't going to do that. Not when that annoying couple wanted to hang around them. Jamal saw Gilbert had gone the other way. He followed suit and proceeded over there, revving up the engine, accelerating to turn. However, he miscalculated the speed of the jet ski at that angle. Angela let out a piercing scream when their watercraft flew into the air and capsized, submerging them under water.

Jamal didn't panic. Besides being a strong swimmer, his life vest quickly brought him to the surface. He looked around for Angela. She wasn't far. Clutching onto the rear of the overturned jet ski, Jamal reached out for her.

"You, okay?" he shouted over the sound of splashing waves.

Angela nodded, coughing out water. Jamal positioned himself to push the jet ski upright. With a grunt of exertion, he turned it over. They both climbed back onto the watercraft. Gilbert had arrived by then to check on them.

"Hey, you good, my friend? I didn't know you were trying to follow me. My mistake."

"Yeah, we're fine. No worries. I didn't give you the heads up," Jamal brushed it off and adjusted his goggles.

Gilbert did a quick, but thorough check of the jet ski to make sure it was still operable. He also expressed relief when he saw that neither of them had been hurt. After he left to rejoin the rest of their group, Angela didn't waste time chiding Jamal.

"I told you to slow down. What were you thinking when you sped up like that?"

"Please, Angela."

"Don't 'please Angela' me, Jamal." She snapped, shaking her head and sending water droplets flying from her hair in all directions.

"Whaddup peeps? You over there doing tricks?"

"Why can't this corny muthafucka take a hint?" Jamal grumbled under his breath, refusing to respond. He didn't bother looking up. There was no reason to pretend. Jamal had no intention of interacting with them. As he'd told Angela, she would have to deal with her new acquaintances. He would not put on an act for their benefit. It was Angela who invited them to dinner without asking him first, and now they were acting like they were best friends. Their boisterous voices and laughter yanked Jamal from his thoughts.

"No. We're fine. Go ahead. We'll catch up with y'all. Thanks!"

What the hell? Jamal turned to look at her and barked. "Now, why did you just tell him that? We're not catching up with them. Unless you plan on hanging out with them by yourself."

"What is your problem, Jamal?"

"My problem is you, Angela. Did you come on this trip to be on an island surrounded by bama muthafuckas or be with me?" Jamal's voice rose in anger.

"I can't believe you're yelling at me right now. It's not that serious."

Chapter 5

"It is. I told you I didn't want to be around them. He's annoying, and his wife eggs his ignorance on."

"All I wanted was to enjoy this weekend. You're ruining it arguing with me over something so stupid."

"I'm not ruining anything. You are. And you could've enjoyed yourself if you had followed these four simple rules. One: don't invite random people to join us for dinner. Two: make sure I'm okay with it first. Three: set an alarm or get out of bed on time so we won't be late for the activity *you* planned. And finally, no new fucking friends!"

"Wow. I'm sorry for being late. But we made it here, right? I just wanted to have a good time. Is that so wrong? And they're not that bad."

"Yes! It's wrong on all levels. And what do you mean, not that bad? Have you somehow forgotten they were already drunk and kept asking for more drinks? Even after we told them no and that you stopped drinking, they still tried to offer you something. You shouldn't be around the temptation. And I hate being late. That shit grinds my gears, Angela. And for the last time, I thought this trip was about us."

"This trip is about us. Stop making it about them! I didn't think it would be this big of a deal, Jamal. They seemed nice, and I thought it would be fun to have dinner together."

"You thought wrong. It's a big deal because you went out of your way to be friendly without being considerate of my feelings."

The tears welled in Angela's eyes. "I didn't realize it would bother you so much, Jamal. I promise I wasn't trying to disrespect our time together."

Jamal's expression softened a bit once he saw the distress on her face. However, his emotions remained the same. He had no intention of spending any time with that couple from Alabama. All he wanted was to make it through one more day on the island and return home. Jamal placed a hand on her arm, speaking in a gentler tone. "Sweetheart, it's important that we communicate about these things and make decisions together."

After brushing away a stray tear, Angela nodded. "I understand, Jamal. I'll be more mindful in the future and talk to you before making plans."

Before Jamal could respond, a loud whistle pierced through the air. He saw Daniel signaling for the group to gather. It was time to head back to the dock. Angela didn't say anything but leaned in and wrapped her arms around him. Jamal navigated the jet ski to stay with the rest of the group. While everyone else yelled and cheered in excitement, Angela remained quiet with her head resting on his back. Jamal figured she was still upset. Oh well. None of this would've happened if she had left that couple alone.

The silence between them continued even as they boarded the bus to return to Royal Suites. Jamal plugged in his headphones and listened to a podcast while Angela mindlessly scrolled through her social media feeds. Once they arrived at the resort, Jamal rushed them off the bus to avoid talking to the couple. He was glad Angela didn't put up a fuss about it. But as soon as they walked inside their bungalow and Jamal closed the door, Angela spun around on him. She marched right up to him, getting in his face and pointed an accusing finger.

"I can't believe you would embarrass me like that! What in the hell has gotten into you, Jamal? I'm so sorry I didn't talk to you and ask if they could kick it with us. And sorry they weren't bougie enough or up to your standards. Mack and Kema are actually cool as hell. But you wouldn't know that 'cause you thought they were country. Okay, they were loud. So what! Who don't we know from the south that isn't? And I know we were here so we could spend time together alone, but people come on vacations and meet new people from all over the world! What did it hurt having dinner with them, Jamal? It was just dinner! They weren't forcing drinks down my throat, as you put it. And they weren't trying to hang out with us. We just happened to run into them. What you did out there just to avoid them was totally uncalled for. All because you couldn't stand to be around them. We could've gotten hurt!" Angela shouted, her chest heaving.

Jamal swatted her finger out his face. "But we didn't get hurt, did we? No. And I'm going to stand by what I said. You wanted this weekend getaway, so it was supposed to be about us. Nobody else. Not even for dinner," he retorted.

Chapter 5

"What is wrong with you?"

"I already told you. This weekend would've been perfect. We would've been great. But you fucked it up when you had to go and invite them bama muthafuckas. They ruined my whole mood."

"Do you even care about what's going on between us anymore?"

"Now what are you talking about?" Jamal huffed, throwing his hands up.

"I'm talking about us!"

"Don't yell at me, Angela. Talk to me in a calm manner. You can get your point across without all this attitude."

Angela rotated her neck and rolled her eyes. "Don't tell me how to talk to you, Jamal. Not when you been getting loud and poppin' a funky attitude with me since we've been here. There's obviously something going on between us that we need to talk about."

Jamal understood fully what she was referring to, but he played along, cocking his head to the side. "Like what?"

"Like, when was the last time we fucked, Jamal?"

"If you think I keep a calendar of that, no. I don't know, but what're you getting at?"

"That's the fucking problem! Do you even realize that you've barely touched me in weeks! I wanted to come here so we could spend some time alone together."

Jamal didn't bother holding back the snort. "Now, that's funny. Because if that's what you wanted, some dick, I couldn't tell with you being up in *Mack* and *Kema's* faces last night."

"Ugh! Why are you back on them?!"

"I'm not saying another word if you keep yelling at me."

"I'm upset right now, Jamal! What do you expect? We used to talk all the time. Even when you were married, we talked more. Now? I barely get to see you, let alone talk to you anymore. You think I didn't notice the last time when you couldn't get it up? Yeah. It never took you long to get hard. So, who are you fucking Jamal? And don't gimme that bullshit about how work is stressing you out!"

And this is precisely why I got rid of your brother's nagging ass. Jamal retorted, "Perhaps you're feeling on edge now that you can't drown it in a bottle. But you're going to stop yelling at me, Angela." Jamal folded his arms across his chest and gave her a serious look.

Angela's jaw dropped before she clamped it shut. She shook her head. "That's real fucking low coming from you."

"Yeah, well, I'm not sure how to take the high road here. I've never had my woman do the shit you've been doing. Keep track of time better because I hate being late. When it's supposed to be just us, let it be just us. And all this shouting? I'm not okay with it. So, stop it. I don't know the type of men you've been with before, but now that we're together, it's not happening. My ex-wife didn't act like this. And neither will you."

"I-I-I don't even know what to say anymore. You're acting like a completely different person right now," Angela scoffed, storming off toward the bedroom.

Yeah, well I am. Get used to it. Jamal was unfazed. The juggling act was tiring him out. He wanted a simpler solution to his dilemma. Now that Angela was back home and in her usual routine, she wasn't as fragile as he'd presumed. She would be fine. Another man would be better suited for her. His goal now was to have her end the relationship on her own terms. Jamal figured if he became a less-than-ideal boyfriend, Angela would decide to break up with him, sparing him the task.

Angela stayed in the bedroom for another hour without coming out. Jamal didn't see the need to check on her. Instead, he concentrated on devising a plan to leave the suite. He needed to chat with Christian. Knowing Angela's routines, eventually she would come out to eat and soon after, head to bed. Checking his watch, a smile formed across his face. It wouldn't be long. He just had to be patient.

Minutes later, Angela emerged. As expected, she stepped out to contact the butler for room service. When their dinner arrived, they ate in silence. Jamal had nothing else to say. Angela seemed perfectly content eating and watching television. After finishing her meal, Angela showered and retired to bed without uttering a word to him. That was his cue.

Jamal slipped from the room. He headed directly to the bar, downing several shots to calm his nerves after the argument and the earlier events of

Chapter 5

the day, before proceeding to the business center for an uninterrupted video call with Christian. It had been over twelve hours since their last conversation. He missed Christian terribly. Jamal wished he had a private space to indulge in some phone sex, and he hated having to lie about being stuck in a late meeting. Even though he wished he could talk to Christian all night, Jamal kept their conversation short.

"And what're you doing when you get back?" Christian asked with a grin on his face, as he peered into the camera.

With a mischievous grin playing on his lips, Jamal answered, "As soon as I step off that plane, I'm coming straight home to slide up in you."

6

TRAINING STARTS TODAY

"Ang, you two were supposed to be going away to reconnect and figure out what's going on between y'all. How could he blame you for turning it into a complete disaster?" Mia asked, gesturing with her toiletry bag toward the screen.

Angela didn't respond. Instead, she watched Mia toss the bulky pouch into her suitcase before moving on to gather piles of clothing from around her room, arranging them on the bed. Her best friend was busy packing, preparing to join her husband in Las Vegas. Twirling a lock between her fingers, Angela sighed. She had no answer to Mia's question—at least, not one that felt right. After the jet ski incident and the argument that ensued, she and Jamal barely said two words to each other. Angela didn't understand what the issue was with her introducing herself to that couple and inviting them for dinner. She didn't think it should've been such a big deal to speak to them the next day either. Jamal's behavior was uncalled for. No. It was an embarrassment. Their argument had escalated into him speaking to her in a way she'd never heard before. And it wasn't her fault. He was the one that turned their romantic getaway into one of the worst trips she'd ever been on.

After returning from Curaçao, things went back to the way they were before—long days with extra shifts and emergency surgeries for Jamal. Angela hardly saw him. She didn't want to accept that they were growing apart. But the writing was on the wall. Her anxiety grew as the weekend approached. Jamal was leaving for another conference and wouldn't be back until the following week.

"So, how was it your fault?" Mia's question interrupted Angela's thoughts. "Better yet, y'all came back and he's been ghost. He's gonna bounce again this weekend, addressing nothing that happened last week. What's up with that, Ang?"

She didn't respond. She didn't get the chance. Her mother stormed into the living room, unleashing a barrage of cuss words in Spanish and English.

"That hijo de puta took her outta the country just to embarrass her. Pendejo! He thinks 'cause he's this doctor or whatever, he can talk to her any ol' kinda way. I know she ain't from no bougie ass . . ." Bianca paused for a beat. She looked at Angela and asked, "Where the hell you said he's from in Jersey?"

"Glen Ridge, Mamá," she answered, shaking her head.

Bianca waved a dismissive hand and continued on her rant. "Lo que. Anyway, he acts like he's better than mi bebé. Que se joda!"

"Mamá!"

"No, Angela! Fuck him! You say that Tré knew him. Cómo? I don't believe he did. 'Cause he never would've let this stuck up puto treat you like this."

"Exactly Mamá! He's a stuck up puto!" Mia interjected enthusiastically. "I could tell that when I met his bougie ass. And you know she's right, Ang. Tré would've done his background check on him. I wonder if he found something suspicious, but never got the chance to tell you," she mused, wagging a designer sunglasses case at the screen.

Her best friend caught her off guard with that comment. The memory of Tré's warning replayed in her mind: *"You can keep hiding whatever it is about him you don't want me to know, but the truth will come out. And when it does . . ."*

Chapter 6

If Tré had discovered that she was in a relationship with one of his married friends, it was hard to predict what his reaction might've been. Her brother's tendency to bully others and the thought of him finding out about Jamal's infidelity and their secret affair made her shudder. She was well aware of the lengths Tré would go to to protect her reputation. He undoubtedly would've told their mother about it, which would've only escalated the situation.

Bianca spoke, breaking through Angela's reverie. "Mia's right. Tu hermano would've handled this with a background check by now. But no worries. Simeon's looking into it. He'll take care of that puto."

"What do you mean, Simeon is looking into it? And how will he take care of Jamal, Mamá? What did you say to him?"

"Wait, did I miss something? Who's Simeon?" Mia asked, moving in closer to the phone screen.

Her mother turned, raising a brow. "You didn't tell her about *our* friend?"

Angela's cheeks grew warm as a flush spread across her face. It was undeniable that her childhood friend had an effect on her. But what was Simeon looking into? Angela shook her head.

"No, Mamá. I didn't tell Mia about him. Now you tell me, what is Simeon doing looking into my man?"

"That right there is why! El es un chico. He's not a man! No man would've treated the woman he loves like this. Tu eres el premio. You hear me, mija? *You* are the prize. If he was *your man*, he would put in the work and figure out how to fix this. Y'all haven't talked all week! What kinda bullshit is that? He hasn't even tried," Bianca criticized, making a point to roll her eyes.

It was difficult for Angela to defend Jamal, especially when her own mother continued to bring up his flaws and disrespect in their relationship. All she wanted was for things to go back to the way they were before Tré died. Just then the doorbell rang. Angela hopped up, her eyes widening in disbelief.

"Mamá, is that—"

"Sì!" she replied with a mischievous grin. Angela couldn't stop her in time. "Espera un momento. Be right back," Bianca tossed over her shoulder, darting out of the living room.

Angela's eyes rolled to her iPhone screen, meeting Mia's inquisitive stare. She had some explaining to do. After all, she had kept her in the dark about Simeon. But what could she say? Except that her childhood friend had grown up to be a fine-ass man that was educated, successful, funny, and now he had Angela and her lady parts struggling to remain loyal. After that trip from hell and not getting her back blown out, the idea of hooking up with Simeon crossed Angela's mind for a split second. However, she quickly dismissed the notion.

"Umm, hello? Wanna tell me who this Simeon character is? Mamá sure seems excited about him."

Sighing, Angela shrugged but looked back before quickly replying. "There's nothing to tell. Simeon's nobody really."

"Oh, he's somebody if Mamá is acting like that."

"That's because he's been coming to check on her. I've known him since I was a kid. He's a little older than me, but we grew up around here together. So, of course she likes him over Jamal. But I ain't hardly studying Simeon. Mamá's doing the most 'cause she don't want me with Jamal."

"Wait. That's him with the deep voice speaking Spanish?" Mia's eyebrows shot up.

Their voices had carried into the space, also getting Angela's attention. She turned to face the entrance of the living room and quietly confirmed, "Yeah. That's *him*."

A few seconds later, he appeared, ducking to clear the doorway, and stepped into the living room. Simeon's tall frame didn't stop moving until he was standing right in front of Angela, invading her personal space. The scent of his manliness flooded her senses. Angela's pussy gushed in excitement. She discreetly squeezed her thighs, wishing she had worn a pantyliner.

"Hey, Angela. How're you?"

"Umm, I'm good, thanks. You?"

"I'm good too, no complaints." Just then, an audible cough came

Chapter 6

from her device propped up on the coffee table. He flashed Mia a genuine smile, greeting her, "Oh, hi. Sorry, didn't know you were on a call."

"Don't be rude, mija." Bianca motioned toward Simeon and urged Angela, "Introduce our friend to her."

Angela peered up at Simeon. He blessed her by widening his mouth to reveal thirty-two teeth and those pits in his cheeks, which caused her heart to do a backflip. Feeling the heat warm her face, she quickly tore her eyes away.

"Uh Mia, this is Simeon Ingram. Like I told you, we grew up together. Simeon, this is my best friend, Mia Harris."

Simeon dipped his head in acknowledgement. "Nice to meet you, Mia."

"Likewise, Simeon," Mia replied, smiling back at him. Her glance slid to Angela—quick, deliberate—followed by a not-so-subtle nod and a wink.

What was that for? Angela thought to herself, but out of her peripheral vision she caught sight of her mother gesturing behind her.

When Angela turned, Bianca's movements halted, and she diverted her attention from them, acting as if everything was normal. But when Bianca and Simeon made eye contact, he didn't hide his smug grin. It dawned on Angela her mother was still trying to play matchmaker for her and Simeon. She'd actually convinced Mia to join "Team Simeon" without Bianca even saying a word.

Simeon spoke up with excitement, "So, you're best friends with the senator's daughter, who is also the wife of one of my favorite wide receivers. That's pretty dope, Angela."

"Yep, that's my girl. We've been thick as thieves since our days at Spelman. But I'll let her fill you in on all the details." Mia beamed proudly before addressing Angela. "I need to finish packing, Ang. I've got a plane to catch at the crack of dawn. But make sure you call me later. Love you Mamá!"

After their video call ended, Angela pocketed her phone. Her mother and Simeon were both standing there, watching her silently. An awkward pause stretched for a few seconds too long. Angela tucked a lock of hair behind her ear, pushing out a nervous laugh.

"Well, umm, I guess I'll get going, Mamá. Sorry I didn't plan on staying for dinner tonight if you and Simeon already had plans. Maybe I'll catch up with y'all next time."

"Mija, he's not here for my dinner. Are you, Simeon?"

"No, Mamá I'm not." His eyes remained on Angela when he replied in a tone that suggested more. "I'm here for you. Or rather to ask: would you care to have dinner with me?"

Yes! Wait. No. I can't! Angela's eyes bounced back and forth, torn between her mother's encouraging smile and the eagerness on Simeon's face. Conflicted, she was unsure of what to do next. It all seemed so unfair. She wasn't supposed to be attracted to anyone other than Jamal. However, she struggled miserably in that area. It was hard not being drawn to Simeon. So to avoid any complications, Angela decided it would be best if she didn't travel down that road. She finally shook her head from side to side.

"I don't think that's a good idea. You know I have a man. How would that look, me going out with you?"

Bianca scoffed, opening her mouth, ready to argue, but Simeon squeezed her arm, silencing her. "Mamá tengo esto. Don't worry. I got this. Te llamo mas tarde."

"Sí, okay. Let me finish dinner and give y'all some privacy. Gracias por todo, Simeon."

"You don't have to thank me Mamá. But you're always welcome." He bent forward giving a peck on her cheek.

Bianca responded with a soft pat to his face before turning to Angela. She hugged her tight and whispered, "Te quiero muchísimo, mija."

"I love you too, Mamá. You have a good night. Call you later, okay."

"Tú también. Qué tengas buenas noches."

Once they were alone, Angela was acutely aware of the charged atmosphere in the air. It was as if electrical currents were pulsing between her and Simeon. But she shouldn't allow herself to feel this way. What about Jamal? The thought screamed in the back of her mind. But Angela

Chapter 6

couldn't deny that her relationship with Jamal was falling apart. Ever since her brother's death, they had grown distant, and their bond had weakened. She was partly to blame for pushing Jamal away. Turning to the medications and wine to cope with Trè's death, she'd become unavailable emotionally and physically. He had been so patient with her, even saving her from a potential overdose that one night. After her brief stay in the psych ward, he remained with her throughout her time in rehab, which only strengthened her love for him. But now, she wondered if his feelings had changed. Was he cheating? She refused to accept that, especially when he was under so much pressure at the moment. Angela would not let lack of communication ruin what they had built together. To do that, she had to focus on repairing their relationship instead of entertaining lustful thoughts about another man.

"So, what do you say to that?" Simeon's soothing baritone broke through Angela's musings.

"I'm sorry. Say to what?" Angela asked, realizing she hadn't even heard his question.

Simeon let out a low throaty chuckle, holding up his phone. "I asked what do you say if we did a lil' rock climbing? And then I take you out for a bite to eat." Angela opened her mouth, but Simeon quickly added, "No strings attached. Look, I heard you loud and clear. You got a man. I can respect that. But Mamá is worried about you. I promised I would at least make sure you were really okay."

"First off, you don't need to make sure of anything. I'm good." She folded her arms under her breasts and joked, "But rock climbing? Who does that?"

"I do. Besides being a total body workout, it offers plenty of other benefits."

"Like what?"

"It helps reduce stress. It's great for mental health because it challenges the mind and enhances brain function. You might find it interesting. You're looking at a real-life Spider Man here."

"Boy, bye. I'll believe your big ass climbing a wall when I see it."

"So, that's a yes then?"

He said no strings attached. Angela shrugged, but then answered with a nod, "I guess. I'm not doing anything else."

"Great. Let's go. Just follow me."

Angela did just that. She followed Simeon's lead, keeping up with his confident strides. She also gave him a slow once-over, taking note of his easy gait and his wide shoulders. *Real-life Spider Man, eh?* Given his size, he could probably scale walls and beat hers up too. She bit her lip, shaking her head to dismiss the lusty thoughts of him. Her mother suddenly appeared from behind the wall that separated the living area from the rest of the house. With wide eyes, Angela realized she'd been caught ogling Simeon. Bianca's satisfied grin made it obvious that she had spied and eavesdropped on their conversation as well. Naturally, her mother would be thrilled about them going out together, but Angela needed to set things straight.

"Not happening, Mamá. I already got a man," she emphasized, shutting the door before her mother responded.

∼

The drive to the rock-climbing gym took less than thirty minutes. Angela parked in the space next to Simeon's black Silverado. After killing the engine and grabbing her purse from the passenger seat, she pulled the lever to open her door, but Simeon pushed back, closing it. She shot him a confused look. Shaking his head, he pointed to where her fingers were around the handle.

"Let it go."

Angela playfully cut her eyes at him but did as he instructed, allowing Simeon to be a gentleman. He'd done the same in front of her mother's house when they were leaving. Once Simeon opened the door, Angela placed her hand into his outstretched palm, which was double the size of hers. It was neither callous nor overly soft, but smooth and a perfect fit. He squeezed, giving a gentle tug to help her from the car. A chill traveled up her arm and rippled throughout her body, causing her skin to pebble. She snatched her hand away. Thinking it'd been too abrupt Angela stole a

Chapter 6

peek at him. His attention was on what was in front of them. She relaxed some, relieved he'd been oblivious to her reaction to his touch.

Simeon led her through the parking lot toward two industrial structures with gray vinyl siding. Etched onto the glass doors in white were the words "Crawl the Wall" and a graphic of a climber on a boulder. He held open one side of the entrance, allowing her to walk in ahead of him. Angela's eyes bounced around the spacious establishment, noting the lively atmosphere. The energetic beat of Imagine Dragons' "I Don't Know Why" filled the air from the surround sound system, adding to the bustling vibe of the gym. Small clusters of people were scattered throughout, engaged in conversation. A handful of children darted past them, their laughter filling the air. In the distance, climbers scaled the walls while their spotters kept a watchful eye below. This further piqued Angela's interest in Simeon's hobby.

"This whole place is indoor rock climbing?"

"Yep. We've got over thirty thousand square feet of climbing terrain in here. And that second building on the back is where the taller walls are," Simeon explained while guiding her to the reception area.

They walked past a workout room with floor-to-ceiling glass walls, showcasing various types of workout equipment. A few people were running on the treadmills, others were lifting weights on the benches, and one person was doing pull-ups on the bars. While in a typical gym, the air would be thick with the pungent aroma of sweat, here a subtle hint of deodorizer masked the combination of scents from chalk powder, rubber matting, and mild foot odor. Before they reached the large U-shaped desk, a man had emerged from an office door behind the receptionist. He had a lighter brown complexion, but the man's facial features, height and stature were very similar to Simeon's. He greeted them with a welcoming smile. Simeon had his hand out and his mysterious look-alike clasped it, pulling him in for a quick hug. They stepped back from each other, and Simeon made the introductions.

"Angela, this is my cousin Rocco, the owner of this gym. Roc, meet Angela, she's a friend of mine from the Mist."

"Aight, cool. Nice to meet you, Angela."

"You as well." She returned a polite smile. After looking around at the bustling gym, Angela confessed, "I've never been to a rock-climbing gym. I'm surprised to see there's a lot of us in here. Not trying to be funny, but this isn't exactly a 'Black' sport," she gestured with her fingers, making air quotes.

Compared to her, the two men looked like giants. They exchanged glances before erupting in laughter. Puzzled, Angela wondered what they found so funny.

"Hey, can I get in on this joke? Just so long as it's not about me."

"Sure, and it's not entirely about you. But we hear that all the time—people saying Black folks don't climb. That's a lie. Roc makes it his mission to challenge that idea every time he meets someone Black. And between the two of us? Let's just say we've got enough charm to make it real hard for anyone to turn down an invite," Simeon replied, touching her arm lightly.

Again, a tingling sensation shot through Angela's body the instant his palm made contact. Even after he removed it, the warmth lingered, and she longed for it to return. Angela covered the spot where his hand had been and rubbed, wondering how such a simple action caused so much stirring within. She fought to push it aside, telling herself it was nothing.

Just then, Roc's voice broke through Angela's thoughts. "Which is why I came out of the office to see my cuz. Here you are, this beautiful woman that I've never seen him with. Knowing that you're likely a new climber he's talked into coming, I know we've got work to do. But trust that it'll be fun. We just need to get a pair of climbing shoes on your feet. What do you say?"

She stole another look at the walls, noticing their varying sizes. People of all ages and genders were climbing at different points, some high up and others closer to the ground. It appeared to be a strenuous sport, but also potentially fun. Angela shook her head and shrugged, still unsure.

"First, thank you for the compliment, but I don't know. Looks like you need a lot of upper body strength for all of that," she gestured toward the bouldering area.

Chapter 6

With a chuckle, Simeon disagreed. "Not entirely true. And over there is a perfect spot for you to begin your training."

"My training? Are you serious?"

"As a heart attack," Simeon confirmed, nudging his cousin.

Roc held up a hand and presented his argument. "Angela, I was just like you. I thought this was a 'white' sport, but nah. This is for us too. There's plenty of us in this community. But it's not enough of us representing. After doing a little research, I found historically it's because of location and cost. As you can see, we're just outside of the city's loop, which is great. Not a lot of traffic, right?" He paused, waiting for Angela to respond. Once she nodded, Roc went on explaining, "Here at CTW, we've tried to make this affordable for everybody. So, I wanna see more of us out here. I'm gonna make sure of it. But yeah, you're in the best hands with Za. It's because of him there's a CTW. He's the one that showed me the ropes and crags. The rest is history."

Her eyes darted between the cousins and once more at the walls. *Oh, what the hell?* Angela finally nodded and joked, "Okay, Za, I guess I'm ready to start my training. When do we come back?"

Once more, Simeon and Roc shared a laugh amongst themselves. She didn't see what they found funny until Simeon tipped his head in the opposite direction. Angela looked that way when he announced.

"Your training starts today, angel."

Angel? The unexpected nickname caught her off guard and made her heart skip a beat. She pushed aside the flustered vibe and concentrated on his words. Angela turned back to him and squealed, "Today? You mean like right now? Nah uhn, Simeon. No. I'm not dressed to go climbing no walls."

"Good thing we have a store," Roc interjected, pointing to another area on the other side of the sprawling gym.

"Wow. You even have your own store. Guess I'm not getting out of this now, huh?"

"Nope. It's there for that very reason—for people like you who think that you can't start today. Za, why don't you take her to get the gear, and I'll have Shanti get her paperwork ready."

"Did y'all just bully me into this without my consent?"

"Never that. And we're gonna get that consent. See y'all in a few."

Roc disappeared behind the reception desk where he spoke to the girl that Angela assumed was Shanti. She looked up from her computer and gave Angela a genuine smile. Angela reciprocated with a friendly nod. Simeon motioned for her to follow him to the Crawl the Wall shop. Since she was new to the sport, Simeon told her the only thing she would need for their session today was shoes.

"But knowing Roc, he wants me to go all out. So, I'll get everything you'll need from here on out."

"You don't have to do all that, Simeon. This will probably be a one-time thing."

"Except it won't be, angel. That's non-negotiable. This will be your first, but certainly not your last time. Now, come on. Let's get your shoes taken care of. Then you can pick out a couple of outfits."

Disregarding Simeon's ramblings about what she needed, Angela homed in on one thing: he had called her "angel" again. What was that about? Instead of asking, she watched his broad back and long legs while he made his way to the shoe section on the other side of the store. After a pause, Simeon turned around, holding up a single climbing sneaker by its laces.

"I think you'll like—hey! What're you doing over there? We'll look over there after we get the shoes. C'mere."

"I couldn't resist. He has some really nice stuff in here," Angela reached out to touch the sleeve of a shirt.

In reality, she was only pretending to browse through the racks, stopping to glance at a few more items on her way to Simeon. It was a convenient cover for the whirlwind of thoughts and emotions swirling within. Deep down, Angela realized she wasn't fooling herself. Simeon had gotten under her skin. She struggled to see him as just a friend. He claimed to respect her relationship with Jamal, but Angela doubted whether she even had one anymore. Though her situation with Jamal was rocky at the moment, that wasn't the real issue for her.

She was attracted to this man. From their initial chat to his courteous

Chapter 6

behavior at her mother's house, everything about him had left a significant impression on her. Even his choosing pink sneakers without realizing it was her favorite color had an effect on her. Simeon sparked mixed feelings in Angela, and she was uncertain how to handle it. He was causing chaos in her heart and mind.

"Which ones do you like?" Simeon asked, holding up another shoe that was multi-colored, but predominantly neon pink.

Without hesitation, Angela reached out and grabbed it. "This one! The pink in it is just right. Oh, I guess I should tell you, pink is my favorite color," she mentioned sheepishly while inspecting the shoe.

"Yeah, I kinda figured," he replied with a smirk while turning back to return the other one to the shelf. He added over his shoulder, "You wear it a lot. I bet Vicky's PINK hate to see you coming."

Angela found his comment surprising. She wasn't even sure if Jamal had noticed her love for the color and the Victoria's Secret line. After taking a peek down at her pink t-shirt and matching sneakers, she jokingly thought to herself, *another point for "Team Simeon."* Shrugging it off, she redirected her attention toward getting some help. Almost as if hearing her thoughts, a store clerk approached them. Angela gave the young girl with lemonade braids her shoe size and then joined Simeon by the display wall full of helmets.

He handed her a neon pink and black protective hard hat. "Perfect match."

"Are you sure it'll fit? Shouldn't I try it on?"

"C'mere. Let me do it."

"Okay. But hang on. I gotta pull this out of the way," Angela motioned to her hair.

After gathering it into a low ponytail, Simeon placed the helmet on her head, adjusting the straps and buckles under her chin, tightening them. "How does it feel?"

Angela gave him a thumbs up. "Perfect fit."

"Excuse me. Here are your shoes."

It was the store clerk. She handed Angela the box containing the climbing shoes. Simeon brought her to a bench near a wall mirror. In no time, Angela took off her sneakers to try them on. The shoes coordinated well with the helmet and were also a perfect fit.

"What do you think?" Angela asked, standing in front of her reflection.

Simeon came up and stood behind her, nodding his approval. "I think you're ready to get started on bouldering. Let's get you a CTW outfit."

Angela picked out a white t-shirt with the printed statement: "Climb the Wall" and black yoga pants featuring the gym's logo embossed down the leg. They proceeded to the counter to make the purchase, which Simeon handled. He then guided her to the locker rooms to change clothes. Once Angela was in her new outfit, she met Simeon again at the receptionist's desk, where Shanti had the consent forms ready. After Angela completed the paperwork, Simeon led her to a less crowded area of the gym. The walls here were shorter but still had many of the colorful handholds. Angela was eager to find out what Simeon had planned for her.

"Look, I'm not expecting you to be Spider-Girl today. But eventually, I need to see you up there," Simeon pointed to a wall which extended to the top of the exposed ceiling.

"I think not. But I wanna see you do it."

"Been there and done that. Now you gotta do it."

"How about you show me what I need to do, and we can start right here, Za," Angela joked, gesturing to the spot where they were standing.

Simeon chuckled and outlined how they would begin. "We're going to try bouldering today, which doesn't involve using any ropes. We'll start with some stretching, focusing on your legs since you'll be using them a lot."

He gestured to a cluster of wide, red handholds, then climbed up six of them with ease. Angela licked her lips, observing how it was a simple task for him to grip the lightweight, flexible resin in his gigantic hands and pull his muscular frame upward. He placed his foot on one hold and began climbing, his sculpted thighs flexing against his relaxed fit jeans. She gulped hard. Her twat must've swallowed some air too, as she felt a sudden rush of arousal between her legs. Angela shifted on her feet, her mind

Chapter 6

filling with images of him in another way. Just then, Simeon jumped down, interrupting any dirty thoughts.

"These are VB holds, which are meant for beginners. This essentially is a ladder. You just climb up it. And don't worry about falling. The mat down here is to cushion your landing."

Angela listened intently to the rest of his instructions. She then spent the next hour climbing the wall, taking spills while laughing uncontrollably as Simeon taught her the ins and outs of the sport. By the time she finished, Angela decided she would come back without a doubt. She even revisited the store to pick up a few more outfits in pink. Simeon dropped the shopping bag with her newly purchased climbing gear and equipment into her trunk, closed it, and turned to face her. "Did you have fun?"

"I did. Thank you."

"Roc's glad to hear you'll be back. So am I. Ready to get out of here and grab a bite to eat?"

"Yes. After trying to be Spider-Girl, I'm starving."

"Good. Come on." Simeon moved to the driver's side and opened the door. He waited until Angela got in before saying, "I know a spot that's not far from here. And it's early enough where it won't be too crowded. Follow me."

Less than fifteen minutes later, Angela parked next to Simeon in front of a beige building with red letters spelling out "*Cobb Kitchen & Bar.*" He helped her from the car, and they walked into the restaurant, which was nearly empty as he'd predicted. At Simeon's request, the hostess seated them in a booth near the back with a view of the city's skyline. After placing their drink orders, they perused the menu and engaged in light conversation.

"I really had a blast today. Thank you again for inviting me," Angela stated, flashing him a wide grin.

Simeon smiled back, his dimples showing. "That's exactly what I was hoping for. I'm happy you enjoyed it, and you're welcome."

"Hey, I didn't ask earlier. But what is Za short for?"

"Zaire, my middle name."

"Nice. I like it."

"And I like hearing you say it, angel," Simeon confessed with a wink.

Why do you call me that? Instead of asking, Angela crossed her legs tight, trying to quell the sudden rush of desire coursing through her body. Taking a gulp of water, she hoped it would cool her down. It was no use. The heat rose within her loins. Her poor kitty wouldn't stop fluttering. Angela tried to focus on something else, clearing her throat before changing the subject.

"How did you get into rock climbing?"

"This guy I play ball with. One day I hit him up to shoot some hoops, and he told me that's what he was doing. I went to see what it was about. I got hooked after the first time. When I'm not shooting hoops, I'm on a wall."

"That's pretty cool."

"So, other than climbing, what do you do in your free time?"

"You're funny. Since when did climbing become one of my hobbies?"

"Today, when you told Roc you can't wait to come back and do the ropes." Simeon then leaned forward, locking eyes with her as he asked, "Now, other than climbing, what else do you do for fun, angel?"

Jesús! This man is too fine. "Umm well, I love crafts—pottery, weaving, and quilting. But mainly painting is my thing. I just like being creative with my hands."

He opened his mouth, but their server arrived at the table with their dinner, interrupting him. For Angela, it was a welcome distraction from Simeon's intense gaze. She needed a moment to compose herself and regain control. Did he realize the effect he had on her? With their meal before them, Simeon rested his hands palms-up on the table.

"Do you mind if I bless our food?"

"No. Not at all. Please do," Angela bowed her head, intertwining her fingers with his.

Another point for Team Simeon. He'd done the same the night they had dinner with her mother. Angela remembered what Bianca had told her. She said Simeon was a devout man, attending services with his family, which was another quality Angela found appealing. This trait was one of the many she

Chapter 6

wanted in a partner. While she didn't attend church regularly, Angela desired a partner with some kind of spiritual faith. She had never seen Jamal pray, not even once. Pushing the thought to the back of her mind, Angela focused on Simeon asking for God's blessings on the hands that had prepared their food. After giving thanks, they engaged in a friendly chat with Angela sharing her excitement about becoming a licensed practical nurse.

Simeon pointed out with admiration, "Remember when they had that race on your street? Lijah, Junior, and I think three other boys crashed into each other? You jumped into action making sure none of them had broken bones and everybody's 'boo boos,' as you called them, had band-aids. I always knew you were destined to be a doctor."

"Oh my god, you remember that. Yeah, I guess you can say that was the start of it. I was always caring for some bruise or injury Junior had when Mamá wasn't around. I never wanted to be a doctor, but I wanted to help people. I enjoy helping in a way that goes beyond what doctors can offer. Building trusting relationships with my patients is something I take pride in. I like knowing that they can count on me to advocate for them and their families."

Simeon nodded and carried on, describing his experience as a marketing director. His master's degree and commitment to his field really impressed Angela. As a relatively young man in his thirties, he had already accomplished a lot. Angela was curious why he didn't have a woman. Before she could ask, the tone of their conversation changed when Simeon revealed his true intentions for inviting her to join him.

"I know you said everything's okay, but Mamá might have a different opinion. Is there a reason why?"

Angela took a sip of water from her glass before setting it down and letting out a long sigh. "Wow, that came outta left field. Hmm, well since you've been hanging around my mother so much as of late, you should know how she is. She's always gonna have something to say because that's Bianca Washington for you. Now, I'm not sure what she's told you or why she wants you to check into my man, but you can stand down. We're good over here."

"Are you really though? From what she's told me, I'm not so sure. Do you think Tré would've been cool with him?"

Good question. Would he? Angela's lips tightened into a straight line. She stared at Simeon for a few seconds and then lowered her sight to the stuffed chicken breast, grilled asparagus, and roasted red potatoes remaining on her plate. Everything had been so good. But Angela didn't want anymore. Her appetite was gone. A gnawing churned in the pit of her stomach while she pondered over her brother's relationship with Jamal. According to Jamal, they knew each other. They were good friends. But would that have been the case once Tré learned his good friend who was married was seeing his younger sister? No. Her brother would have never been okay with it. Tré would have told her to end it. She finally brought her gaze up to meet Simeon's and lied. "I'm not sure, but they knew each other. I found that out. The thing is Jamal knew him as 'Rico.' They never talked about me, which isn't surprising since Tré wouldn't have. He never told his friends he had a sister. Talking 'bout he didn't want any of them trying to holler at me."

"Yeah, I know. He didn't want nobody talking to you. Anyway, Mamá said you went out of town with this guy and instead of having fun, all you two did was fight. What's up with that?"

Angela frowned at hearing her mother had been sharing her relationship woes with Simeon. She quickly shot back, "That's not true."

"So, what happened?"

"We had a disagreement." Angela explained, though unconvinced herself. She noticed the skepticism in Simeon's expression and quickly raised a hand in defense. "Don't give me that look. Okay. Maybe, he blew things way out of proportion. And I can't figure out why."

"What was the issue?"

What does it matter? This isn't your business. Angela thought. Yet, curiosity got the better of her. She decided to share to gauge Simeon's reaction. Perhaps by getting a man's point of view, she might better understand where Jamal was coming from.

"I invited another couple to have dinner with us. But I didn't think it was that big of a deal. I mean, I kinda get why he was upset. This trip was

Chapter 6

supposed to be just for us. Jamal said these strangers, who were loud and drunk, ruined everything for him. When we went jet skiing, we ran into them again. To avoid them, he ended up flipping us over in the middle of the ocean. We argued right there and again when we got back to our room. After that, the trip was an epic fail. We've barely said two words to each other since we've been back," Angela concluded, fiddling with her straw.

Simeon lifted an eyebrow and gave a disapproving shake of his head. "Hold up. It's about to be a week. Y'all still haven't talked about it? You mean to tell me he's still upset?"

Angela gave a half-hearted shrug and nodded, but no words came out. There were none. They hadn't talked about it. The only justification she could give was that Jamal had been at work. "Jamal's been under a lot of pressure at work and—"

"Don't do that, angel. Don't make excuses. You know that's bullshit. It doesn't matter if your man is under pressure and stressed out. That's what you go on vacation for, to unwind and relax. Why bother going somewhere if you're gonna be a dick and a grump? And since y'all been back, he still hasn't tried to make things right? What's up with that?"

Again, Angela had no answer. She didn't know why Jamal hadn't made time for her. They needed to fix things between them. Rocking her head from side to side, she replied, "I don't know. We just haven't gotten a free moment to talk. He's been busy with work."

"Mamá ain't feeling a lot of the shit he's done, and neither am I. I don't have to check into dude to know he ain't somebody Tré would've been good with. If my girl got sick, I'm taking the time off. Mamá told me he owns the practice. Is that true?"

Angela gave a small nod.

"I'm not putting you in no facility, angel. Fuck that. But that's just me."

"Is there anything else you need? Takeout boxes?"

Their server had returned. Angela glanced down at her half-eaten meal, unsure if she wanted to take it with her. The conversation's abrupt change of subject to her love life completely occupied her thoughts.

Simeon spoke up. "Yes. Could we get a couple? And could you also pack up a slice of chocolate cake for both of us to take home? Thank you."

When the server left, Simeon leaned forward, piercing Angela with a serious look. He didn't say anything for the longest beat, his intense espresso stare holding her attention and prompting her to stay still and silent. *What was going through his mind?* Angela then questioned whether their friendship could remain strictly platonic. His next words only added to her mixed feelings about him.

"I'm a man of my word. So, I'll respect that he's your man. For now. But respect doesn't mean I'll stand idle while he diminishes you. Don't mistake my restraint for weakness, angel. He's got one chance left to fix things between y'all. One."

7
I'M FINALLY LIVING IN MY TRUTH

The neon marquee reading ***Himeros*** pulsed above the entrance, illuminating the sidewalk with vibrant colors including pink, green, blue and purple. The rhythmic beat of "Blinding Lights" by The Weeknd echoed from within, drawing Jamal closer. As he approached, a brief thought crossed his mind: if Angela hadn't been sick with a stomach virus, she would have insisted on being there. Thankfully, she was home, recovering. He glanced down at Christian, whose grin spread wide across his face.

"Ready?" Jamal asked, gripping the handle of the metal barrier.

"As long as you are."

He stepped to the side, gesturing for Christian to walk ahead of him. "Let's go do some schmoozing then."

Shimmering chandeliers lined the ceiling, their soft glow casting deep crimson hues over the expansive venue, creating an atmosphere of temptation and mystery. Staffers greeted Jamal and Christian when they strode in. With their names checked off the list, they proceeded further into the lavishly decorated space. Glossy, contemporary leather furniture lined the room in black, oxblood, and midnight blue, each piece positioned for intimate conversation. Guests were already enjoying drinks and appetizers offered by the attentive servers.

This highly anticipated gala aimed to raise funds for advanced dementia support technologies and spotlight innovative solutions. Leading donors, researchers, healthcare executives, and collaborators from across the nation would be in attendance. Jamal was eager to network and hopefully establish some valuable financial connections for the future. However, he also had to be careful since he wasn't the host of the event. There were a few frenemies among the attendees who could cause trouble for him if given the opportunity.

Jamal surveyed the area, recognizing the familiar faces of notable colleagues who threw subtle glances in their direction. As they weaved through the crowd of tuxedos and designer dresses, Jamal overheard whispers about his personal life: the horrific accident involving his ex-wife Desiree that had made the news, how she left him for the music and business mogul Derrik Carter who was with her in the crash. Each remark sliced through his carefully maintained exterior. He forced a smile and nodded at acquaintances as he passed, but inside, anxiety swirled. What would they think of him now? Could he project an image of authority and inspire credibility?

Christian reached out and placed a hand on Jamal's arm, causing him to slow down. "Jamie, is everything okay?"

"Yeah, I'm fine. Let's go grab a drink," he responded flippantly, steering them away from their original path and toward the bar.

A bartender stood poised behind the counter, dressed in a sharp black dress shirt with rolled-up sleeves, showcasing his muscular, tattooed forearms. Behind him, a deep red backsplash glistened under the pendant lights like liquid fire. Shelves lined with top-shelf liquor stood in perfect alignment, displaying a range of rich bourbons, smooth tequilas, aged scotches, and clear vodkas. Each bottle exuded elegance with its sleek design and embossed labels. Jamal ordered his usual whiskey without the chaser. However, he asked for a double shot. Christian decided on a mojito. After downing the whiskey and requesting a second one, Jamal relaxed. With his third shooter in hand, he teased Christian for choosing

Chapter 7

the Cuban punch instead of something stronger. "I thought you wanted to get fucked up tonight. That cute drink is not the way to go."

Christian checked around them before he quipped. "It's too many dicks on the floor. I need to be on point with these highbrow know-it-alls."

"You know, I'm one of those highbrow geniuses you speak of." Jamal leaned in and whispered, "And the only dick on this floor you need to be concerned about is mine, Chris."

"I am, Dr. Edwards, but with you I never know what kind of trouble we'll get into. One of us needs to be sober. It should be me."

"The audacity. Didn't I get my first misdemeanor messing with you?"

"And didn't my friend get it dismissed?"

Jamal opened his mouth to argue, but it would've been pointless. Even though it had been a few months prior, he still hadn't forgotten. They had been caught in an alley, near a club having sex. Jamal would have never imagined engaging in an act like that before. Certainly not in public. But when it came to Christian, Jamal let all his inhibitions go. And he was right. His friend had made sure their records did not show any evidence of their shameless tryst. Jamal shrugged indifferently. "Yeah. So—"

"So, it's water under the bridge. We're free and clear of that. Moving right along." Christian bumped his shoulder against Jamal's, flirting. "Now, this place doesn't have an adjoining hotel. But I see what looks like a rather wide and long balcony outside. We can always improvise, Jamie."

"Chris, I know you're not thinking about—"

"Edwards! There you are! We've been looking all over for you."

Ugh. I'm gonna need something stronger than this to deal with his ass. Jamal thought to himself as he turned around.

Ian Taylor stood before him in a black custom-fitted tuxedo with intricate jacquard patterns, and of course, a dramatic cape billowing at his back. It was classic Ian: bold, theatrical, and never one to blend in. Jamal wasn't surprised in the slightest. After all, the event, a pure spectacle, was being hosted at one of Atlanta's most exclusive and high-profile venues. Rumor had it Brielle Stephens, Desiree's best friend, had planned the whole affair, which tracked. But the real showstopper was Ian himself, not just attending but hosting this gala with his usual flair. He was always extra, always center stage, and still, somehow, always managing to get under Jamal's skin.

His biggest competition for the position of head of surgery, Ian was a persistent pest who kept showing up at the most inconvenient times. Just the sight of him filled Jamal with anger. It took everything in Jamal's power to keep his emotions in check. He had to stay composed and not let any sign of weakness show or else Ian would take advantage without hesitation.

With a slight nod and a forced smile of his own, Jamal greeted him. "Good evening, Taylor. And why, may I ask, were you looking for me?"

"Naturally, I was curious when I saw you had a plus one. I was wondering who you'd be bringing, especially since you're newly divorced," Ian broadcasted, his lips curling into a sinister smirk. His gaze then swung to Christian and lingered a moment too long before he purred, "And who might this be?"

It wasn't lost on him where his rival's attention had fixated. Fully aware of Ian's sexual orientation, Jamal's muscles tightened throughout his body. He cleared his throat to make the introductions. "This is, uh, Christian Hilcrest . . . a friend of mine. Christian, this is Ian Taylor. One of the doctors I work with at Northside," Jamal replied, avoiding Christian's eyes.

Under the judgmental stares of his coworkers, he couldn't bring himself to say boyfriend or partner. It just didn't seem appropriate. Sensing the piercing side-eye from Christian, Jamal averted his gaze.

"Why, hello, Christian. It's a pleasure to meet you." Ian extended his hand.

Christian accepted it, responding coolly, "Likewise."

"I must say, you have impeccable taste, Christian. Your suit is absolutely stunning. I don't think I've ever seen anyone pull off this combination of brown and green. And it takes a certain kind of man to pull off such bold colors. It definitely compliments your skin tone," Ian remarked, his eyes unabashedly roaming over Christian's figure.

"Well, I am a buyer for Gucci."

Chapter 7

Is he really entertaining this guy? Jamal groaned when he noticed Ian hadn't let go of Christian's hand. Christian didn't pull away either. Heat rose from Jamal's neck to his ears. He couldn't shake off the discomfort bubbling up in his gut. Was it jealousy? He tried to brush off the notion. However, Jamal's unease only grew stronger with each passing second that he watched them together. Was Ian eye-fucking his lover in front of everybody? But then again, Jamal hadn't officially claimed Christian as his own. Suddenly, Jamal regretted inviting Christian to join him.

"Would you happen to fancy fine art?"

"I would."

"Is that so?" Ian murmured, a hint of a smirk playing at the corners of his mouth. "Well, Christian, I'm sure you'll find the art collection we have here tonight quite fascinating then. In fact, I've arranged some exclusive entertainment for our esteemed guests tonight. Would you care to join us?"

"Sure. Sounds intriguing." Christian nodded, finally removing his palm from Ian's. He let out a fake chuckle. "I'm sure my friend won't mind if I go with you all. Right, Jamal?"

Friend? What? I'm your man! Jamal's fingers twitched at his sides, an involuntary reaction to the green-eyed monster fighting to get to the surface. He had referred to Christian as a friend, and now he was making him pay for it. Jamal sighed quietly and shook his head.

"No. Not at all. I see a few people I need to chat with anyway. Enjoy yourself. Catch up with you later."

"Don't worry, Edwards. He's in very skilled and capable hands with me," Ian taunted, his voice dripping with sarcasm and amusement. Ian winked at Christian and held out an outstretched arm, motioning for him to follow. Teeth gritted, Jamal helplessly watched as Ian and his associates swept Christian away, their laughter reverberating in the expansive ballroom.

Struggling to keep his emotions in check, Jamal clenched his hands into tight fists. He navigated his way through the crowd, desperate for a brief reprieve to allow him to gather his thoughts.

"Edwards," a familiar voice called out. Jamal turned his head to find Dr. Mitchell walking toward him. "You look troubled. Need a drink?"

"Yeah. As a matter of fact, I do."

"Come. Let's sit."

They found a lounge area tucked away from the buzz of the main hall and settled into the comfortable, oversized armchairs. Dr. Mitchell shifted in his seat, the fabric of his perfectly tailored tuxedo pulling across wide shoulders hardened by years in the field. His salt-and-pepper hair, cropped close to his scalp, gleamed under the low lights. No judgment lived behind those deep brown eyes, only the quiet steadiness of a man who'd seen too much to flinch now. Dr. Mitchell lifted a hand, signaling a nearby server to come over. Less than five minutes later, the drinks arrived. The two men raised their glasses in a quiet salute before sampling the aged liquor.

Dr. Mitchell took a slow draw, then fixed Jamal with a look that cut through the noise of the gala. His voice rumbled low, steady as a heartbeat. "Don't let Taylor rattle you, Edwards. This gala's all for show. The real decisions? They happen behind closed doors, and you've already done the work to earn your place."

Jamal lowered his tumbler and shook his head, "No. Never that. It's just been, well . . . it's already an overwhelming evening."

"Ah, well, you know these affairs can be quite intense. I see several fresh faces in here. Nothing you can't overcome," Dr. Mitchell mused, his gaze scanning the room before returning to Jamal. "But I sense there's more on your mind than just the gala tonight."

"You're right. It's not just the gala," he admitted. Jamal took another swallow from his glass and set it down on the table in front of them. His voice was barely above a whisper when he confessed, "I've been living a lie, Mitch. For years. And now, it's finally catching up to me."

The older man didn't prompt him or ask questions. He simply waited in silence. That was one thing Jamal appreciated about his mentor. Dr. Mitchell would never pressure someone to share something before they were ready. He understood the weight of unspoken things.

Their bond had formed years ago when Jamal was a fresh-faced intern navigating the chaos of Northside Regional. While other attending physi-

Chapter 7

cians barked orders or ignored him, Dr. Mitchell saw something in Jamal and took him under his wing. He taught Jamal what medical school and textbooks never could: the nuanced rhythm of hospital life, how to speak to patients like people instead of charts, when to push and when to pause. And when personal struggles bled into professional life, Mitch never judged—he simply listened.

Jamal took a moment to collect his thoughts. They were alone. And as the silence stretched between them, Jamal had a sense of comfort knowing he could confide in Dr. Mitchell about what was weighing heavily on his mind. "I didn't bring Angela."

"I noticed."

"She couldn't come anyway. A stomach virus has kept her in bed. You know, when I met her, Desiree had just started traveling a lot for work. She said it would only be temporary, but it never slowed down. I hardly saw her. A man has needs, Mitch. Can't no woman act like their husbands won't be tempted, especially Black men in this profession, with beautiful women throwing themselves at you every single day. And I was still faithful. Yet, I felt like she was punishing me for being a good husband. Why was I the bad guy for wanting to start a family? I thought that's what she wanted. What we both wanted." Jamal paused for a beat. He picked up the tumbler, taking a sip and went on, "Anyway, things between Angela and me, like most couples having an affair, moved fast. Way too fast. Before I knew it, I was helping her buy a condo. Then I upgraded her out of a Honda and put her in a Mercedes. But then I found out she was my boy's sister. Man, nothing is ever as it seems. Like I said, I've been living a lie. Pretty much my entire adult life."

"Damn, you do have quite a bit on your mind."

"Yeah, and I know you're not my therapist, Mitch. So, I appreciate you letting me get this out."

"Of course, Edwards. Anytime you need it, I'm here."

Jamal nodded and continued. "I did everything by the book. I graduated from Ivy league schools. Got married to a beautiful wife. We both had amazing careers. And that big ass house in Buckhead? I was living the so-called American Dream. Hell, if she wasn't holding out on the pussy, we probably would've had our two-point five kids by now. That's what I was supposed to do, right?"

"Not supposed to do, but I can understand societal norms and pressures for where they think we should be."

"Well, regardless of all that, it would've all been a sham, Mitch. All of it."

"Edwards, what are you saying?" Dr. Mitchell asked, his brows furrowing while he searched Jamal's face.

Jamal drained his glass and set it down on the table with a thud. "It happened in college, the first time. I was confused and ashamed of what Sean and I did. I didn't know how to deal with my emotions. Part of me liked it and I was curious, but another part knew it wasn't acceptable. How could I ever share that with anyone? I couldn't go back home and tell my family I had feelings for men. And definitely none of my close friends. That would've been social suicide." He let out a sigh, remembering how he tried to hide it. "So, I covered it up by sleeping with as many girls as I could. It worked for a while. Until it didn't. That's when I met Christian, right when Angela was going through the loss of her brother. It might sound fucked up, but Christian came into my life at the perfect moment during the worst time. I can't change that. Angela didn't deserve to lose me on top of everything else, but I can't keep leading her on either. And just last year, people saw me married to a woman, but now I'm here with Christian, a man that I deeply care for. Yet, I'm too afraid to admit it publicly. If I don't come out completely, I'm going to lose him. Mitch, I'm at a loss," Jamal trailed off, searching Dr. Mitchell's face, hoping to find understanding and assurance that his feelings were valid and he wasn't crazy for feeling this way.

A quiet moment rested between them, and finally, Dr. Mitchell placed a reassuring hand on his shoulder. "Our lives are often dictated by what society expects of us, isn't it? We lose sight of our true selves in pursuit of acceptance and success. It takes courage to live authentically, to embrace all aspects of ourselves. Living our truth can be one of the most difficult and courageous things we do. We fear losing the respect of those we admire, but ultimately, the only person we need to answer to is ourselves.

Chapter 7

Tell me, Edwards. What do you truly want?" he asked, never breaking eye contact.

Jamal opened his mouth to answer, but the words got tangled in his throat. "I . . . I umm, well, honestly, I didn't know what I wanted until . . . *him*. I don't know if I should. All the embarrassment it'll bring. Is it really worth the risk, knowing what I might lose?"

"Edwards, you have nothing to lose that you haven't already lost. Don't you deserve to be happy as well? You're an exceptional surgeon. Don't let anyone take that away from you. And don't let societal pressures define your worth. Stay true to yourself and everything else will fall into place. Remember, people admire you for your skills, intelligence, and dedication to your patients. Those qualities will never change, regardless of who you love."

Jamal stared at the smooth, reflective surface of the floor, taking in Dr. Mitchell's words. A newfound sense of determination sprouted within him, fueled by his mentor's unshakeable belief in him. He understood the path ahead would not be easy, but for the first time, he could picture a life without the secrets and lies.

With a deep breath, Jamal stood up from his seat. "Thanks, Mitch. As always, your guidance means more than you know."

"Stand in your truth. Embrace who you are meant to be, Edwards," Dr. Mitchell offered one last nod of encouragement before Jamal disappeared into the crowd.

His mentor's words struck a chord, challenging him to face his fears head-on. Could Jamal be honest about who he was? Would the medical community still respect him if they knew the truth? A spark of defiance ignited in him. Jamal had one goal in mind as he marched further into the spacious venue: to find Christian and confront the reality that had been buried in his heart for far too long.

"Where are you?" he muttered under his breath, his gaze sweeping across the throng of guests. He caught sight of Christian on the balcony, engaged in an intimate conversation with Ian. His rival leaned in closer, his hand resting briefly on the railing near Christian's. Jealousy stirred, but Jamal pushed it down. This wasn't the time for theatrics. Straightening his jacket, he approached them calmly, purposefully. Not storming, but stepping up with quiet confidence.

"Christian," Jamal said smoothly, his tone polite, yet firm enough to draw attention without causing a scene.

Christian turned, brows lifting in surprise. "Jamal?"

Ian's gaze flicked toward Jamal, his lips parting in mock curiosity. "Well, look who it is. Dr. Edwards," he said with a sugary lilt, eyes scanning Jamal from head to toe. "Something we can help you with?"

Jamal ignored the tone but nodded respectfully to Ian. "Actually, yes. I wanted a quick word with Christian. Won't take long."

Ian's brows arched with theatrical interest. "Oh? Anything *we* should know about?" he teased, clearly fishing.

Jamal let out a short breath, then turned to Christian with sincerity. "Also . . . I owe you an apology. I should've introduced you properly earlier. As my man."

Christian blinked, appearing stunned for a beat before the corners of his mouth slowly curved into a smile.

Ian let out a dramatic gasp. "Well. This just got interesting."

Jamal looked him dead in the eye, unbothered. "Excuse us."

He gestured for Christian to step away for some privacy. Jamal didn't need his rival hearing anything regarding his and Christian's relationship. Christian followed Jamal a few steps away, out of earshot. The chatter of the party continued behind them, but in that moment, it was just the two of them.

Jamal didn't flinch. "Chris, baby, I meant what I said. I've spent my entire life hiding who I am because I was afraid of losing my success and the respect of others. But tonight, I was thinking about the whole idea of societal norms. What is truly normal? I realized that none of it matters if it means losing you. So, right here and now, I choose to live my truth." He paused, swallowing hard as he fought to keep his tone even. "I apologize for earlier. I will never be ashamed again to let it be known you are more than my friend. You're my partner and the person I love."

Christian's eyes widened, but a smile danced on his lips as he moved

Chapter 7

closer. He reached for his hand, the contact sending a shiver down Jamal's spine. "Oh, Jamie, I never imagined you'd be so bold. I love you too."

"Neither did I. Thank you for being patient with me." Jamal breathed out a sigh of relief, letting go of some of the tension that'd been building inside him.

A familiar voice chimed in behind them, laced with a teasing sweetness. "Well, well. Friends to lovers, huh? Edwards, you do know how to keep a girl guessing."

Jamal turned to see Ian standing a few feet away, one brow lifted, lips curved in a knowing smile. There was no bite in his tone this time. Just curiosity layered under charm.

"I've gotta say," Ian continued, eyes flicking between them, lingering just a little longer on Christian, "I never would've guessed. But . . . it's kinda hot, not gonna lie."

Jamal kept his chin high, unmoved, his focus still on Christian. "It's not about shock value, Taylor. I'm just finally living in my truth."

Ian pressed a hand to his chest with playful flair. "Oh, darling, no judgment here. I live for a good reveal." He glanced at Christian with a teasing smile. "Guess that explains why you never batted an eye in *my* direction. Can't say I blame you, though. Clearly, your type was standing right in front of you all along."

Christian chuckled, shaking his head. "You're a mess, Ian."

Jamal's smirk deepened, confidence radiating from him. "Come on, Chris. Let's get out of here. There's someone I want you to meet. Someone who actually matters. I've got nothing to prove here, and nobody's walking away with what's already mine."

Christian laughed, squeezing his hand tighter. "Well, as always, I'm following your lead, Dr. Edwards."

With Christian beside him, Jamal walked past Ian, his posture relaxed, head high. No tension, no shame. Just freedom. The air around him felt lighter, unburdened, and finally his own.

Jamal introduced Christian to Dr. Mitchell and several other esteemed colleagues of his. The evening progressed with no hiccups. However, the highlight of the night came when a wealthy benefactor approached Jamal and expressed his interest in donating to Northside Regional. The distinguished gentleman overheard his declaration of love to Christian and insisted on making a private donation on one condition: it had to be for one of Jamal's programs, not Ian's. This generous contribution would significantly advance neurology research. The networking event had been a success, and with a confirmed sponsor, Jamal was ready to head out.

"Did you plan to leave this early?" Christian asked while they were settling into the drive home.

"Yeah. This was Taylor's event, and the less time I'm around him the better."

"I see. Well, Jamie, what you did back there . . . I know it wasn't easy for you."

"Neither is living a lie. For the first time in my life, I feel free."

Christian reached over to rest his hand on Jamal's thigh, his touch warm and grounding. "I'm really proud of you."

"Once again, thank you, Chris. For everything," Jamal said, sneaking a look at Christian, who met his gaze with a knowing twinkle in his eyes.

Christian unbuckled his belt and dipped his head past his waist, murmuring, "Now let me thank you . . . for everything."

8

WE CAN'T CHANGE THE PAST

"But you promised!"

"I know, sweetheart, but what do you want me to do? It's an emergency surgery. They didn't have enough surgeons on staff today and—"

"Damn it, Jamal! Why is it always an 'emergency surgery'? You're never here when I need you!" Angela shouted into the phone, tears pricking at the corners of her eyes.

"Hey! I've been there for you, and I'm always there for you. This is my job, Angela. It's my duty to save lives. I can't just walk away from a patient who needs me."

Her patience had worn thin. Angela was unable to restrain herself. She clicked her teeth together in frustration and retorted, "Of course not. But I need you too. Your job shouldn't be your entire life! Can't you see history is about to repeat itself?"

"What're you talking about?"

"You were complaining about this same thing with your ex-wife. Wasn't she always traveling? That's what you've been doing a lot of lately. Emergency surgeries, and then it's all these extra shifts. Does this sound familiar to you now?"

"No, because I'm not her. If anybody understands my job, it should be—"

"Understand? I've been more than understanding for months now. Jamal. You get this position as head of surgery and how's it gonna be? Let's not forget about your practice. I'll never get to see you then."

"You'll get to see me. And I'll make it up to you, sweetheart. I promise. Just let me get through this surgery, and we'll have the entire weekend together."

The rhythmic sounds of the hospital machines filled the air, creating an ever-present backdrop. But the long, exasperated sigh Jamal released didn't escape Angela. His pleading tone didn't help either. How could he be so selfish when *she* was the one dealing with him not coming home?

"You know what, Jamal? That's all I keep hearing from you. Promises. Always promises. Promises don't keep me warm at night. I'm tired of being alone." She exhaled, trying to keep her emotions in check. Feeling defeated, Angela replied, "Fine. Do what you gotta do."

"Look, we'll talk about this when I get home."

"Sure, whatever, Jamal. Go save another life while you neglect ours."

"I'll see you later," he declared and ended the call.

Angela stared at the dark screen. His excuses had become a regular occurrence, and she wasn't able to shake the suspicion that something deeper than emergency surgeries was going on. How had they drifted apart? Was he growing tired of her? Was there someone else? Something was happening with Jamal. It was time to confront the truth, whatever it may be.

Her fingers hovered over the phone's display, contemplating her next move. She needed to talk to someone. Anyone to help her make sense of her spiraling emotions. Without hesitation, she dialed Mia's number. After several trills, the call went to voicemail.

Instead of leaving a message, Angela sent a text. Knowing Mia was in Las Vegas with Troy now, she didn't expect a quick response. She scrolled through her list of contacts, this time stopping at Simeon's name. Angela paused for a second and then tapped the call button, her heart fluttering with excitement when he picked up.

Chapter 8

"Uh hey, Simeon, you busy?"

"Nah. What's up, angel? You good?"

That name again. Angela brushed it aside and answered, "Yeah. I'm fine. I was just wondering if you had any plans tonight. I'm kinda bored. And I could use some company." Before he had the chance to suggest it, she quickly added, "But no rock climbing, please."

Simeon's light chuckle echoed in her ear, causing Angela to bite into her bottom lip, stifling the schoolgirl giggle that threatened to escape.

"Okay then, no rock climbing today. But next week, I have another session planned for you and you're not getting out of it."

"Fine. I'll be there. Now, where you at? And what're we doing?"

His laugh rumbled on the other end of the line, the deep vibrations sending an electrical current straight to her core. Angela squeezed her thighs together, attempting to control her body's response to the sound of Simeon's voice dropping an octave.

"Bossy, huh? I like that. If you're that bored, angel, I'll be wherever you need me to be."

The double entendre was clear to her. She rolled her eyes, whining, "Simeon! Stop playing! I'm being for real. I don't wanna spend another night cooped up in this house."

"Okay. Okay. I was heading out to this art show tonight."

Angela perked up, but then she began fussing. She'd told Simeon about her love for art and painting. She hadn't heard of any exhibits happening in the area. "Seriously? I didn't know there was one going on today."

"Yep. It's called the *Black Girl Pop Yo Art Show*. They hit all the major cities in the US. I thought you would've known about it."

"I know about them, but I guess I haven't been keeping up with a lot these days. My mind's been elsewhere..." Angela trailed off.

"So, you wanna go?"

"Hell yeah! You know I do."

"Aight. It starts in a couple of hours. I'll shoot you the address."

"Okay, then. See you in a few!"

After hanging up, Angela rushed to her bedroom, shedding her work clothes for a quick shower, and slipping into something casual, yet stylish. She chose a white fitted top with a pink blazer and paired it with distressed jeans that hugged her curves just right. To finish the outfit, she threw on gold accessories and wedge sandals. Thanks to watching Mia's stylists for years, she had learned how to do her own makeup and gave her face a light, natural beat. Angela pulled her hair up into a messy bun and was ready to go with plenty of time to spare. While she drove to her destination, Dave Hollister's "Take Care of Home" played in the background. Just as she was getting into the groove, her mother called. She pressed the button on the steering wheel to accept the video call.

"Hola mija ¿Cómo estás?" Bianca's cheerful voice echoed throughout the cabin.

She looked at the screen, noticing her mother's bright emerald eyes and a wide-toothed grin. It was like getting a quick glimpse of her brother again. Angela returned a genuine smile and greeted her, "Hola Mamá, estoy bien ¿Y tú?"

"Bueno. ¿Y adónde vas? I see you're out in all that traffic."

"I'm meeting up with Simeon. We're going to this art show in the city."

"Really? A second date? Go Simeon! I like him for you."

"It's not like that Mamá, so cut it out," she muttered with a playful eye roll. Her mother was relentless about Simeon. Angela stood her ground, saying, "Mamá I love Jamal, and I'm committed to our relationship. Simeon respects it. You should too. I just needed to get out of the house. I was going out whether or not Simeon took me."

Bianca let out a loud, pointed tut, her eyes narrowing with the kind of judgment only a mother could deliver. "Dios mío, ese hombre, he no good for you, mija. You think I'm mean when I say this, but I just don't get it. How can he be this doctor, but not take care of his woman? You are not his priority. How can you not see that? He puts his career first before you. Do you really want a man like this, Angela? And you want a familia? Ha! Then you must be okay with having a husband who doesn't come home. 'Cause how can you possibly see a future like this with him? I didn't raise no fools. Your brother would never let you act like this behind no man!

Chapter 8

You listen to me and pay attention to what I'm saying. Jamal says he despises being late. So, I'm sure he knows how to manage his time. He's too dedicated to that job, or someone else other than his patients are occupying his time, mija. Either way, it's not a good sign. Because if he truly wanted you, he would find and make the time for you."

Angela remained silent. No argument there. Jamal would've made time for her. At least he did in the beginning. But those days had vanished. With a heavy heart, Angela acknowledged that her love wasn't receiving the same level of devotion it once had from him. What they once shared felt like it was fading away into nothingness at an alarming pace. How did they end up here? How was she going to rekindle the flame between them that had died?

The loud honking of a horn jolted Angela out of her thoughts and back into the chaotic traffic. She tried to refocus on the surrounding cars, but her mother's words singed the corners of her mind like a freshly burned memory. Bianca's message had been clear and unforgettable. With a nod, Angela finally responded.

"Sí, Mamá. I've been thinking about that. You're right. He would. But I know what it's like being in this field. There are a lot of pressures that come with this job. I'm sure once he gets this head of surgery position, it'll be fine."

"Don't make excuses for him, mija. I didn't do it with Tré's father, God rest his soul, and I swore I wouldn't do that for you and Junior's daddy. I've raised my children to know better than to be somebody's sloppy seconds."

"I know, Mamá."

"Okay, and that's why I think you should give Simeon a chance. You never know. He might be the one who can give you what Jamal can't. Or rather won't."

Her mother just wouldn't stop pushing the idea of her dating her childhood friend. But "might be" wasn't a compelling argument for Angela to end things with Jamal over communication problems or without solid proof of him cheating. It simply wasn't enough. And she was over it. Angela didn't want to talk about her relationship anymore.

Keeping her eyes on the road and her attitude in check, Angela politely dismissed her mother.

"Mamá, I'll call you later okay. I gotta focus on this traffic. Love you."

Ending the call, Angela spent the rest of her drive lost in deep thought. Her relationship with Jamal had grown cold in the past few months. She no longer recognized the man she had fallen in love with over a year ago. This replica didn't dote on her the way her man did in the beginning. After her brother's death, Jamal had been there for her in every way possible, being the supportive and loving partner she needed during her time of grief. But now, all of that had stopped. Jamal's replacement didn't make her breakfast sandwiches and coffee in the morning. Nor did he bring her flowers. This version of Jamal had no interest in the new painting she'd finished last week. Her mother's advice made sense, but could she really move on from Jamal and embrace the possibility of a future with someone else? The lyrics of "Unlove You" taunted Angela while she struggled with her feelings. She murmured to herself, staring at her reflection in the rearview mirror after parking. "Tonight isn't about your issues with Jamal. Just relax and enjoy yourself."

Angela exited her Mercedes coupe and strutted toward the black brick building nestled in the heart of the industrial district, its towering structure silhouetted against the neon glow of Metro Atlanta. The distant hum of machinery and the sporadic hiss of steam vents added to the atmosphere, combined with the steady sound of her sandals scraping over the uneven pavement. Streetlamps flickered, creating distorted shadows along graffiti-streaked walls, while the city's bright lights bounced off the metal structures around her, painting the night in a shimmering blend of gold and silver.

It was as though Angela stepped into a different realm entirely when she entered the building, mesmerized by the vibrant colors and diverse textures. Surrounded by beautiful artwork, she'd entered a new dimension where her worries melted away.

"Angela!"

A commanding voice broke through the chatter of the bustling gallery. Angela turned to find Simeon striding toward her.

Chapter 8

"Traffic was insane getting here, right?" He greeted her with a chaste kiss on the cheek.

Angela tucked a strand of hair behind her ear, pushing out a nervous laugh. "Yeah, I just took a shortcut. No big deal."

"Well, I'm glad you made it. I hope you're ready to check this place out. I took a quick look around. There's something I want you to see."

"Lead the way."

Angela followed him deeper into the gallery. After walking past a few exhibits, Simeon stopped in front of a large canvas depicting a Black woman standing at the edge of a cliff. Angela thought the woman's haunted eyes seemed to follow her when she moved.

"What do you think about this?"

"Her eyes. They're so ... so ..."

"Intense?"

"Yes! Like she's about to make a life-changing decision but can't quite bring herself to take the leap."

Simeon nodded, his gaze following hers. "I've always admired artists who can express such depth in their creations."

"Really? Sounds like somebody's an art critic."

"If my opinions counted, I'd write reviews. I just love it. Isn't it amazing how they can make us feel so connected to their art?"

"Yes, there's something powerful about an image that can evoke emotion without words."

"Me? Who's the art critic now?"

She waved him off. "Hardly. But I know what speaks to me."

"Same here." Simeon admitted, turning to face her. His expression softened when he asked, "Wanna know what I see in this painting?"

"What?" Angela asked, her heart thudding in anticipation.

He met her stare with unwavering focus, saying, "Strength. No matter what life throws her way, she'll rise above it. She'll jump right into the unknown."

As Simeon's gaze held hers, she wondered what might happen if they took a leap into the unknown together. Angela cleared her throat, returning her attention to the painting. "Yeah, that's exactly what I was thinking."

"I knew we'd see it the same way. Aight, come on. Let's keep exploring."

They meandered through the crowd, pausing before canvases that captured worlds within frames. Angela pointed to a painting, the disarray of colors that somehow found harmony. Tilting her head, she mused, "Feels familiar."

"It's messy as fuck. Like life. But we love it anyway."

"At least we can learn to make peace with it."

"Come on."

Simeon guided her to another piece showing metal entwined strategically with a woman's body. After observing the artwork, he gave her a once over then commented, "How about this one? I get strength and elegance."

"Contradictions coexisting."

"Ha! Okay then. Well, have you ever tried painting yourself?"

A faint blush colored Angela's cheeks, and she finally admitted, "A year ago. But I lacked the patience and skill to make it anything meaningful like this. Maybe I should give it another try. Who knows, maybe I'll create something worth hanging on these walls one day."

"Or at least on your fridge," Simeon quipped, grinning broadly.

Angela shoved his shoulder. "Boy, I got skills. And I can do something better than this."

"Aight, I'd love to see it. Tell you what. I'll pay for it and put it on my fridge, courtesy of Angel Picassa."

"Okay then. Deal," Angela agreed, her laughter mixing with his as they continued their journey through the gallery.

Simeon's humor and wit were just what she needed, lifting her spirits despite the heaviness she'd been under earlier. For once, she was comfortable expressing herself freely, knowing that Simeon was truly interested in her favorite hobby.

The vibrant hues of the walls shimmered under the dim lighting, casting a hypnotic glow on them as they moved from one exhibit to another. Angela became lost in the artwork, each piece pulling her

Chapter 8

further into a world of untold stories and unexplored emotions. The conversation flowed easily between them. It was like they had known each other for a lifetime, rather than having only recently rekindled their friendship.

Angela and Simeon paused before a particularly striking painting that depicted two figures, their forms intertwined, caught in an eternal dance of light and shadow.

"Did you know . . ." Simeon began, leaning in close enough for Angela to catch a whiff of his cologne, ". . . that the artist who created this series believes that true beauty is found in the struggle between chaos and order?"

He could only know that if he truly appreciated art. "Is that so?" Angela replied, her sight fixed on the canvas.

The swirling reds, browns, and oranges floated across the surface, both chaotic and captivating. As Angela studied the piece, the invisible threads that bound her to Simeon tugged at her heart, drawing her even closer to him. She drew parallels between the painting and her own life—a constant tension between expectations and her true desires.

Redirecting Angela's attention back to him, Simeon continued, "Absolutely. This piece captures life's duality. We experience order, then chaos. Light gives way to darkness. There's a rhythm, an ebb and flow, a push and pull. Yin and yang. It's strikingly profound, wouldn't you agree?"

His smoldering, dark brown eyes bore into hers, causing warmth to bloom in her chest. In that moment, Angela felt seen, truly understood by the man standing beside her. It was a sensation that had been sorely lacking in her life with Jamal.

Touched by their shared viewpoint, Angela agreed. "It's like no matter how dark things get, there's always a glimmer of light ready to break through."

"Exactly. And sometimes, all it takes is one person to help us find that light." Simeon commented, his expression thoughtful. After a brief pause, he asked, "Can I ask you something, angel?"

Apprehensive, yet curious, she returned a wordless nod.

"Do you ever wonder what might have been if things had been different?"

"In what way?"

"If Tré was cool with it and you ended up with me instead of him, the guy you're with now?"

Simeon's words hung in the air, a question left unexplored due to the separate paths they had chosen in their teenage years. As kids, she never regarded him as anything more than one of the neighborhood boys. Simeon probably thought little of her too. Or did he? Angela's throat tightened with emotion as the gravity of the moment settled on her shoulders. The endless possibilities stretched out before her like an unwritten story. She looked down at the shimmering stars reflected on the floor and shrugged.

Angela eventually replied, unsure if he heard her over the surrounding conversations. "We can't change the past, can we?"

"No. But perhaps we can alter the future." He hooked a finger under her chin, lifting it. Simeon's expression softened, his husky tone coaxing her. "Angel?"

"Za," she breathed, dragging her eyes up to meet his.

Simeon leaned in closer. Their lips brushed for a mere second before he pulled back, creating a respectful distance between them once more.

"I'm sorry. I shouldn't have," He licked his full kissers and gave her a gentle smile, murmuring, "I just... I couldn't help myself."

"Well, neither could I. And it only seems to happen around you," she joked, though her heart was pounding like she'd been running the 100-meter dash. She appreciated Simeon's restraint but couldn't ignore the growing attraction between them.

"I ain't gon' front. It's not easy, but you can trust me. Remember, I won't cross the line unless you want me to."

"Right. Thanks."

Angela took comfort in his statement, knowing Simeon's intentions were pure. But her loyalty to Jamal ate at her conscience. Was it right to stay with a man who always put her second when there was someone else who was willing and able to put her first without distractions?

Chapter 8

As they redirected their focus to the painting, Angela's thoughts whirled, overwhelmed by the implications of the near-kiss and the charged tension between them that hung in the air like a dense mist. Countless questions bombarded her mind, all clamoring for attention, but she couldn't find straightforward answers. What was she going to do? Pushing aside the internal conflict, Angela focused on the present moment, enjoying what she loved most—art.

Throughout the rest of the evening, while they explored the gallery, their conversations continued to flow, revolving around each piece. Angela cherished every second as if it were a vital lifeline. Her time with Simeon had been truly delightful. The exhibit space's recessed lighting dimmed, indicating the night was ending. A pang of sadness suddenly washed over Angela. The realization settled in that their time together was drawing to a close. They strolled together in companionable silence the short distance to her car, with Simeon stopping at his truck along the way.

"I got you a lil' something. It's Cabernet Sauvignon with an herbal twist," he said, pulling out a small pink and black wine tote bag.

Angela scrunched up her face. "An herbal what?"

"Wine. I know you're missing it, angel. One of my boys—his girl, she got into this stuff. It's supposed to give you a good buzz like the real thing. He said she swears by it. Says it relaxes her 'cause it's all natural, if you know what I mean."

Her eyes widened when he unveiled a stunning black wine bottle, its smooth glass gleaming under the light. The beige label bore a tapestry of vivid colors, depicting an expansive tree with winding branches, each bearing bunches of grapes in deep purple, ruby red, and gold, as if freshly picked from a vineyard at sunset.

"Za, you trying to get me high instead of drunk?"

"I'm trying to give you something that supports the choice you've made to leave alcohol behind. And yeah, you're gonna get a lil' buzz, but it'll help you relax too," he replied, returning the THC wine to its holder.

Wow. He remembered. She hadn't gone to treatment for addiction—her battle was with grief. She needed to learn to cope without losing herself again, so she chose to stay away from alcohol.

"Thank you. I really appreciate it. I'm low-key excited to try it now. You've piqued my interest. I just hope I won't start craving the real thing or want to try weed."

Simeon leaned in, pressing a kiss to her forehead. "I doubt it. You're much stronger than that lady in the painting. I know you've got this. Come on. Get in. And let me know when you get home."

He opened her door, and Angela lowered herself into the driver's seat. Simeon handed her the wine, which she placed on the passenger's side with her purse, before peering up at him with a genuine smile.

"Thank you again for tonight, for the wine, and for everything."

"Anytime, angel. Just shoot me a text or call. I'll be here. Or wherever you need me to be," Simeon declared, closing the car door, making sure she was safely inside before walking away.

Less than an hour later, Angela found herself in an empty house. With a sigh, she headed to the cabinet, took out a silver bucket, and filled it halfway with ice, carefully placing the bottle of cannabis-infused wine that Simeon had given her inside. While waiting for it to chill, she changed into her pajamas. Before she forgot, Angela sent Simeon the message that she'd arrived home safe. Returning to the kitchen, she uncorked the bottle. At first, the aroma of weed was potent in the air, but it quickly dissipated. Angela poured a serving and made herself comfortable on the living room couch. As she sipped the semi-fruity flavored beverage, memories of their stolen moments together flooded her thoughts. His masculine scent, the almost-kiss, and his laughter replayed in her mind. The spark of desire ignited in the gallery still lingered. Angela sighed, wrestling with the conflicting emotions of loyalty, longing, and love.

The buzz from Angela's phone on the coffee table shattered the quiet in the room, jarring her from her thoughts. Assuming it was a reply from Simeon, she eagerly reached for it, only to be let down by Jamal's text illuminating the screen.

> Sorry sweetheart, I'm taking an extra shift. Won't be home tonight. ~Jamal

Chapter 8

. . .

Does he even care anymore? A single tear slid down Angela's cheek, the salty trail reflecting her internal struggle. She clutched the phone tight, her anger and hurt flaring to life.

"You deserve better," Angela murmured shakily. Her mother's advice echoed in her ears, urging her to choose herself and embrace the possibility of happiness with Simeon. "I do," she admitted softly, as another tear followed the first. "But how can I let go of something that was once so good?"

While the question hung in the air, her thumb hovered over Simeon's name. Calling him would be acknowledging irreparable damage to her relationship with Jamal. But it would also provide her with the solace and understanding she so desperately craved. Angela stood at a crossroads, the path before her obscured by shadows of uncertainty.

She knew one thing for certain: things in her life were changing, and it didn't feel like it was for the better.

9

LOVE TAKES CENTER STAGE

Jamal rested against the balcony doorframe, taking in the quiet majesty of Paris at dawn. The first light of morning painted the rooftops gold, transforming the zinc and slate into a glimmering ocean of silver and blue. The streets below buzzed with café owners arranging chairs on sidewalks, delivery trucks rumbling over cobblestone, and lone cyclists weaving through the waking streets. In the distance, the Eiffel Tower appeared hazy through the lingering mist. The city was like a dream, ageless and vibrant. He glanced back at the suite's entrance while speaking into his phone.

"Why aren't you in bed? It's late."

"We haven't talked since you've been there. I figured if I called you at an odd hour, I might hear your voice. Is that alright? Or are you rushing me off so you can get back to whoever you're there with?"

Yes. But you're not catching on. Jamal thought silently as he moved to the middle of the room. He had hoped by this point they would have had another argument, prompting her to end things. His former mistress-now-girlfriend wasn't giving up on them that easily, though. He had to give her credit for that. Angela dealt with a lot of drama he intentionally put her through, more than his ex-wife or any other woman. Her pride ran deep, and Jamal understood she probably felt obligated to him for all the support he provided after her brother's death. She wasn't ready to abandon the fairytale she envisioned for their relationship. Unfortunately, she would have to. Jamal's dreams for his future didn't include her.

He let out a dry laugh. "I'm here with my colleagues, sweetheart. You know that."

"Do I? You act like *we* weren't at conferences while your wife was back home, Jamal. I'm not stupid."

"You certainly aren't. But jealousy doesn't suit you either. There's no reason for accusations. I'm going to assume you're just cranky because you're tired. It's past your bedtime."

"I can't believe this. I'm trying to talk to you, and you're telling me I need to go to bed. What's really happening here? Can't you see how things have changed between us? I just want my man back. Is that too much to ask for?"

Yes, because your man is not yours anymore. Looking at the door, he answered plainly, "No, it's not. And yes, I see the changes. But nothing's happening, except the usual demands in the life of medical professionals like us. You knew what you were getting into, Angela. This isn't new to you. I won't apologize for progressing in my career to secure the future. What I really need is for my partner to have my back right now instead of nagging me, causing added stress."

"I'm sorry, babe. You're right. I just miss you, and us. That's all. I don't mean to be a nag."

Jamal looked at the door to the suite again and reassured her, "All of this will settle down and be over soon enough. Be patient."

"Okay. I will. But I wish I could see you right now. Can we video chat later?"

"Maybe, since it should be an early night. I'll call you when we get out of the last session," Jamal lied, having no plans to call Angela later. "Listen, I need to go so I can get some rest. Love you."

"Love you more," she replied, ending the call right as the suite's lock disengaged.

Chapter 9

Christian breezed in, carrying an assortment of breakfast delights from a nearby patisserie. The aroma of fresh espresso and buttery croissants wafted through the room as Christian placed the treats on the round table by the window.

"I hope you're hungry."

"Famished, to be honest," Jamal replied, unable to resist a grin as he took a seat across from Christian. He watched Christian pour out two cups of rich, dark espresso, the steam curling upward like wisps of smoke.

"Here's to waking up to another beautiful morning in Paris with my love," Christian declared, lifting his cup in a toast.

Jamal tapped his small mug against Christian's, savoring the coffee's aroma before taking a sip.

While Christian discussed the upcoming fashion show that evening, Jamal wrestled with his dilemma. How could he part ways with Angela and fully embrace this life without hindering her progress? Would he end up holding her back? Maybe he was overthinking the situation and Angela would be perfectly fine.

"Jamie, you seem distant. Everything okay?" Christian asked, pulling Jamal out of his reverie.

"Oh yes, I'm fine. Thinking about the fashion show. I'm getting excited just listening to you."

"Good, because it's going to be a spectacular event. I hope you enjoy it."

"I'm sure with you there, I will."

～

Later that evening, the fashion show venue pulsed with energy, its strobe lights casting an electric glow over the throng of stylish guests. Jamal and Christian stepped inside, and the hum of conversation wrapped around them, a medley of laughter, clinking glasses, and hushed gossip in many accents. The air was thick with the scent of high-end perfume, a heady mix of jasmine, citrus, and warm vanilla, blending with the subtle musk of designer leather and freshly ironed fabric. They settle into their seats. The anticipation was almost tangible, crackling like static in the air, with each camera flash contributing to the night's heightened excitement.

"How're you feeling?"

Turning his head, Jamal admitted, "I never imagined I'd be in the front row at a Paris fashion show."

"I'm happy to be the one who popped your cherry," Christian flirted, taking hold of his hand.

Right as Jamal was ready to respond, the room erupted in applause, drawing their attention to the long, narrow catwalk in the center. As the lights dimmed, the first model strode onto the runway, his tall, slender frame draped in a breathtaking Dolce & Gabbana suit. The fabric, a luminous shade of gold, shimmered like molten metal under the spotlights. With his back straight and shoulders poised, he exuded quiet strength, his eyes locked ahead. His arms swung in a controlled rhythm, the detailed lines of the suit accentuated by his confident stride. It was truly art in motion.

Jamal's fascination with the designs grew as the show continued. The clothes themselves seemed to narrate a story, reflecting both historical richness and modern influences. He and Christian exchanged brief comments, their mutual appreciation for couture strengthening their connection. In that moment, nothing else existed—just Paris, fashion, and the two of them. When the lights rose for intermission, Jamal and Christian joined the throng of attendees mingling in the venue's opulent lobby.

"There's someone I want you to meet." Christian guided him toward an impeccably dressed man standing near a cluster of photographers. "This is my friend Sisko. You might recognize him from *Baller Bizness*. Sisko, here's my babe, Jamal Edwards."

With a slight nod, Jamal extended his hand. "Nice to meet you, Sisko."

"Same here. It's good to finally put a face to the name of the man who's captured the heart of my friend," Sisko said, gripping his palm and giving it a firm shake.

While the two friends chatted enthusiastically about the night, Jamal thought about how Christian had introduced him as his babe—a label

Chapter 9

that would have previously unsettled him. Yet here, in this enchanting city, surrounded by individuals who celebrated love and creativity, he was free to be himself. The anxiety and insecurity that once held him back were gone, replaced by a newfound sense of acceptance. Right then, Jamal was caught off guard by a burst of camera flashes, white hot and exploding in rapid succession.

"Smile for me, gentlemen," a photographer requested.

Jamal slipped his arm around Christian's waist, pulling him closer. Jamal's smile was so wide it reached his ears, causing his eyes to wrinkle at the corners.

"Wow! You two look fantastic together. Thanks!" he complimented them after snapping a few more shots.

Before they could walk away, a crowd swarmed the couple, eager to capture more pictures. They bombarded Jamal with questions about his career, especially whether he was in the fashion industry.

"Jamie, you're a natural," Christian whispered, so close the warmth of his breath was against Jamal's ear.

"I am?"

"Do you see how you've captured everyone's attention here? They see it too. My man is fine as fuck. And look at how you ate down in this suit. Yes, boo, you're definitely a natural at this," Christian confirmed, squeezing his arm. "I don't know if being a surgeon is truly your calling. You might need to reconsider your career path."

Shaking his head, Jamal let out a belly laugh. "Yeah, no, that's not happening. Patients are my calling, and they need me more than these fashion enthusiasts." He peered around the room before looking back down at Christian. "This has been an amazing evening. I know I've said thank you for inviting me to come, but again, I appreciate you expanding my palate, especially in fashion."

Christian peered up at him. Without a second thought, Jamal lowered his head and devoured Christian's soft, welcoming lips. In that instant, bursts of bright flashes erupted around them. Christian withdrew but remained close. Jamal noticed a group of bloggers crowding around, murmuring in admiration, asking questions and ready to capture another special moment. But he paid them no mind, focusing entirely on Christian, who now felt like the only person in the room. Thankfully, the intermission ended, and their attention had to shift back to the runway inside.

When they got back to their suite after the fashion show, Jamal was still buzzing with excitement from the evening. Once the door shut, he walked Christian back until he hit the wall. Jamal placed his hands on either side of Christian's shoulders, caging him in. He pressed his mouth to Christian's, their kiss igniting with a heat that was both urgent and aching—hungry for connection, desperate to forget everything else. They nibbled and slurped from each other, their combined moans vibrating through a brazen kiss that held nothing back. Jamal slowed their fervent tongue of war to light pecks. He reached in between them, taking his time to unbutton Christian's jacket and then his shirt. His index and forefinger found a taut nipple. He was less than gentle.

"Ssss oww!" Christian exclaimed. He opened his mouth to complain, but Jamal latched on, suckling happily like a babe on its mother's breast. "Oh my god, Jamie. Yes! That feels so good."

Christian ground his body against Jamal's, their swollen members colliding. Jamal grunted at the intimate friction. He pulled Christian away from the door. Hands clawed at clothing, pulling and tearing, until nothing remained but skin. Shirts, pants, and jackets fell to the floor, leaving a haphazard trail leading to the bedroom.

Jamal's desperation grew, fueled by more than lust. It was everything, all at once, a fire that refused to be quenched. He kissed Christian again, deeper this time, his tongue delving into Christian's mouth while stroking him. Christian met him with equal fervor, his touch igniting an inferno within, his breath hot and urgent against Jamal's neck. The room spun as they fell onto the bed, tangled together in a mess of limbs and desire.

"Fuck, I need you, now!" Jamal groaned. He slid his hand down to grip Christian's hair-roughened thigh. "Turn around."

Christian obeyed, arching his back and tooting his butt up. Jamal wanted to feel every inch of Christian's tight hole as he took him from

Chapter 9

behind. Grabbing the tube of lubricant from the end table, Jamal squirted a line on his shaft and a dollop right in the middle of Christian's ass. While coating his firm flesh, his eyes roamed over the expanse of muscles, veins, and skin. He could barely contain himself. Jamal pressed the tip at Christian's puckered entrance, shivering with anticipation. He pushed inside, slow and steady. The stretch was delicious, like biting into a ripe peach.

"Mmm, Jamie. Give it to me hard," Christian purred, grabbing onto the sheets.

Jamal leaned in to kiss Christian's shoulder, his teeth nipping him softly. "You like this rough stuff, don't you?"

Christian nodded, arching his back and jutting his hips toward Jamal. His breathing turned more erratic as Jamal delved deeper, harder. With a teasing pause, Jamal withdrew and coaxed, "Say it."

"Yes," Christian cried out. He slammed his fists against the mattress. "God yes! I fucking love it! Harder, Jamie! Harder!"

Jamal plunged back in, burying himself to the hilt. Christian's gasps turned into screams when Jamal began a relentless pounding, his hips smacking against Christian's ass with each powerful stroke. Jamal felt the column of Christian's throat flexing as he moaned against his neck. He reached around to grope Christian's leaking member, jerking it in time with his thrusts. Christian whimpered, throwing his head back and bucking his hips up to meet Jamal's strokes.

"I'm fucking you so good," Jamal panted into Christian's ear. He licked the hot piece of flesh, tasting salt and sweat.

"Harder! More, Jamie!

Jamal wanted more. He pounded away at Christian's ass with a heated emotion that matched their desire. Every moan, cry, and shout from Christian fueled him, fed his need. Their movements grew more urgent, more desperate for release. The sensation swelled within Jamal, building to an unbearable crescendo. It was unlike anything he'd ever known, a world he never dared to imagine, and now he couldn't imagine living without it.

"Shit! I'm gonna come," Jamal warned.

Christian urged him on with an enthusiastic shout, "Yes! Yes! Give it to me!"

Jamal pulled out and shot his thick load all over Christian's back and legs. He collapsed on Christian, who was panting heavily beneath him. After catching his breath, Jamal gave him a gentle kiss before rolling off. He glanced over at Christian, who lay there sweat-slicked and spent, yet radiating contentment. Pulling him into his arms, their hearts pounded in unison, breaths mingling in quiet harmony. In the soft silence that followed, Jamal's mind raced with questions: Was this connection real? And could it survive the chaos of his life? For now, he would cherish this moment and not worry about what might come tomorrow.

Morning light spilled through the window, brushing the edges of the room with a soft, golden haze. Jamal blinked awake. Christian remained snuggled under him. He extricated himself from Christian's embrace, careful not to disturb his slumber, and reached for his phone on the nightstand. He wanted to capture this moment. As he unlocked his phone, a flurry of notifications caught his eye—text messages, news articles, and social media alerts. His curiosity piqued, Jamal opened one article, only to be confronted by a familiar image: himself and Christian at the fashion show, their smiles wide and genuine, their hands intertwined.

His heartbeat sped up, scrolling through more articles, the headlines announcing their debut on the global fashion scene. *"Jamal Edwards and Christian Hilcrest: Fashion's Newest Power Couple"* proclaimed one, while another declared, *"Love Takes Center Stage at Paris Fashion Week."*

"Is this really happening?" he muttered, his eyes darting between the screen and Christian's sleeping figure beside him. Jamal realized the disruption these photos could cause back home, threatening the life he had meticulously crafted. But the secret was out. He had no choice. He would have to deal with Angela now. Jamal's jaw tightened, looking down at Christian's peaceful form, the rise and fall of his chest so steady. So unaware. A surge of defiance burned through him, but beneath it, something darker coiled.

With a slow exhalation, he closed out of the browser tabs, swiping away the evidence of the mayhem unfolding. Beyond the window, the city

Chapter 9

stirred, the first traces of dawn stretching across the skyline. Yet, the prospect of a new day felt heavy and inescapable. A change was on the horizon.

Jamal didn't know it yet, but the storm he had tried to contain was already raging across the Atlantic, spreading like wildfire, setting the stage for consequences he would never see coming.

10

THIS TEA IS PIPING HOT TOO

"Hey, y'all! Heeeeey! What's happening?"

Clapping erupted from the audience as LaLa sashayed across the floor of the studio. Instead of her signature afro, she'd opted for a sleek ponytail that ran down her back. The tall, brown-skinned woman donned a black, sleeveless ruffled top with burgundy leather capris and her usual platform red bottoms.

She waved to the studio audience. "Welcome to another episode of *Baller Bizness* with yours truly, LaLa."

"Annnnd your lovely co-host, Sisko! I'm back, baller babes!"

The audience erupted into more cheering and applause as Sisko entered from the other side of the studio. LaLa laughed heartily and joined the crowd in clapping. "Yes, yes, Sisko is back from Paris, y'all! Love your fit, boo!"

He turned in a circle and bowed. As always, Sisko was stylishly dressed in Tom Ford. He wore a blue oriental floral, velvet jacket, lavender button-down shirt, plum-colored slacks, and black loafers. The bright lights behind the video cameras illuminated the stage, as the hosts moved towards the oversized armchairs in the center of the studio. They playfully embraced and shared French cheek kisses before taking up seats opposite each other.

Lala grabbed one of the coffee mugs from the table that sat between their chairs and took a sip before speaking. "Mmhmm, yes indeed! So glad you could join us today as we dish out all the juicy drama going on with the ballers around the world. I'm excited because my co-host Sisko is back from his trip to Paris. Oh, you must tell us how it was."

Sisko popped his lips. "Girl, it was an ahh-mazing trip. I hung out with some of my fave models and designers while touring the City of Love. So much fun. But before we get into that, can we please get an update on Troy Harris? On my return flight home, I saw all this stuff going on with him. I know you know what's going on. Spill it."

"Well, I can't confirm what I know. I think I've been blocked. Anyway, we all know he's now in Vegas on the Raiders' roster. The season's starting up and, well, everyone is wondering how he's going to do with this new team."

"And what about Mia Harris?"

"What can I say about Atlanta's biggest socialite, except now she's a part of the Vegas scene. A couple months ago I saw her promoting a few brand ambassador collaborations. However, as of late, I haven't seen any new posts."

Sisko laid a hand on his chest and leaned back. "Whaaaat? But she's always posting on the Gram."

"I know. Makes me wonder if this tea I have has something to do with her sudden absence. My sources say she and Troy have been seen around Vegas, and Mia appears to be sporting a baby bump." LaLa smirked while pointing to one of the jumbo screens.

"Girl, you know we have to do some digging. Baller babes, when we do find out, we'll let you know."

LaLa winked and nodded, then waved her hand dismissively. "But enough about them, before you tell us about Paris, I do have some hot tea to spill about one Atlanta native that, ahem, seems to like his women seasoned."

Chapter 10

Sisko picked up his mug and leaned back. He sipped while peeking over the rim. "Go on, I'm listening."

"Remember when I went to Miami for the BMA Awards?"

Sisko nodded. "Yes, I remember."

"I ran into my good friend, Derrik Carter, who happened to have a beautiful woman on his arm. He made it very clear that she was a business associate. I was trying to figure out where I'd seen her before. Then it hit me when I saw her this past weekend. Girlfriend, Khloe Dillon loves to make her rounds at the parties of young business tycoons. She's finally snagged herself one fine, young stallion."

"Who she done snatched up out of Atlanta?"

"Bakari Woods, the CEO of BWoodz Systems. He's on the list of up-and-coming business tycoons to watch. They were awfully chummy at this charity event he sponsored in Midtown. When I asked him, he was proud to say she's the love of his life. Congratulations, you two!"

Sisko grinned and placed his mug back on the table. "She definitely snagged a rich and fine one. Congratulations, boo!"

"Now what about this trip to Paris? Tell us more. Anything exciting to report on?" LaLa leaned in, smiling.

Sisko popped his lips and clapped his hands. "As I've already said, it was an ahh-mazing trip. If you haven't checked out my posts, make sure you do by following me @PettyPrinceATL. I posted just about every single day I was in Paris. But y'all, how about while I was over there, I had the pleasure of meeting another ATLien. Well, he's a transplant from Jersey. But nevertheless, he's a doctor—no, excuse me—surgeon from Buckhead who has his own practice and works out of Northside Hospital. The cameras caught him in all his fineness, and his pics went viral. From what I heard, he's been getting offers from all over. The fashion world is wondering if we'll eventually have a surgeon-turned-model who will grace us with his presence on the runway."

"And who is this surgeon?" LaLa raised an eyebrow.

Sisko popped his lips. "Now LaLa, girl it's funny 'cause the baller's business we 'bout to be up in is your boy's."

"My boy? Who?" LaLa picked up her mug and leaned back.

"Derrik Carter."

LaLa choked. She sat up straight and placed the mug on the table. "I'm sorry, what did you just say?"

"Yep, this tea is piping hot too." Sisko popped his lips again. "So, you know I did a little digging and found out our sexy surgeon, Dr. Jamal Edwards is the former spouse of none other than Derrik Carter's wife, Desiree."

LaLa clutched her chest. "I know you lying."

"Am not. It's public record. But girl, there's more. The math ain't mathing on the dates of them gorgeous Carter twins being born and the Edwards' divorce."

LaLa's eyebrows shot up. "Wait, are you saying Derrik and Desiree Carter were having an affair?"

"I'm not saying anything, but we need to make some calls." Sisko pointed to his left at the jumbo television screen on the wall. "I had the pleasure of speaking with Dr. Jamal Edwards about going viral. Now, he's modest y'all. The good doctor didn't want all of this attention, but he can't help that he has a handsome face and whew, the body these fashion designers look for. Personally, I'm excited because he's dating one of my favorite Gucci buyers, Christian Hilcrest. I just love them together."

LaLa snapped her fingers. "Maybe we can get an exclusive. I'll have to put in a call to my friend. Now, before you share the rest of your trip, we have to take a quick break for a word from our sponsors. Y'all get your mugs because we're serving up some more hot tea on a possible new couple alert, Jamin Love and Shayla Starr. Yes, from the group Love in Minor Keyz better known as LMK. That's right, the R&B group under Derrik Carter's BlakBeatz Entertainment label. Stay tuned! We'll be right back!"

11

THAT MAN WAS NO GOOD FOR YOU

Angela sat motionless on the couch, the remote clutched in her hand like it was the only thing tethering her to reality. Through the speakers, the sound of Mariah Carey's "Breakdown" filtered out, the lyrics resonating with the ache in her chest. Although the exclusive footage had aired hours ago, she remained glued to the screen, unable to tear her gaze away from the slow-motion betrayal.

Jamal. In Paris.

Smiling, relaxed.

His hand resting intimately on another man's thigh.

Not just any man. His lover.

Angela blinked back the burn of tears, forcing herself to watch again as the gossip hosts dissected every detail. They displayed images of Jamal whispering in Christian's ear, his hand lingering at the small of his back, as they gazed at each other. Then came the kiss. Listening to the commentary was brutal and unforgiving, but none of it compared to the voice in her own head. *This can't be happening.*

And yet, it was—proof, playing on an endless loop.

She'd watched the clip at least a dozen times, searching for some logical explanation, some way to convince herself she hadn't just watched her boyfriend parading another relationship across a Parisian runway like a damn trophy. But no matter how many times she tried to rationalize it, the truth remained: Jamal hadn't just betrayed her. He had flaunted it. Like she didn't exist.

Angela had spent the last hour trying to talk herself down, logicize, and make sense of what felt senseless. Was it real? Could there be an explanation? Had she missed the signs? The questions swirled, relentless. *How long? How many lies? Did he think I'd never find out?*

Her mind replayed the last few months, dissecting every moment with Jamal, every excuse, every time he brushed off her questions about his sudden trips, emergency surgeries, his late-night calls. *Was I blind or just stupid?* And maybe the worst thought of all—*Did he ever love me, or was I just a convenient cover?*

Angela let out a shaking breath and pressed the heels of her hands to her eyes, forcing herself to stay calm. She had already let herself cry. Hot, angry tears had burned down her cheeks the moment the video started trending.

Her jaw clenched. The worst part wasn't the cheating. It was the public humiliation. She reached for the remote and turned off the TV, leaving the room filled with the melody of a song that captured everything she was experiencing. At that exact moment, Mariah's voice crooned sweetly in the background, asking what a person should do when someone they've been really loyal to suddenly stops loving them.

Angela let out a bitter laugh, shaking her head. "Damn. Really, Mimi? Did you have to hit me with that?"

She tightened her fists, refusing to let the sting of Jamal's betrayal turn into self-pity. No, she wouldn't let this break her. Jamal was in for a surprise if he expected she would simply fade to black quietly.

Her hands shook with frustration, fumbling for her phone, dropping it twice before finally holding it securely. She swiped across the screen, dialing Mia's number. The phone rang twice before her best friend came on the line. Angela's words poured out in a frantic rush.

Chapter 11

"Mia, I told you! I knew it! I fucking knew it! Jamal—he was cheating! But this? Hell no! I didn't see this coming! And it wasn't with another woman!"

"Ang, I'm gonna need you to breathe. Slow down and explain what happened."

"LaLa and Sisko with their messy asses is what happened! Jamal wasn't even at a fucking conference in D.C. He was in Paris parading around with some buyer from Gucci named Christian! He's fucking gay, Mia! Gay! But do you wanna hear the fuck shit? I hope you're sitting down for this."

"I am. Lemme hear it."

"Why was he married to the same hoe that was fucking on Troy and Derrik!"

"I'm sorry, come again?"

"You heard me. Jamal's ex-wife fucked your husband and his best friend. Sisko said the math wasn't mathing. But Desiree had twins, and you said Troy doesn't have twins running in his family, right?"

"No, he doesn't. Not on either side. But wait, Ang, back this up. You found out Jamal is gay and that his ex-wife is Desiree all on *Baller Bizness*? When?"

Angela ran a trembling hand through her hair and blew out a deep breath. "A couple of hours ago. They talked about Troy playing for the Raiders, you not being online anymore, and the rumors around your pregnancy. But it was brief. Since LaLa knows Troy, she said she was gonna be calling for an exclusive. I would've called you already, but I've been trying to get in touch with Jamal. Here he was acting like it was just Tré when he's the one that's gay too! I should've known with his ass running up to that country club all the time. Now it makes perfect sense. Everything Tré was saying about them hanging out there. I'm the fucking fool, Mia."

"Ang, listen, I need to make a quick call. Let me get my head wrapped around what we can do about Jamal. I'll think of something. Just relax and stay put. Don't do anything! Do you hear me?"

Angela stared at the phone for a second, confused by Mia's response.

She needed her best friend's help in figuring out what to do, and she was blowing her off. But she was also aware Mia was trying to fix her troubled marriage. Her own issues with Jamal had to take a back seat. Dejected, Angela replied quietly, "Okay, fine. I won't. But hurry up please."

"Alright. I'll call you back."

Angela ended the call with a slow exhalation. The living room had a suffocating feel now, the walls threatening to close in with every passing second. She needed a moment before she completely lost it. Dragging herself up from the couch, she padded into the kitchen. The light from the range hood cast a soft glow over the space, the familiar scent of her mother's cooking still hanging in the air. Angela moved on autopilot, grabbing a glass from the cabinet and filling it with water from the fridge. The first sip was crisp, enough to soothe the dryness in her throat. She took another, slower this time, trying to center herself. But before she could even put the glass down, she heard the sharp intake of breath behind her.

"Lo sabía! I knew it!" Bianca stood in the middle of the floor with her hands on her hips. She scoffed, "I knew that man was no good for you. But you, you never listen. Nunca escuchas. You never do."

Angela sighed, rubbing her temples to ward off an impending headache. "Mamá, por favor—"

Bianca lifted a hand, cutting her off. "Por favor, nothing. You ignored every red flag, every warning. And now, look," she pointed to the living room, shaking her head. "The whole world found out before you did."

Angela fought the sting behind her eyes. She wanted to be angry, wanted to snap back, but the truth sat between them, undeniable.

I just needed some water, not a lecture. She sighed, running a hand down her face. "Mamá, I didn't come in here for this. And now's not the time to hear 'I told you so.'"

"¿Y cuándo es el momento, mija? When? Tomorrow, huh? Next week?" Bianca shot back, her voice rising with every word. "¿Por qué no? I tried to warn you, but you still let that snake slither his way into your heart, and look what happened!"

Angela leaned against the cold marble countertop, her grip tightening

Chapter 11

on the edge. She stared back at her mother and retorted, "I didn't let anything happen. And I always listen to you, but you don't get it. Jamal wasn't like this. It was different in the beginning. He was kind, loving and supportive. I don't know what changed. We were truly happy."

"Happy? ¿Cómo? How can you say that when it's obvious he was cheating on you from the start? And not with one but two people. He had a wife and then a man. I know I raised you better than this!"

"I didn't know, okay! He made me feel special, loved. I thought we were building a future together. Do you really think I would've stayed if I knew he was doing *this*? It sucks, Mamá, but I had to find this out myself... no matter how embarrassing and hurtful it is."

"You learned exactly what I was trying to tell you, right? That pendejo was lying to you all this time and playing right in your face."

"Yes! That's what I learned. Dios mío, Mamá, you think I didn't notice? I confronted him! And every single time he made me feel crazy for even asking. Like I was the problem! He lied to me, okay. But I also learned that I can't let you run my life!"

"Run your life? That's what you got out of this? I've been trying to protect you, mija!"

"Protect me or control me? More like control, 'cause you've never trusted me to make my own decisions. You or Tré!"

"Because you never made the right ones! Mira lo que pasó con Jamal! You picked another man who was gay, mija! Tré could see that shit from a mile away."

"Oh please! Tré couldn't see anything. He just assumed every man with nice shoes was gay."

"Now we know why," Bianca pressed her lips together, eyes narrowing as she gave Angela *that* look—the one that said *mmhmm, girl, don't play dumb.*

Okay, Tré was in the life. He would know. Pushing the thought to the back of her mind, Angela shrugged indifferently. "Well, he got lucky that time."

"And this time?"

"Jamal wasn't gay when we met!"

143

"Doesn't matter, Tré must've known. Why do you think he was doing background checks?"

"Nobody asked him to! It was none of his business. And it's none of yours! I never asked for this!"

"Mija, por favor, just listen to me! I've been trying to tell you what I know because I've lived more life than you. Men like Jamal, they don't change. They just get better at hiding. You think I don't care how you feel right now? You think I wanted this for you? To see my daughter humiliated on national television? I wanted you happy! I prayed every night I was wrong about him. It hurts to see you suffer like this."

"What hurts most isn't even the cheating. It's that everyone knew. Everyone but me, Mamá. But I have to be the one who lives with this. Not you. Can't I do that for once in my life?" Angela replied softly, wiping away a stray tear.

"Angela, you have always been so strong and capable. I'm not happy you're hurting. I would trade being right for your happiness any day. This shame you're feeling? It's not yours to carry. A man who lives in shadows will always cast them on the people closest to him. That man . . . he was never going to give you what you deserve. And you've been through so much. First you lost Tré, and now this man you believed was going to be your husband one day. I worry for your mental well-being. So much loss, so much pain. It's not healthy. I don't want you to go back to that dark place again."

"I won't. I'm never going back there. Yes, Tré's death broke my heart, and I made some poor choices in how I dealt with it. But I survived that, and I'll survive this too. Now that I know the truth about Jamal, I can finally move on. And I will. On my terms. Not yours."

"Okay, mija. I hear you. Ven aquí." Bianca spread her arms wide. Angela stepped into her mother's warm embrace as she promised, "I'm here for you, no matter what."

"I know. Thanks, Mamá," Angela whispered, squeezing tighter.

Bianca let her go, and Angela moved over to the kitchen window, her attention locked on the swaying branches of the oak tree outside. The wind had picked up, mirroring the storm brewing within her soul. She

Chapter 11

wrapped her arms around herself, not for warmth, but for something to hold on to. Something solid. Because everything else—the love she thought she had, the future she'd imagined with Jamal—had crumbled in an instant. The truth sat in her chest like a stone: Jamal had never been hers. Not really. But now she was past that. Past the tears. Past the initial shock. What she needed to do next . . . she wasn't sure yet.

As if Bianca had read her mind, she gave Angela a knowing look. "Mija, at least now you can be with someone who loves all of you, not just the convenient parts."

"No, Mamá. I'm not jumping into something else because things didn't work out with Jamal."

"Who said anything about jumping? All I'm saying is that you deserve someone who treats you right, and not like his dirty little secret."

"When he comes around, I'll deal with him then. Right now, I'm not thinking about nobody."

Bianca narrowed her eyes, challenging her. "I think you have been. Simeon has proven himself to be dependable time and time again. Why not him?"

"No! You're only saying that because you like having him around. I just went through a humiliating breakup. How can you possibly think starting something with Simeon would be a good idea?"

"Have you ever stopped to compare them? Simeon is successful, caring, and every time you call, he's there when you need him. Dependable, unlike Jamal. And I saw you looking at him that day, mija. You're not blind. That man is attractive and quite the charmer. A gentle giant, really. Bigger than Jamal in every way: height and personality . . ." Bianca paused, a cheeky smile appearing on her face when she added, "And I bet you he's big down there too."

"Mamá!" Angela's cheeks flushed with embarrassment, but she couldn't stop the naughty grin tugging at her lips. Unlike the emptiness Jamal had left behind, the notion of Simeon had sparked a fiery need inside.

"He's a good man, Angela. The kind of man who will love and cherish you."

"How do you know?"

"Don't play with me, mija. I know his parents. That boy was raised right."

Angela rocked her head back and forth. "I don't think I'm ready for that."

"Ready or not, life goes on. And you need to get over your ex, so why not get under the next?"

"Mamá, I know you did not just suggest I get over Jamal by sleeping with Simeon?"

"Yes, I did." Bianca snapped back with a neck roll. She moved to stand in front of her, resting both hands on Angela's shoulders. "Mija, listen to me. You have someone who cares about you, who wants to be there for you. Simeon has been by your side through everything lately. Give him a chance. What could it hurt?"

Angela stared at the floor, mulling over her mother's question. She appreciated Simeon's support and friendship, but could she open herself up to someone else? Shaking her head, she answered her mother.

"What if I'm just trying to escape my feelings for Jamal, and I make another mistake? I don't want to hurt Simeon if he's a rebound."

Bianca held Angela's face, raising her chin to meet her gaze. "Choosing happiness is never a mistake. You deserve someone who will stand by you and love you unconditionally. And from what I've seen, Simeon is that person."

Tears brimmed in Angela's eyes. She took a deep breath and nodded. As her thoughts drifted to Simeon, hope and trepidation fluttered in her chest. Perhaps it was time for her to embrace a future that promised love, support, and understanding. She owed it to herself to find out if Simeon was the right person.

Angela finally conceded, her words slow and measured. "I guess it couldn't hurt to see where things could go with him."

"It won't. Remember, you deserve happiness, mija. Love doesn't wait for us to be ready. Whether or not you believe it, love can bloom from the ashes of a heartbreak. You just have to be open to it." Bianca gave her hand a comforting squeeze and then walked away.

Chapter 11

Once her mother exited the kitchen, Angela pulled her phone out of her pocket and typed a message to Simeon:

> Hey where are you? ~Angela

> Wherever you need me to be ~Simeon

> I need to be with you ~Angela

> Meet me at Omarosé ~Simeon

12

NO REGRETS

ANGELA MADE HER WAY TO THE ENTRANCE OF OMAROSÉ. SHE noticed Simeon coming out of the lounge, his towering frame blocking her view of the inside. The thudding beat of Diddy's "Last Night" reverberated against the closed door behind him. He met her gaze, concern visible in his expression. Angela mustered a faint smile and offered a small wave. Simeon closed the distance between them, drawing her into his muscular arms. His intoxicating scent overwhelmed her senses. She buried her face in his chest, taking another whiff. He smelled amazing.

"Hey, you look upset. What's wrong?" Simeon murmured in her hair.

Taking a step back, Angela met his worried eyes. She hesitated, searching to find the right words. But finally blurted, "It's Jamal."

"What's up?"

"He cheated on me."

"C'mere. Let's move from this door."

Angela followed him to the parking garage where Simeon led her to his truck, which wasn't far from where she'd left her car. He stopped and turned around, his handsome face now marked with frustration. The crease between his eyebrows deepened, but his voice remained calm.

"Now, tell me. How did you find out?"

"*Baller Bizness*, with their messy asses."

"*Baller Bizness*? How in the hell did he end up on there?"

Angela smoothed the edges of her hair and took a few steps before exploding in an angry rant. "That arrogant pendejo was playing in my face the whole time! Lying! He told me he was in D.C., but he was in Paris at a fashion show with some Gucci buyer! Their pictures are all over the Internet. Fashion's hottest new couple. Tuh! This is so fucking embarrassing! And all this time, I've been asking what's wrong and fighting for our relationship. It was all for nothing! Nothing! And Mamá acting like I knew about this or something. Do you really think I would've stayed with him if I'd known? Hell no!"

"Whoa, okay. Okay. Slow down, angel. Look at me. I need you to take a deep breath."

Simeon drew her back to stand directly in front of him, his large hands rubbing her arms to ease the storm of emotions threatening to take over. Following his instruction, Angela took several deep breaths. She finally looked up into his dark brown eyes, finding her center. He nodded, coaxing her to continue.

"Okay, so truth be told, when we first got together, I knew he was with someone else. He was . . . he was married. Our affair went on for a year. You can think I was wrong, but he wasn't happy with her. Well, that's what he claimed, because she was barely home and didn't want to start a family. The irony is, like her, he started traveling. A lot. Anyway, he left his wife for me. But how about it turns out his ex-wife was fucking on Mia's husband and his best friend."

"Wait, what?" Simeon interjected, his eyebrows arching in surprise.

Angela nodded and continued explaining, "It's a long story, but basically *Baller Bizness* got to digging in his background. They found out Jamal's ex-wife is now married to Troy's best friend, Derrik Carter. That's how he ended up on there."

"Damn, that's some wild shit."

"Yeah, but you know what though? It doesn't matter because it was all a lie. Just like my brother, who was out here living a double life. I had to find out Jamal was gay on national television. He's gay, Simeon. Gay!

Chapter 12

How was I supposed to know? And what the fuck did I do to deserve this, huh?"

Simeon blinked before blurting. "Wait—what? Hold up . . . Jamal is gay? Are you serious right now?"

Angela gave a bitter laugh. "Dead serious."

He ran a hand over his beard, eyes wide. "Damn. That's . . . I wasn't ready for that one. And you—God, Angela, you had to find out on national TV? That's foul on so many levels."

She looked away, her body tight with emotion, and Simeon stepped closer, his voice dropping but laced with disbelief and empathy.

"Listen, you didn't do nothing. And you didn't deserve any of that. Not the lies. Not the humiliation. He was a coward and selfish." His gaze softened. "But you're here now. And no matter what he did, it doesn't change who you are. You're strong. You're still standing. I see you, Angela. Every piece."

Swiping away a stray tear, Angela retorted with a sarcastic laugh, "You think I don't know that? Ugh! I just . . . I feel so raw now. I let myself fall for him. Maybe I'm just not meant for love."

"Ay, don't talk like that. I know you got a lot of love to give, and you deserve to receive it too. But ain't none of us immune, angel. Love involves risk for everybody. Sometimes we get hurt, but that don't mean we stop trying," Simeon replied softly, his thumb tracing soothing circles on her arm.

"But what if I can't trust my own judgment anymore? What if I keep making the same mistakes over and over again?" Her eyes searched his for reassurance.

He nodded in acknowledgment. "What if you don't? You won't learn, right? It was Maya Angelou that said something about having the courage to trust love one more time and always one more time. You can be careful. But don't let your past define your future relationships. Eventually, you'll learn to trust again. Time heals all, right? And you know you're not alone on this journey. I'm here for you."

"Talking to you does make me feel a little better. Thank you for listening," she whispered with unshed tears pooling in her ducts.

Simeon gathered her in his arms, his embrace offering comfort from the chaos within. He murmured into her hair, "You don't have to thank me, but anytime. And Jamal never valued you. He wasn't deserving of you. It's okay. You just ended up loving the wrong person."

Angela clenched her hands into tight fists, her breathing growing heavier with emotion. The woman standing on the cliff in the painting came to mind. *It's now or never.* Angela was ready to take the leap. She just hoped Simeon would be there to catch her. "No. Don't talk about him anymore!" Angela snapped, wrenching herself away from him. She stepped back, her eyes burning with defiance. "I don't love him. That feeling's gone 'cause I . . . I-I want you!"

Simeon tilted his head, as if questioning her bold declaration. But Angela meant what she said. Jamal had been stringing her along for months. Although she had loved him, that love no longer lived in her heart. It had vanished and was now replaced by a bitter hatred. Silence surrounded them, thick with unexpressed desire crackling in the air. It was as though time had halted, amplifying the heat between their bodies.

Without responding, Simeon advanced, closing the distance. He grasped the back of her neck and pulled Angela to him, capturing her lips in a kiss so intense it seemed to sear through her very soul. With each sweep of his tongue against hers and every gentle nip at her lower lip, Angela found herself more entranced by Simeon.

She craved him.

She needed *him*.

Her hands roamed over Simeon's broad shoulders, reveling in the tautness of his muscles under her fingers. She slid her palms down the front of his firm and bulky frame. As their kiss deepened, Angela's reservations crumbled, replaced by the firm conviction that her place was here, with Simeon. When they finally broke apart, their foreheads rested together while they caught their breath. Angela's eyes fluttered open, meeting his gaze.

"I've been wanting to do this for weeks."

Simeon let out a deep sigh, a faint smile curving his lips. His thumb brushed along her jawline, the calloused pad grazing her skin so lightly it

Chapter 12

sent a shiver racing down her spine. His voice was low and gravelly when he replied, "And I've been thinking about this moment since you walked into Mamá's kitchen. Every time I saw you, my childhood crush on you just kept growing."

"So you've had a crush on me since we were kids?" Angela inquired softly.

He drew back a bit, studying her face as though committing every curve and freckle to memory. "Ever since the day you brought Junior over to play with my brother Lijah. You don't know how much I've been holding back. I wondered if you'd ever feel the same."

Her lips parted to speak, but at first, no words came. Instead, she reached up, her fingers brushing over his wrist near her jaw. The warmth of his skin beneath hers grounded Angela in a way nothing else could. She tightened her grip, as if to anchor herself to him. "I felt it. Whenever you're near me . . . I feel it."

"I could see it in your eyes, the way you've held back."

"I couldn't get you out of my head. But I would never cross that line."

"You don't need to explain. I understand why you couldn't allow yourself to feel anything before." He moved his other hand up to cradle her face and leaned closer. "But what about now? What do you want, angel?"

The nickname rolled off his tongue like a whispered prayer. Her heart responded with a furious thud that echoed in her ears. Angela was certain he could hear it too. What did she want? Was she really ready to take this leap with Simeon? He was everything Jamal wasn't—rough around the edges, dominating, and utterly irresistible. Yes. She wanted to be claimed by this Alpha male who made her feel alive again.

"What do you want?" Simeon pressed again, interrupting her reverie. His thumb moved gently against her cheekbone in a slow stroke that sent heat pooling in her stomach. His voice dropped even lower, almost coaxing now. "Tell me."

"I-I . . ." Angela took a shaky breath as she tried to gather herself. Words felt inadequate compared to the depth of what she was feeling, but she forced herself to speak before fear or doubt stole this moment from her. "I want you, this. I want us," she answered, the words spilling out before she had time to second-guess them.

But once they were out there, they felt right. They were true.

"Say it again," he urged, his tone now tinged with something fierce and desperate.

Angela reached out, gripping the front of his shirt, and declared with more conviction, "I. Want. You."

"You got me, baby. I'm all yours," he replied with a wide grin spreading across his face.

Simeon eliminated the small gap between them, their foreheads touching once more. He kept soothing her with gentle caresses. Every nerve ending in her body seemed to come alive under his touch. She smiled despite the tears welling up in her eyes. They weren't from sadness, but from being overwhelmed by emotions.

"So, what happens now?"

Simeon drew back a little, his gaze roving across her face as if searching for something, wiping away a stray tear that had escaped, streaking her cheek. She shuddered when his mahogany eyes darkened with passion. His hand glided down to rest on her waist, drawing her closer to him again. He tilted her chin up, his thumb brushing over her bottom lip. "From now on, we don't hold back. Just be present with me. Right here, right now."

"I'm not going anywhere." Angela offered a small smile, teasingly adding, "Unless you make me wait weeks for another kiss like that."

"You're mine, angel. Ain't no more waiting."

And with those words, his lips were on hers again. Not rushed, but slow and confident, as if every moment before had been leading to this. The low drone of the parking garage faded into the background, with the far-off screech of tires and the muted thud of car doors closing, overshadowed by the mesmerizing way he molded his body to hers. Angela leaned into him to keep her balance after his brazen, deep kiss that made her feel as though the ground had shifted beneath her feet.

Simeon eventually broke away, pausing to rest his forehead on hers before releasing a deep sigh. "Let's go home."

Chapter 12

Angela blinked up at him, lips still tingling. "*Your* house?"

"That a problem?"

"Not unless you're planning on making me wait again once we get there."

His chuckle was low, rumbling through his chest as he laced his fingers with hers and led her to the other side of the truck. "I don't repeat foolish mistakes." A loud beep echoed when Simeon unlocked it. He opened the passenger door and ordered, "Get in. We'll come back for your car later."

Angela's breath was wobbly as she slid inside. The interior still held a lingering trace of his cologne. She barely had time to settle before he shut the door and rounded the hood. He glanced at her with a comforting smile before starting the engine.

Aside from Chris Brown singing his hit "Feel Something," the drive started out quiet. The city lights streaked past, their glow bouncing off the windshield while she stole glances at him. Simeon drove with one hand on the wheel, the other resting on his thigh, fingers tapping idly like he was working through something in his head.

"So, umm . . . are you always this intense?"

Simeon cut his eyes to her, a smirk tugging at the corner of his lips. "You don't like it?"

"I didn't say that." She shifted in her seat, crossing her legs. "Just . . . I don't think I've ever been kissed like that before."

"Well, I aim to stand out from the crowd."

Angela clicked her tongue against the roof her mouth, but she couldn't fight the heat creeping up her neck. She let out a breathy laugh, shaking her head. "Mission accomplished."

"And you really are beautiful when you blush."

"Thank you." Angela attempted to calm down, focusing her attention on the R&B sounds of Silk's "I Can Go Deep." But it was no use. She began fidgeting with the hem of her shirt, gathering her thoughts before speaking up. "So, what's your story, Simeon? A man with all that you have to offer . . . I find it hard to believe you're single. Why aren't you in a relationship?"

"Ah, the million-dollar question. Let's just say I've been through my fair share of ups and downs. Relationships demand a level of commitment and sacrifice I wasn't ready for . . . until now, that is."

"Oh, really? And what changed your mind?"

"Running into someone who challenges you in unexpected ways tends to shift one's outlook," Simeon answered cryptically.

Curious, Angela couldn't resist asking, "Am I that someone?"

"You might be."

Her face split with a wide grin at the suggestion. Angela unintentionally leaned closer, drawn by the moment's magnetic pull. They were wrapped in a thoughtful silence, teeming with unvoiced questions.

Looking around at the unfamiliar surroundings, she asked, "Where do you live?"

"Just a few miles away. Feeling nervous?"

"No," she replied quickly, her fingers curling in her lap.

He hummed, the corner of his mouth tugging up. "Already fibbing?" he teased. Angela scoffed, but her pulse betrayed her, thrumming faster when he reached over at a red light and ran his knuckles down her thigh. "No need to be nervous, angel. I got you."

The light turned green, and just like that, his touch was gone, replaced by the steady roar of the engine as he maneuvered through the streets. A few minutes later, Simeon parked in the driveway of a modest, ranch-style home with dark brick and large windows. He turned to her, his gaze intense, unreadable.

"You ready?" His voice was low, serious now.

Angela met his eyes. She gave a slight nod and a clear answer. "Sí. I am."

Something flickered across his face—satisfaction, maybe relief. He tipped his head, then got out and came around to her side, opening the door before she had the chance.

"Come on," he murmured, offering his hand.

She took it, stepping into the crisp night air, into him, into whatever this was about to be. Angela walked beside him up the stone path leading to the entrance. The house loomed before her, its brick exterior softened by the glow of strategically placed lights along the walkway. Simeon

Chapter 12

unlocked the door and pushed it open, moving aside to allow her to enter.

The moment they were inside, the home's warmth replaced the coolness. A rich aroma of amber, leather, and musk hung heavy in the air. The modern space was breathtaking and luxurious. The living room stretched before her, its open floor plan flowing directly into the kitchen. Recessed lighting created a soft glow across the hardwood floors, showcasing the room's rich textures.

Angela's gaze swept over the expansive living room, taking in the details. It was masculine, but sophisticated. A black leather sofa, loveseat, and armchair formed a stylish seating area centered on a glass coffee table. Huge windows were framed by heavy slate-gray drapes, a low-profile entertainment unit and state-of-the-art sound system sat against the wall, and a single abstract painting hung above the fireplace, its dark swirls of color oddly hypnotic.

"This is . . ." Angela turned to him, struggling to find the right word. She took a cursory glance of the area and decided on, "Unexpected."

Simeon arched an eyebrow, casually shrugging off his jacket and draping it over the back of the armchair. "That a good thing or a bad thing?"

"Definitely good," she admitted, after handing him her lightweight coat. Angela strolled further into the room and made herself comfortable on the sofa. "I just figured you for more of a simple setup kind of guy."

A low chuckle rumbled from him as he moved toward the wet bar near the fireplace. "I like my space to feel like me. And I think you know by now I'm far from a simple kind of guy." He went into the fridge and grabbed a bottle of the cannabis infused wine, then held it up in offering. "Drink?"

Angela wished it were the real thing. She needed to take the edge off. But the wine sans alcohol wasn't so bad, and it still gave her a buzz. She eyed the bottle, shrugging with a small smile. "Sure, why not?"

Simeon poured them each a glass and then switched on the surround sound system. The soft melodies from Raheem Devaughn's "Customer" floated through the room. Angela took a slow sip before setting the low-ball glass down on the coffee table. Once more, her gaze darted around Simeon's cozy haven, taking in its masculine ambience that was as heady as the wine they were enjoying. Her eyes roamed over his silhouette illuminated by the low-lighting, his broad shoulders straining under his shirt, and his chiseled jaw, partly hidden by a rugged beard that hinted at delicious friction. Suddenly, their eyes clashed.

Simeon leaned against the bar, watching her with that same unreadable expression. "You good?"

"Shouldn't I be asking you that? I mean, you just brought a woman you hardly know into your home."

A slow smirk played on his lips. "For starters, I never invite someone I barely know over. Besides, I know you well enough to welcome you here. Since I bought this place, you're the only woman besides my mom and sisters who's stepped inside."

"Well, I'm flattered then. Maybe I should feel special."

Simeon pushed off the bar, his steps slow and purposed as he crossed the room. He stood before her, extended a hand to help her up, and declared, "You should always feel special, angel. Especially around me."

Angela peered up at him, searching for any signs of doubt or hesitation in his eyes. Instead, she only saw a firm, unshakeable confidence that made her own anxieties seem trivial and ridiculous. Unable to hold back, she asked, "Is this really what you want?"

"More than anything." He stepped closer, his hands gently cupping her face. Simeon gazed at her with adoration and confessed, "I've wanted you for so long, Angela. But I'll wait as long as it takes for you to be ready."

"I'm ready."

Simeon smiled, his thumb tracing the curve of her cheekbone. "I hope so, because I've been waiting for the day when I could finally express how much I care about you. Let me love you, my angel. Let me show what it feels when a man genuinely loves you."

The room seemed to shrink, the space between them charged with something electric, something inevitable.

She swallowed, her heart thudding hard against her ribs. "Simeon . . ."

Chapter 12

Words eluded her, especially with the way he gazed at her, as if she were the center of his universe.

"If you don't want this, tell me." He murmured, still stroking slow circles against her skin. "But if you do . . ." His fingers slid under her chin, tilting her face up to his. "Let me in completely."

Angela exhaled, a tremor in her breath. She wasn't used to this—the patience, the reverence in his touch, the way he made her feel valued, not just wanted. "I don't want to say no."

"Then don't."

Simeon edged closer, his warm breath caressing her skin. He paused cocking his head slightly as if giving her a silent opportunity to retreat if she wished. But she didn't. She couldn't. Instead, Angela leaned in, closing the distance between them, her fingers gripping the soft fabric of his shirt. Their mouths met in an intoxicating kiss that was both fervent and languorous. His tongue slid against hers, wet and eager, stirring a heat that spiraled low in her belly. Meanwhile, his hands explored her body with a surety that made her knees weak.

"Off," he muttered against her mouth, his voice raw, commanding.

Angela didn't protest, lifting her arms for him to strip the fabric off her. Her bra was next, his fingers fumbling with the clasp for only a moment before it fell away. He unbuttoned her jeans and helped her slide them down her thighs until they bunched around her ankles, and she kicked them aside. Simeon's hand snaked its way down Angela's spine, stopping just above the edge of her lace panties. With a devilish grin, he pressed lightly against her crack, and she shuddered in response. She moaned into his mouth, encouraging him to continue. Simeon slid her flimsy lingerie piece down her legs. Instead of tossing them aside, Angela watched as he tucked them into his pocket and stepped back a couple of feet.

"Cristo, Angela, eres tan hermosa. So fucking beautiful," he gritted out, before quickly undressing himself.

Angela found herself face-to-face with a Zulu warrior. Simeon was undoubtedly the most beautiful man she'd ever seen, his muscular chest and arms adorned with permanent ink that spoke of a life rich with culture and experience. His well-defined abs and powerful thighs promised strength and stamina beyond what she could imagine. Angela's gaze drifted, tracing the contours of his torso until they reached the sharp dip of his hips—the unmistakable "V". Her throat went dry. Her eyes hovered there for just a second too long.

"You're staring. See something you like?"

Angela blinked rapidly, heat rushing to her cheeks. "I wasn't," she protested, but her words faltered. She swallowed hard. "Okay. So, maybe I was staring. You're very . . . fit."

"Fit?" he repeated with mock offense while giving his thick, veined shaft a tug. "Is that all you can say about it?"

How was she supposed to respond? How could anyone think clearly when faced with such a magnificent sight? She hadn't had many lovers, but enough to recall each one, and none were this size. Her mother was right. Simeon was indeed a big boy. As she stared at him, his dick twitched a little, her own wetness intensifying. Unable to resist any longer, she reached out to touch him.

Her hands wandered, tracing the rugged planes of his chest, fingers gliding over the defined ridges of his muscles flexing under her touch. Angela raked her nails lightly over his abdomen, reveling in his staggered breaths and how his body responded to her like he had been waiting, aching for this moment as much as she had. Motivated by his reaction, Angela's fingertips ghosted over his length, the silky smooth skin stretched to rigidity, causing her pulse to quicken. She bit her lip, captivated by the girth and weight in her palm.

Simeon grunted, closing his eyes in pleasure. He pressed into her hand, the heat of his erection throbbing with need, demanding more. Angela brought her gaze up, locking with his, recognizing the desire burning bright in his eyes. His grip tightened at her waist before sliding lower, kneading the swell of her hips. She arched into him, her pebbled nipples brushing against his solid form. A little moan escaped her lips when his mouth trailed along the column of her throat, his teeth grazing the delicate skin just enough to send heat pooling in her core. His fingers threaded through her hair, tilting her head up, and their lips met in a

Chapter 12

hungry kiss that left them gasping for air. She whispered his name in a hoarse voice.

He pulled back slightly to look at her. "You want more?"

Angela nodded eagerly, unable to form words. He guided her to sit on the edge of the leather couch. She observed Simeon taking a knee between her legs. His muscular arms slipped under her thighs, opening them wide like a flower, anticipating the sun's warmth. Angela watched him dipping his head toward her vertical folds and extending his tongue to explore her. He traced slow circles around her entrance, teasing the soft, puckered skin. She undulated her hips closer to his mouth, and Simeon latched onto her protruding nub. His fingers plunged into her slick, soaked pussy, curling just right to make her thighs tremble. In pleasure, Angela's back bowed off the couch while he probed inside her.

"Joder, Za," she gasped in Spanish, her nails digging into his broad shoulders. "¡No te detengas! Don't. You. Fucking. Stop."

"¿Te gusta ese? You like my fingers fucking you deep?" Her hips jerked in want, unable to say it. His thumb pressed into her clit, spinning tight, maddening circles. "I like to talk, baby. You need to tell me."

"Sí! Dios, sí! Más. Please, more," Angela panted, her chest heaving.

Simeon didn't waste a second. He yanked her legs wider, spreading her like a feast, and dove in, his tongue skillfully caressing her bundle of nerves with a wicked accuracy that made her scream out her appreciation.

"Fuck! That feels so good."

He pulled back just enough to give her praises too. "You taste so good, angel. Like forbidden fruit drizzled in honey." His fingers sank deeper, pumping in and out. The wet squelch of her hot and sticky center filled the room.

Angela's body quivered at the brink. She whimpered, "I'm so close. Soooo fucking close. Por favor, Za, I wanna—"

She couldn't finish her sentence. Simeon had latched onto her sensitive nub once more, sucking while his fingers plucked at her G-spot until she came undone. The first orgasm ripped through her like a wildfire. As a powerful sensation of pressure coiled in her belly, her inner muscles tightened around his long digits. Her body shook with continuous waves of pleasure. Simeon didn't let up, swirling his serpent-like tongue back and forth over her swollen button until she was squirming and writhing beneath him.

"Okay, okay, it's too much. Too much!"

Simeon leaned back a bit, his lips and beard glistening with her juices, a feral grin spreading across his face. He teased, his voice dripping with mockery. "Too much? For who? Not the same girl who just begged me for more?"

Angela glared at him, but there was no heat in it, just unadulterated lust. "Shut up and kiss me," she demanded, pulling him up to meet her lips.

Simeon didn't need to be told twice. He kissed her fiercely, his hand sliding down to grip her ass, squeezing hard. The flavor of her own arousal on his tongue sent a fresh jolt of desire through her. Angela playfully bit and pulled at his pillowy kissers, their mouths fervently engaged in a heated exchange.

He murmured against her mouth. "You're mine, now. All fucking mine."

"Prove it," she challenged, lowering her eyes to his thick, swollen masterpiece.

In one fluid motion, Simeon flipped her over, shoving her face-first into the plush leather couch. Simeon had her ass high in the air, presenting her pussy already glistening, the slickness dripping down her inner thighs. Angela heard the noises of a packet being torn apart. While sheathing himself, Simeon leaned close, muttering the filthy things he intended to do to her. An involuntary shiver coursed through her, electrifying every inch of her being, from the crown of her head to the bottom of her feet. His free hand slid between her legs, fingers spreading her pussy lips. Simeon rubbed his engorged mushroom tip up and down her slit, teasing at her entrance. The friction was maddening.

Desperate for him to plunge into her, Angela rocked back, hissing, "Stop fucking teasing."

"Shhh . . . patience, angel," Simeon replied with a low, rough grunt.

But he didn't make her wait long. He drove into her with one forceful

Chapter 12

motion, burying himself completely inside her. Angela cried out, the sound muffled by a throw pillow, the stretch and burn sending shockwaves through her body. He didn't give her time to adjust. His hips pounded into her with a rhythm that made her toes curl. Each pump was deep, relentless, his dick hitting that sweet spot inside her over and over again.

"You wanted me to fuck it up, right?"

"Uhn, yes! Oh Dios, por favor, Za! Fuck it up!" she screamed out in Spanish and English, her nails clawing at the couch cushions.

Simeon wasted no time in obeying her command with powerful, piston-like strokes, increasing in intensity. With every pump, her walls clenched and relaxed around his massive girth. The obscene sounds of him plunging into her sopping pussy were punctuated by the slapping of his meaty glutes against her ass cheeks. Angela dipped lower, her butt jiggling with every deep thrust. Sweat poured down Simeon's chiseled torso, dripping onto her back as he hammered into her. In and out. He had stretched her so wide, Angela thought she might split in half. But she didn't want it to stop. She wanted more.

Simeon tangled his fingers in her hair and yanked her head back, nipping at her earlobe. "Fuck, Angela. Tu coño is so sweet and so tight. I could fuck you like this forever."

Him talking dirty to her in Spanish sent a thrill through her. Angela begged, her pants short and shallow. "Por favor, Za. Harder! Don't stop."

He groaned, withdrawing and guiding her into the next position. "C'mere, baby... I need to see your thick ass ride it."

Simeon lowered himself onto the leather cushions. With a sly smirk, Angela straddled him like a queen claiming her throne. She steadied herself with one hand on the back of the couch and used the other to guide him between her slick folds. In a slow, grinding motion, she sat down, taking in every inch until she was fully seated on his lap.

He let out a strained grunt. "Fuuuck."

"You like that?" she taunted, rolling her hips in slow, sensual donuts.

"Sí, angel. Me encanta. I fucking love it. This tight little pussy was made just for me," Simeon groaned through clenched teeth.

Angela leaned forward, giving him access to her breasts, which Simeon grabbed and fondled. He pinched one of her nipples hard enough to make her gasp before drawing it into his mouth, sucking greedily while thrusting upward. This time, he didn't slow down. His dick was like a piston, driving into her with a force that left Angela breathless. He gripped her thighs, his fingers digging into her flesh hard enough to leave bruises. She didn't care, she wanted those marks. Her hands roamed over his chest, nails scratching his skin as she rode him. Simeon growled dirty words into her ear, calling her names only lovers used and promising things only they would do for each other's bodies.

"Uhn, fuck! Yes! Yes! Ay dios mío, I'm 'bout to come!"

"Yeah, that's it. I can feel you gripping my shit. Give it to me, angel. Gimme that nut," he murmured against her neck.

Angela's orgasm hit like a freight train. Her inner muscles tightened around his shaft so tight he had no choice but to follow. Angela screamed his name and Simeon groaned hers, it was explosive, messy, and so fucking perfect. Worn out, Angela collapsed against his chest, both of them panting. Sweat drenched their skin, and the air became infused with the combined scent of their lovemaking. Beneath her, Simeon's heart thudded against her cheek, a soothing rhythm that made her want to stay tangled with him forever. Slowly, she lifted her head, meeting his heavy-lidded dark chocolate gaze. There was satisfaction there, but also something deeper. Possession. Reverence. Certainty. Like she wasn't just a woman he had touched, but a woman he would never let go of. He rubbed lazy circles along her spine, his touch sending fresh waves of pleasure through her already spent body.

"You good, angel?"

Angela didn't answer right away. Instead, she let her fingertips roam the sharp planes of his jaw, mapping the rough stubble, memorizing every detail under the lamp's gentle glow. She finally responded with a question of her own. "Why do you call me angel?"

"Even before I knew your name meant that, you were the most beautiful girl I'd ever seen. The only way I could only describe you was as a real-life angel. My earth angel," Simeon caught her exploring hand, bringing it

Chapter 12

to his lips before capturing her mouth in a kiss that was neither hurried nor desperate, but deep and searing.

When he drew back, his voice dropped to a murmur. "I'll never hurt you, Angela. I swear it. You'll never regret letting me love you."

Something in her chest clenched tight, unfamiliar. She didn't want to be the kind of woman to let her heart lead, but with Simeon, resistance was pointless. She wasn't sure what tomorrow would bring, but for now —for *this*—there was no room for doubt. Her lips curled into a knowing smile after she settled against him once more, her body fitting to his like they had always belonged this way.

Angela pressed a kiss to his bare chest, letting the steady rhythm of his heartbeat soothe her. She whispered, "No regrets."

13

I NEED TO GIVE YOU SOME CELEBRATORY HEAD

Jamal drummed his fingers against the polished mahogany desk, grinning as he reread the email from the hospital's administration:

> *Congratulations, Dr. Edwards. We are delighted to announce your appointment as Chief of Surgery at Northside Regional Hospital, effective immediately. Your extraordinary contributions and proven leadership have set a high standard of excellence. We look forward to your continued success and the positive impact you will have on our institution.*

A wave of relief washed over Jamal. His personal life being shown on *Baller Bizness* was insignificant. This achievement was always in his destiny. He should've been celebrating and basking in his success. But he couldn't.

Not quite yet.

An unresolved matter loomed over him, something that should have been resolved by now.

Angela.

Jamal hadn't spoken to her since Paris. He had ignored the slew of calls and texts that flooded his phone after *Baller Bizness* broke the story about his budding romance with Christian. She'd been begging for the truth and demanding an explanation. As if she deserved one. But didn't she?

What could he say? That Paris had been liberating? That Christian had given him something she never could? That he was sorry she had to find out this way? No. That wasn't his style.

She should've taken the hint. Jamal relaxed in his chair. The fact he was spending less time with her should have been the sign Angela needed to move on. He had more important things to focus on now—a future to build, a life to plan out, and no room for unnecessary distractions. To him, that's all she was now. An inconvenience. A temporary indulgence that had run its course. He was indifferent to her feelings and unconcerned with her misplaced loyalty. But the longer she went without being dealt with, the more unpredictable she could become. And unpredictability was dangerous.

His phone rang, its sharp tone cutting through the recesses of his mind. Jamal grumbled once he peered down, recognizing the number on the screen. *Speak of the relentless little pest.*

It was Angela.

He debated whether to pick up or ignore the call. Deciding it was time to deal with her head on, he tapped the green icon and raised the device to his ear.

"Jamal?"

He replied curtly, "Yes, what do you want?"

"What do you mean, 'what do you want'? I saw you on *Baller Bizness*! Your lying ass wasn't even in D.C.!"

"What have I told you? You can talk to me calmly and still get your point across without all this yelling," Jamal reprimanded her.

Angela sassed back, "Don't tell me what to do. I have every right to

Chapter 13

yell, cuss, or scream if I fucking want to. You lied to me! You were in Paris with another man! So, you've been gay this whole time?"

"No. It just happened."

"Shit like that doesn't just happen overnight, Jamal. You had to be fucking him for a while. Who the fuck do you take me for?"

"Since you see right through me, I don't know what to say," he responded, his tone sounding both defensive and weary.

Angela's voice seethed with bitter anger. "You cheated on me while I was grieving my brother, and all you can come up with is a half-assed 'I don't know what to say'? How could you do this to me?"

"I never intended to . . ." Jamal paused for a beat. He couldn't keep lying to her after misleading her for so long. Shaking his head, he continued, "Look, I never claimed to be perfect. I didn't mean for things to go this far. Things got . . . messy. Complicated."

"Messy? Complicated? That's your excuse? Don't give me that bullshit!"

"Angela, you knew my life was already complicated. If you couldn't handle that, then maybe you should've thought twice about getting with me."

"If I couldn't handle—what? You've been manipulating me since the start. Was anything you said about your wife even true? Or was that all a front for who you really are?"

"No, she was traveling a lot. I think *Baller Bizness* established she was fucking with Derrik Carter while we were still married."

"And what were you doing? Fucking on Christian and using me as a front? That's what you sorry-ass muthafuckas do on the down low. Then you had the nerve to try and gaslight me, making it seem like I was the problem! Now I know I was nothing more than just another pawn in your twisted game!"

"Oh, spare me the theatrics. You knew exactly what you were getting into. You didn't have any issues with being the other woman, did you? No, you didn't. You enjoyed the attention, the gifts, and the thrill of sneaking around behind my wife's back. Who was it that offered to have a baby when my wife refused? You even ended up with a house and a car out of it."

"I never asked for any of that shit! Of course I would offer to give you that. I loved you! But you took advantage of me when I was vulnerable. Had me believing we had a future together when the whole time you were just using me!"

"Don't act like you're the victim here. You were just as complicit in this as I was. But I never promised you anything after I left her."

"I can't believe this! You did promise me that we'd be together! Why the fuck did you tell me you left her and then came to be with me? No. Don't answer that. The joke's on me for thinking we had something real. It doesn't even matter when it's clear you love the Hershey highway. And you know what? I'm so glad I'm not one of your pawns anymore. I deserve better than this toxic-ass mess."

Jamal's tone turned icy, hardening with a calculated coldness. "Toxic? Not at all. Perhaps it was merely your fantasy of us versus reality. It is what it is, sweetheart. I'm sorry it had to end this way, but if you can't handle the truth, that's on you."

Angela said nothing in response. Instead, she hung up, leaving only the harsh echo of his last words.

Without thinking twice, Jamal blocked her number. He wasn't interested in explaining himself to her again, or to anyone. As his love with Christian blossomed, Jamal grew increasingly indifferent to the noise of those who dared question his happiness. After blocking her on all social media, he orchestrated a silent campaign, instructing his office staff and colleagues at the hospital to reject Angela's calls and report any unannounced visits to security. In his carefully controlled world, her feelings were irrelevant, and she was a distraction he would not tolerate.

Hours later, rather than going to the house he shared with Angela, Jamal unlocked the door and entered Christian's upscale condominium. He scanned the expansive, open-plan layout, with its gleaming hardwood floors and soaring ceilings. Natural light permeated the space through vast windows, highlighting the stylish, contemporary furnishings that exuded understated elegance. West Indies-inspired artwork covered the walls, the

Chapter 13

vibrant and rich hues providing a striking contrast to the décor's chic lines. A beautiful crystal ceiling lamp hung overhead like a constellation, each angle catching light and spreading small, star-like reflections throughout the area.

Jamal took in the luxurious and cozy environment, reassuring himself that this was the life he deserved—freedom with Christian. No limits. Suddenly, memories of his discussion with Angela resurfaced, reminding him of his deceit. He had promised her he would leave Desiree so they could be together. However, Jamal never imagined meeting Christian and falling for him. Once more Jamal convinced himself that Angela would eventually find someone else. These thoughts evaporated when Christian's voice cut through his ruminations.

"Jamie?"

He turned to find Christian standing behind him, his doe-like eyes beaming with affection, a gentle smile lighting up his features. Forcing a light tone, Jamal replied, "Hey, what's up?"

"Nothing. Except, I wanted to congratulate you again." Christian stepped forward, pulling Jamal into a tight embrace.

"Thank you," he murmured, allowing himself to melt into Christian's arms.

"You're welcome, but the celebration's just underway. We've got a packed night ahead. Go shower and join me in the dining room when you're finished."

Jamal threw him a side-eye, suspicious of what Christian might be planning. But before he had a chance to question him, Christian shooed him away.

"Go. I'll be waiting for you."

Jamal didn't waste another second. He dashed off to freshen up, his quick shower and crisp shave taking only fifteen minutes, enough time to wash away the stressors of the day. When he stepped into the dining room, his eyes widened at the spectacle before him. A festive atmosphere filled the room, complete with brightly colored streamers, bobbing balloons, and a prominent "Congratulations to the HNIC" sign.

The mingling aromas from the kitchen promised a feast, rich and enticing. Jamal chuckled to himself when he approached the table, where the centerpiece—a luscious, creamy chicken dish Christian had boasted would earn him a ring—sat surrounded by elegant place settings.

"Come. Sit and let me cater to the man in charge tonight," Christian gestured to the chair at the head of the table.

Jamal slid into the seat, and Christian uncorked a champagne bottle, sending a spray of golden bubbles into the air. He poured their glasses and with a big smile and launched into his toast.

"This is proof of just how valuable you are to the hospital, Jamie. You've earned this. Every bit of it. You're outstanding, both as a surgeon and as my man. My man, my man, my man! You deserve all the success and recognition that comes with being the head of surgery at Northside, and believe me, this is only the beginning. I know you'll continue to do remarkable things. Here's to the future of medicine, and to you leading the charge. Cheers, my love!"

Jamal raised his glass, clinking it against Christian's. "Thanks, Chris. I couldn't have done it without your support."

Christian grinned, his eyes dancing with mischief as he cooed, "I love being your personal cheerleader. Always. You know I gotchu, boo."

A wave of gratitude washed over Jamal, not for his career achievements, but for finally being seen for who he truly was. Lifting his champagne flute once more, Jamal prepared to offer a toast of his own, feeling certain that after tonight, the future would be bright for both of them.

"I mean it, Chris. I didn't do this alone. From the moment I told you, you've been my rock, helping me push past every fear, doubt, and challenge. Coming out, embracing who I am . . . it wasn't easy. But you were there, my compass, my anchor, my everything. I'll always be grateful for you being in my corner through it all. I'm excited about our future together. Cheers to us."

"No fair, Jamie. You're about to make this grown man cry. I swear I don't do this emotional shit. But whew, you got me. I'm really choked up right now," Christian sputtered, fanning his watery eyes.

Jamal set his glass aside and rose, closing the distance between them. He took Christian's flute, setting it down and gathering Christian in his

Chapter 13

arms to comfort him. He teased, "Chris, you do know it's okay for grown men to cry, right? I wouldn't dare say that it shows weakness or think that it's gay."

Christian cut his eyes and kissed his teeth. "You're an idiot, you know that? I'm having a moment here."

"Sorry, but no tears tonight. It's a celebration, remember? Now, show me that sexy smile. Or better yet, give me those lips."

Christian giggled through the tears and puckered up. Jamal devoured his mouth, tasting the sweet champagne on his tongue. A minute later, Jamal withdrew but remained close, peppering Christian with light pecks.

"So, are you ready to serve me dinner, or do you have something else planned, Mr. Hilcrest?"

"Fuck that food right now. I'll feed you later. I need to give you some celebratory head," Christian flirted, easing out of Jamal's embrace.

Without breaking eye contact, Christian lowered himself to his knees. He yanked Jamal's pants and underwear down in one swift motion. Jamal grunted when Christian wrapped his lips around his blooming mushroom tip, taking him deep into his mouth. Jamal's hips bucked forward, pushing his dick further into Christian's throat. Every time he drew back, a trickle of hot saliva dripped from the corner of Christian's mouth. The sight of it only fueled Jamal's lust even more.

"Fuck yeah, Chris. Suck this dick like you mean it," Jamal groaned out through gritted teeth.

Christian moaned in response, vibrating his mouth around Jamal's length, increasing the suction. With each downward motion, he took in more, tapping the dangling part every time. His fingers dug into Jamal's thighs. Jamal sensed his balls drawing up tight against Christian's jaw, ready to release his hot seed.

Jamal eased him off, looking down. Cupping Christian's chin, he rasped, "I need to fuck that back hole."

Christian got up from the floor. With his help, Jamal stripped Christian of his pants, freeing his raging erection from its confinement. Jamal directed him over to the side of the dining table where the bench was. Once Christian lowered himself on it and Jamal positioned himself between Christian's thighs. Jamal's fingers traced circles around his sphincter, teasing and tormenting until Christian begged for more. With one decisive thrust, Jamal breached his rectum, filling Christian up completely. The connection was electric. Warmth surged through Jamal as if lightning had struck him while Christian arched off the bench.

Jamal pumped slow, penetrating and stretching Christian's hole with sensual strokes. Christian's prostate massaged his pole, and it took everything for Jamal not to come on the spot. He groaned even louder, picking up the pace, slapping hard against Christian's ass cheeks with each powerful thrust.

"Fuck, you're so tight," Jamal gritted out, his hand reaching out to grope at Christian's manhood, which was rock hard and leaking precum. He wrapped his fingers around it, jerking it while he pounded into Christian's ass. And just like that, Christian exploded in a wave of intense pleasure. His hot seed shot out across his stomach, splattering against Jamal's hand as it continued to pump his dick.

"More," he managed to choke out between pants.

Jamal obliged, slamming into him with such force it made the both of them grunt in unison. His hips snapped forward. He pounded relentlessly, filling every inch of Christian's tight anal cavity.

"Oh shit, I'm about to come."

Christian pushed him off, begging, "In my mouth."

"And you better swallow every drop!"

Christian dropped to his knees and nodded eagerly around Jamal's throbbing member. He hungrily took in every inch, slurping and gagging on Jamal's rigid length. With a guttural cry, Jamal erupted deep inside Christian's greedy throat, filling it up with hot, sticky cum until he drained his nuts. As soon as Jamal had finished shooting his load down Christian's windpipe, he withdrew leaving behind a stringy trail. Jamal rubbed it across Christian's lips, relishing in coating them with their mixed arousal.

"Fuuuck . . . you're so amazing."

"My pleasure, Dr. Edwards. I do aim to please," Christian cooed, peering up at him through tear-streaked lashes.

Chapter 13

They both collapsed onto the bench together, panting heavily. It was messy and crude, but the most satisfying sexual experience Jamal had ever had.

He took a deep breath and blurted, "Chris, I've been thinking... about us, our future together."

"Okay and?"

"And I've decided I'm selling the condo I have on the other side of town. Since I'm here all the time, how would you feel if I moved in with you?"

Christian blinked rapidly, his lips parting for a moment and then a radiant smile lit up his face. "Really? Jamie, are you sure?"

"I know these are big changes happening all at once, but yes. I'm surer than I've ever been about anything."

"Change is good, especially when it's with someone you love."

"And you're my someone. I love you, Chris."

"I love you too. Let's do it. We'll make this place ours, together," Christian stated, reaching out to squeeze Jamal's hand.

The soft melody of Frank Ocean's "Thinkin Bout You" drifted through the air, filling their dining room with its soothing echoes. The song's soulful notes wove their way around the couple, emphasizing the closeness and connection that had blossomed between them.

"Did I ever tell you this is one of my favorite songs?"

"No. But it seems fitting, doesn't it?" Christian replied, a sly smile forming on his lips.

Jamal pulled Christian into his arms, feeling at peace and whole for the first time.

As Jamal sat there, Christian nestled against him, a sense of contentment washed over him. After all that had led him to this point, he'd finally arrived at a place where he could be himself freely without judgment.

"Here's to new beginnings," he murmured, pressing a gentle kiss to Christian's forehead.

14

WORK IN PROGRESS

"*I WOULDN'T HAVE TO IF YOU'D DO YOUR DUE DILIGENCE AND stop being so damn gullible because they're fine or got a big dick."*

"*Just stop it, Tré, please. I know you care about me, but you're going too far. How come you won't respect me as an adult? You're not my dad and I'm certainly not a kid anymore. Just stay out of my business and let me handle things my way. I've got this."*

They exchanged harsh glances before Tré finally spoke, "If that's what you want."

"Yes, it's what I want."

"*Fine. Don't come crying to me if he breaks your heart and you fall on that pretty face of yours."*

"Ouch!" Angela exclaimed, wincing in pain.

Blood gushed from her cut, smeared across the blade, and splattered onto the countertop. Simeon was at her side in a flash, his firm grip securing her wrist as the chef's knife fell into the sink with a clang.

"Dammit," Simeon muttered under his breath, switching on the faucet to let the cool water rush over her wound.

He lathered a bit of mild soap and gently dabbed at it. Angela whimpered from the stinging. She'd cut herself deep, and the bleeding wasn't slowing. Frantically, Simeon snatched a dish towel within reach and wrapped it around her injured fingers. He then guided her over to a chair at the kitchen table.

"Where's the first aid kit?" Simeon asked, placing Angela's covered hand in her lap.

"Down the hall in the linen closet."

Without a moment's delay, Simeon left the kitchen. Within a minute, he returned, carrying a large red bag bulging with medical supplies. With meticulous care, he unwrapped the now blood-soaked towel, exposing the jagged incisions that nearly reached the white flesh of her fingers. Angela flinched as he applied hydrogen peroxide, the fizzing bubbles making the pain spike.

"How did you do this, angel?" Simeon inquired, rummaging in the bag.

Angela blinked, shock settling in that she'd zoned out. Her mind had been on her situation with Jamal. It'd been more than a month since *Baller Bizness* aired out Jamal's dirty laundry. After that last conversation with him, Jamal moved out the very next day while she was at work.

Coward. Angela thought to herself. Instead of facing her, he took the easy way out. Perhaps it was for the better. She didn't need to see his lying ass. There wasn't anything else to say. He'd left behind legal documents that would remove his name from the deed of the condo and information on refinancing her car solely into her name. Jamal had even given her a deadline to have everything filed. Thinking about everything pissed Angela off all over again. That was how she'd ended up cutting herself.

"Baby?" Simeon's deep, but calming voice brought her back to the present.

"I—I was thinking about Jamal," she admitted softly, her eyes welling with regret.

Simeon's eyes locked with hers when he pressed a clean gauze over the fresh, throbbing cut of one finger. "Next time, keep those thoughts away from sharp objects, aight?"

"I guess it's just one more way to feel the pain." Angela managed a small, rueful smile.

Chapter 14

Simeon shifted, his tone turning both matter of fact and reassuring. "Feel your feelings. It's part of the process. This was another loss, angel. And don't forget that he was the one that took your options away by not being honest. Even after you called him out on his fuck shit. So be pissed off if you need to. You're entitled to that. But don't let it consume you. He's not worth your energy anymore. Or is he?"

At that moment, Simeon's words resonated. He'd referred to her as his earth angel, yet here, with his gentle hands and steadfast support, he felt more like a godsend. After Jamal's betrayal came to light, Angela realized she relied on Simeon more than she had acknowledged. From that point on, her life had improved significantly. She was content. She was thriving. And she was determined not to allow Jamal to disrupt her peace.

Shaking her head with a decisive smile, Angela replied. "Of course not. I had a moment. I'm over it."

"That's my girl. Now go relax. I've got dinner covered." Simeon pulled her up from the chair and playfully smacked her on the ass.

Giving him a quick peck, Angela left the kitchen and sauntered into her creative nook. The room was a sanctuary of artistic chaos. An easel stood ready near a window through which the last of the afternoon sunlight streamed in, casting a warm, golden glow over her partially painted canvas. Angela pressed the button on her sound bar and Billie Eilish's "lovely" played quietly in the background, its melancholic melody mingling with the calm of the space.

Grateful that she had cut the fingers on her non-dominant hand, Angela relaxed in her favorite chair. She dipped her brush into a vibrant pool of red paint on the well-used mixing plate and lifted it to the canvas. Every stroke of her brush was intentional, the bristles smoothly moving across the cotton surface. As the colors came together under her skilled hand, she allowed herself to be completely absorbed in the creative process, the gentle hum of the song and the fading sunlight merging to create a moment of quiet transformation.

Without warning, Angela's thoughts drifted into the shadows of her past. The events of the last month replayed in her mind like a twisted movie reel: Jamal's betrayal exposed for all to see on *Baller Bizness*. The sting of the humiliation remained in her spirit, the disbelief turning to anger that burned in her chest. She imagined the mocking laughter of strangers, each guffaw a dagger that underscored every lie he'd ever told her. In the relentless montage, the truth became painfully clear: he had never cared about her, and she was nothing more than a pawn in his game of deceit.

"Focus," Angela whispered to herself, biting into her lower lip as she attempted to channel her emotions into her artwork.

Simeon became the subject of her musings. Her mother had suggested she reconnect with him, and Angela listened. Her bond with Simeon had grown stronger. He became her rock, her confidant. Simeon stepped up, offering a genuine friendship when she needed it the most. A grin broke out on Angela's face, recalling how her mother had been correct in calling Simeon her gentle giant. He was thoughtful and caring in every way imaginable, making him the most attentive lover she'd ever had. His size was big where it mattered and he'd left her pleasantly worn out, satisfied, and fulfilled. Every. Single. Time.

Maxwell's velvety voice now echoed throughout the air, hitting flawless falsettos in "Pretty Wings." The gentle sound of bristles gliding over the cotton was all she heard, blocking out all other noises. Angela immersed herself fully in the painting with every stroke of the brush, her focus narrowing until the world outside the canvas seemed to disappear. The fusion of colors came together like a mesmerizing symphony, forming depth and texture beyond words. Each swing of her arm infused the artwork with her heart, soul, and mind. The completed piece would be far more than a mere painting. It would be a vivid expression of her deepest thoughts and emotions made real.

Angela was completely absorbed in her artwork, unaware of Simeon slipping into the room. Without drawing attention to himself, Simeon placed a tray of fruit and a bottle of cannabis-infused Cabernet Sauvignon on the table close by and watched her from a few feet away.

After a while, Angela needed to clean her brushes. She gathered the round and flat ones she'd been using and, with a quick spin on her chair, got to her feet.

Chapter 14

Simeon's low, deep voice startled her, making her jump. "Hey there, angel."

"Wha—Za! Ay dios mío! You scared me."

"Didn't mean to. You were deep into it, and I didn't want to interrupt you. But I couldn't help watching."

Angela's eyes drifted to the bottle on the table. "Is that wine?"

"Yep. Dinner won't be done for another hour. I figured we could unwind a bit after you finish."

"Perfect. I'm almost done," she declared, dipping the brushes in the container of water.

Simeon lowered himself onto the lounge chair on the opposite side of the room. Angela went back to her painting, once more consuming herself in the flow of creativity. A few minutes later, while she was finishing, Simeon approached her from behind.

"Is this who I think it is?" Angela turned from her work, grinning.

"Yeah, it's me."

She brushed a stray curl behind her ear and admitted, "Thanks to your suggestion, I tried a hand at drawing myself again."

"This is incredible. You've captured something so raw and honest here."

"I'm still working on it, of course, but I've decided to call her 'WIP', you know, for 'work-in-progress.'"

"C'mere. I'll let you get back to it in just a second. I need to tell you something." Simeon held out his hand.

Angela set the paintbrush on the easel and placed her palm in his. He helped her to her feet, and she peered up at him. "What's swirling around in that big head of yours, Za?"

"I got your big head right here," he flirted, pulling Angela closer to his muscular body.

He sure did. Simeon had a lot to handle, but she wasn't backing down. She welcomed the challenge. Grounding her pelvis on his semi-erected dick, Angela purred, "And you should put it right here."

Simeon eased them apart, leaving only inches between them. His voice dropped low as he promised, "I will. Lemme say this first. I'm so proud of you, Angela. I admire your strength and courage. I see your resilience, and you are achieving great things. I believe in your potential. I acknowledge your grief, anger, and fear. But I know you're built for everything you're facing. You are my favorite person, and you are so special to me."

A tear escaped from Angela's eye as she took in Simeon's words of affirmation. It was as if he had glimpsed into her very soul, acknowledging every insecurity and fear that plagued her. Simeon brushed the wetness from her cheek and hooked a finger under her chin, lifting her face. Angela looked up, immediately drowning in the endless chocolate pools. He leaned in, and she met him halfway. Their mouths connected, her tasting the saltiness of her tears mixed with the intoxicating flavor of their tongues sliding back and forth over each other. A couple of minutes later he withdrew from their kiss, swiping his thumb across her now swollen bottom lip.

"My bad. Let me let you finish."

"Nah, fuck that painting," Angela panted out, breathless and eager. Her hands roamed under his shirt. "Finish me."

Simeon growled low in his throat. In one quick move, he tugged his shirt off over his head. Angela acted fast, a flurry of fingers unbuttoning his jeans. Their clothes flew, scattered across the floor like confetti from a wild party, like they couldn't get free of them quick enough. Simeon's laugh was a rumble deep in his chest as her mouth caught his again, full force and reckless. He pulled her down. The couch complained under their weight, a creak and shift of worn leather when they landed in a tangle of limbs.

Pebbles and Babyface crooned out the chorus to "Love Makes Things Happen" while his fingers wove through her hair. Their tongues danced together, twisting and twirling in a sensual waltz that left them both gasping for air. Mouths still locked, they moved against each other with an undeniable rhythm, their hips grinding in perfect sync. Simeon pulled away just enough to capture Angela's bottom lip between his teeth and sucked gently, sending a shudder of delight through her entire body.

His hands roamed over her curves like a starved man at a feast, skimming up her thighs before teasingly brushing against her swollen clitoris.

Chapter 14

Angela arched her back in response, moaning his name as he continued to torment her with gentle touches. Simeon's fingers entered her wetness, finding her G-spot with ease while he rubbed circles on her nub.

Her hands clawed at his shoulders. The pleasure built inside her, demanding release. "Za, please," she pleaded breathlessly.

Simeon dipped below her waist and, using his shoulders, he nudged her thighs open wider. He swiped his tongue up her vertical folds and twirled it around the swollen, protruding bud. Angela bowed her back, pressing herself against him, hungry for more. Her breath came in short, ragged gasps as he took control, driving her higher and higher with each thrust of his fingers and sweep of his tongue. The pressure was building inside of her.

"I need you inside me," she begged.

Without warning, Simeon eased his digits from her wet heat, and he positioned his engorged shaft at her entrance. "Tell me you want it," he growled, his dark gaze burning into hers.

Angela shuddered violently, every muscle in her body tensing in anticipation. "I want it. Please, Za. Fuck me."

He pushed into her, inch by excruciating inch. Angela gasped at the invasion. His size thrilled her. She'd never known such fullness before. With wild eyes, Simeon withdrew and bent down to lap up her arousal that trickled from her core. His tongue swished back and forth, and he gulped her arousal. She shivered in anticipation of when he would slide it in again. Coming up onto his knees, Simeon's enormous member glistened with her creamy essence as he plunged into her depths. He eased from her, sampling her pussy once more before thrusting back inside, stretching her to the limit by his size.

Simeon seized her lips, sharing her sweet nectar, their tongues tangling into a messy knot. Angela whimpered into the kiss, unable to contain the pleasure coursing through her veins. Simeon's muscles flexed beneath her palms, his skin hot and slick with sweat. His breath came out in ragged grunts and moans that matched hers. Their bodies moved together in perfect harmony. Her vaginal muscles suctioned him in, taking him deeper within her wet heat. Simeon groaned loudly, the sound echoing off the walls.

"Ahh shit, this pussy . . . angel, tan jodidamente buena."

"And you're tan jodidamente enorme. I can feel you stretching me out," she purred appreciatively.

"So, you like that?" Simeon grunted, biting down on her neck hard enough to leave a mark. "You want more?" He withdrew, leaving her pussy clenching around nothing before slamming back in again, cutting off any reply she might have made with another groan.

He plunged into her with so much force that Angela screamed. Simeon's hips rotated right to left, meeting her rising need. Angela couldn't believe how much she craved him. How much she enjoyed the roughness of their lovemaking. She wrapped her legs around his waist, drawing him closer, meeting his thrusts with eager moans. Her breasts jiggled with each movement, and she could feel the heat emanating from his skin. His length dragged along the sensitive nerves within her pussy walls. Her eyes practically rolled back in her head. She bucked underneath him. A rush of warmth spread through her lower region, enveloping her in a cocoon of bliss. Simeon clung to her, murmuring loving affirmations against her neck as he continued to move inside her.

"You're so sexy . . . your pussy is nirvana . . . you deserve frequent orgasms. Our sex life is amazing. I'm so lucky to be with you. Thank you, angel."

"Uhn, Za. I'm so close," she whispered against his lips.

As if fueled by her words, Simeon picked up the pace even more. With one hand, he reached between them and stroked her clit, sending shockwaves of bliss coursing through every inch of her being. Angela cried out his name as an orgasm seized her body, writhing beneath him while wave after wave of pleasure consumed her.

"That's it. She's talking to me now." Simeon growled against her neck, "Come for me."

"Don't stop! Please, don't stop!"

And he didn't. The soft flesh of their bellies slapped together. With every thrust, tremors of pleasure rippled through them. Their orgasm hit

Chapter 14

like a freight train, knocking the wind out of them both. Simeon's head dropped back, a guttural groan tearing from his throat, the whites of his eyes flashing as he emptied himself inside her. Angela screamed his name, her body shuddering beneath him as she reached her own climax.

They both collapsed in a sweaty heap on the couch, breathless and shaking from their shared bliss. They lay there for a while, wrapped in each other's arms, basking in the afterglow of their passion until the loud shrill of Angela's phone brought them back to reality. Simeon untangled their limbs to grab it from the easel. While Angela answered, he went to get the washcloths to clean up.

It was Mia. Since Jamal left, she and Mia hadn't spoken. Mia had been preoccupied with planning her upcoming baby shower, attending marital counseling, and traveling with Troy for his away games. This was their chance to catch up on everything they'd missed over the past couple of weeks.

"He just left, Mia. Jamal packed up his stuff and moved out while I was at work. Didn't even leave a note."

"Damn, girl, that's cold."

"After all that waiting around thinking it was gonna be us. When it was him the whole time in the closet. He was really with me *and* his wife *and* living on the DL the whole time."

"Men like Jamal—they're cowards. You're better off without him."

Angela's attention was suddenly drawn to the television playing in the background, and she let out a gasp. "Wait—hold on."

"What, Ang? What is it?"

"There-There's an . . . we have an active shooter! Oh my god, they're up at Northside! That's where Jamal works! I have to go, Mia. I'll call you back."

15

NOT GON' MAKE IT

"Code Silver! Everybody move! Code Silver!"

Someone screamed the hospital's alert for an active shooter as the deafening crack of gunfire ricocheted off the walls. Pandemonium erupted. Patients and staff scrambled for cover, their movements frantic and uncoordinated. Blood exploded against the white tile floor like a violent rainfall. The once-orderly corridors had become a scene of utter chaos, the air thick with the smell of fear and gunpowder. Northside Regional Hospital had become a war zone.

Jamal was making his way through the maze-like halls when the melee broke out around him. His heart pounded in his ears as the routine calm of the day splintered into urgent shouts and the clamor of alarms.

"Get down!" he shouted at a group of terrified nurses and other staff huddled against a wall. "Stay low and move toward that exit!"

A distant voice rang out. "Dr. Edwards, you need to get to the safe zone!"

Before Jamal could fully process the command, a searing pain ignited in his left shoulder. He staggered when another bullet struck him in the side.

He gasped, gritting his teeth. "I'm hit!"

His strength began dwindling when the shock of pain and disbelief set in. Yet, his survival instincts surged, propelling him into a desperate sprint toward the nearest exit. Then, as if the situation couldn't worsen, more gunshots ripped through the chaos. Their brutal staccato echoed down the hall, a thunderous reminder of impending doom. Two more shots struck uncomfortably close, their impact forcing Jamal to the ground. His vision swam in a haze of red and white as he fought to cling to consciousness, every fiber of his being screaming to survive.

"Damn it!" His fingers slipped through the warm, sticky blood rapidly staining his once immaculate scrubs.

"Doc! You're hit!" a nurse cried out, her eyes wide with horror.

He managed to choke out between ragged breaths. "Stay . . . away."

"Dr. Edwards, we need to help you," the nurse insisted, taking a step closer.

"Please . . . just-just . . . get everyone out."

"Alright, but we'll be back for you," she said, casting one last concerned glance at him before disappearing into the fray.

Crimson fluid pooled beneath Jamal, creating a stark contrast against the spotless white tiles. The gunshots had ceased for now, but the residual panic was still in the air. Jamal could hear the approaching footsteps of medical staff rushing to his aid. With every labored breath, he fought to stay conscious, the pain in his shoulder and stomach an ever-present reminder of just how close death loomed. Tears pricked at the corners of his eyes. The ache was unbearable, but it was nothing compared to the thought of leaving Christian behind.

"Christian . . ." Jamal whispered, the coppery tang of blood in his mouth mixing with the bitter taste of regret.

"Dr. Edwards? Dr. Edwards, can you hear me? Dr. Edwards! We're going to get you out of here, okay?" a voice broke through the haze.

"Stay with us, Dr. Edwards," another voice urged.

His panic subsided for a few seconds while he focused on the figure striding toward him, their face marked by urgency and a hint of menace. *Ian Taylor.*

He strode into the chaotic scene with a composed authority that

Chapter 15

seemed to quiet the surrounding commotion. Ian assessed the situation in an instant, his calculating gaze flitting from Jamal to the medical team poised for action. He kneeled beside Jamal to examine his wounds.

"Edwards! Can you hear me?"

"Christian..."

"Focus on me. This isn't about Christian right now. It's about saving you."

"Can't... leave him," Jamal choked out, desperation lending strength to his feeble voice.

Ian shook his head. "Your life is in my hands now."

The words carried an ominous threat Jamal couldn't decipher, and he shook from a feeling unrelated to his pain. He grimaced when Ian applied pressure to the gunshot wound on his side., Jamal's thoughts drifted back to their time as medical students and the bitter rivalry that had developed between them.

"Will you save me?" It was a plea from the depths of Jamal's soul, a quiet admission of the power Ian now held over him.

"You're not dying here, Edwards, if that's what you mean. Not on my watch." Gritting his teeth, Jamal fought to stay present as Ian's voice pierced the noise around them. "Help! We need help over here!"

"Not gon' make it, you asshole," Jamal muttered, struggling to keep his eyes open.

"Edwards, don't you dare close your eyes. You've got too much to lose," Ian warned, his tone icy.

Jamal couldn't help but snarl, the pain in his body now a searing firestorm. "Like what?"

"Your life. For whatever it's worth."

"Thanks for the vote of confidence," Jamal managed, the corners of his vision blackening. The fight was draining from his body, replaced by an irresistible pull toward oblivion.

"Dammit, Edwards, focus! Stay with me!" Ian demanded.

Another voice cut through the mayhem, urgent and commanding. "Where are they? Taylor? Edwards? Are we too late?"

"Over here! He's been shot multiple times."

"Clear the way!" someone bellowed. Other medical staff were racing toward them, their white coats billowing like sails in a storm.

The noise of the hospital—the shouts, the alarms, the pounding footsteps—all faded into silence as Jamal surrendered to the darkness clawing at his consciousness. It consumed him, leaving only the faintest echoes of whispers. Each breath was a struggle. The void was tempting, promising relief from the agony that wracked his body.

"Pressure's dropping!" someone else shouted.

"Edwards, come on! You're not doing this." Jamal heard Ian's voice crack with urgency, echoing from far away, lost in the cold, dark grip around him.

"We're losing him!"

"Get him prepped for surgery now! Trauma room two, I want IV fluids started stat," Ian ordered, his gaze locked onto Jamal's. "We need to stop the bleeding and stabilize him now. Alright people, let's move!"

Jamal's limbs grew weightless, as if he were floating in a void. In the darkness he clung to fading memories like a drowning man grasping for debris. Amid the chaos of shouts and gunfire, a flicker of awareness cut through the fog—if he woke up, the pain waiting for him would be worse than the fear of taking another bullet.

In that suspended moment, one question loomed: *Would he see another sunrise?*

16

A LONG ROAD AHEAD

Where am I? Jamal's eyes snapped open to blinding lights above him. His first instinct was to sit up, but the moment his muscles twitched, a searing pain tore through him like a serrated blade. Fire spread across his ribs, abdomen, and back, every nerve screaming in protest. He froze mid-motion, teeth gritted, body locked in place.

What the hell happened? A strangled groan formed in his throat but never emerged, swallowed by the sharp sting radiating down his side.

The muted beeps of monitors filled the room. He didn't need to see the IV line in his arm or smell the faint antiseptic tang in the air to know where he was. But why? His mind clawed at fragments of memory, searching, scrambling for answers. Testing his limits, Jamal attempted to shift again. The pain punched through him with ruthless accuracy causing a guttural sound to escape.

He squeezed his eyes shut, willing himself to stay calm. *Focus.*

Forcing slow breaths, Jamal opened his eyes again, scanning the room without moving his head. Various tubes ran down his limbs, tethering him to machines he couldn't see. Restraints. At least, that's how they felt.

Trapped.

Vulnerable.

He hadn't experienced those two states before. And it pissed him off.

I need to get out of here! Jamal roared inwardly.

Ignoring the persistent throbbing throughout his body, Jamal gritted his teeth and tried to sit up. But his body betrayed him, refusing to cooperate. A drop of sweat slid down his temple. Discomfort mixed with frustration fueled the burning sensation in his chest. He despised being helpless, lacking control. This wasn't like him. Yet here he was, battered in a way he couldn't fully comprehend.

The door glided open with a swoosh, its noise cutting through the continuous hum of the machines. Jamal's gaze snapped toward it. A figure stepped in, tall, with sharp features, and purposeful in his movements. *Ian Taylor.*

He moved with measured steps and an air of authority to Jamal's bedside. The faintest squeak of his sneakers on the tile grated in Jamal's ears.

"Edwards," Ian called out, tablet in hand. His eyes flicked down at Jamal, then back to the device, as though taking inventory. There was no friendliness or warmth in his tone; his manner was brisk and detached. Clinical. "Glad to see you're finally awake. I wasn't sure you'd pull through."

Jamal's throat tightened as he tried to speak. Nothing. Not even a rasp. Panic clawed at him, his mind screaming commands his body refused to obey. He willed his jaw to move, his lips to part, but they remained unmoving, locked in defiance. A sharp, labored inhalation rattled through his nose, the only sound he could manage.

His body jerked in a desperate, instinctive spasm. A raw, choked sound clawed its way upward, only to be stifled into a strangled silence. The tube lodged deep in his airway made every breath an agonizing, searing pain. His lips moved in vain once again, each futile gesture intensifying the sense of being trapped in silent suffering.

"Don't!" Ian commanded, stepping forward. "You're intubated, so don't try to speak. It's actually a good thing for both of us, considering how much you enjoy the sound of your own voice. I can get through this without your insolence."

Chapter 16

"Get out," Jamal wanted to say. Instead, all he managed to do was glare at Ian, his eyes burning with a deep resentment.

Ian surveyed the machines surrounding Jamal. The steady beeping of the heart machine provided an eerie soundtrack to the scene. He bent over him, his shadow stretching across Jamal like a predator closing in. "Seriously, Edwards, don't strain yourself. You're only going to make it worse," Ian warned. His eyes shifted to the monitors, then back to Jamal's face. "Your injuries are quite extensive. Shoulder shattered. Two bullets grazed your spine. And a ruptured spleen that required immediate surgery. We almost lost you twice on the table."

Jamal blinked hard. Shoulder. Spine. And a ruptured spleen. Revived twice. The words slammed into him like blows, each one heavier than the last. His chest rose and fell faster now, the tight band of fear pressing harder against his ribs. Memories of those chaotic moments unraveled into fragments, scattering his thoughts into disarray.

Shot.

He'd been shot.

"Yes, you're lucky to be alive. Fourteen hours in the OR," Ian stated matter-of-factly. He continued, swiping across the tablet he held, "But don't mistake luck for recovery. Your mobility has been compromised. For now. You know, these are the most crucial days ahead. You'll be dealing with the aftermath of this for months, possibly longer. If you make it out of here."

If? Jamal thought bitterly, wishing he could wipe that smug expression off Ian's face. His nostrils flared, frustration rolling beneath his skin as he tried to force a word past the tubes. His eyes met Ian's, begging for answers. It was as though Ian had heard his thoughts when he began speaking again.

"I bet you're wondering how you ended up here. Well, some idiot off his meds and his friend came back and sought revenge on your boy Mitch. Lucky for him, he wasn't here. Unlucky for you, and the other six people they injured. Truly unfortunate for the woman who didn't make it. Do you want the bad news now? Yeah, you probably do." Ian paused long enough to data enter notes in Jamal's chart and then he carried on without looking up, "While repairing your shoulder, the MRI showed some nerve damage. And your spinal cord has also been severely fractured. I'm afraid you might be paralyzed from the waist down."

No! This can't be. No matter how much Jamal willed his limbs to move, they remained stubbornly still, betraying him.

"Your recovery will be long and arduous. But with time and effort, you may regain most of your mobility," Ian carried on, his tone devoid of sympathy.

May? The word screamed through Jamal's mind, setting off a whirlwind of panic and fury. This couldn't be happening. Not to him, not when there was still so much left to do.

"Focus on getting better. Right now, you're in no position to worry about anything else," Ian advised, his expression unreadable.

Like hell I'm not. Jamal seethed inwardly, his determination flaring like a beacon in the darkness. He would not be beaten—not by this, and certainly not by the likes of Ian Taylor.

The door opened again. This time the footsteps were softer.

"Jamie?"

Jamal's gaze shifted, settling on Christian's handsome face, which was tense with concern. He wanted to pull Christian into his arms and reassure him that everything would turn out fine. Quitting wasn't in Jamal's DNA. Just as he encouraged his patients to persevere, he intended to face his own challenges head-on.

"Ahh Christian. Perfect timing," Ian said, waving a hand in Jamal's direction with a hint of indifference. "He's conscious, but as you can see from the tubes, he won't be able to speak right now. Allow me to update you on everything."

"Please, go ahead." Christian's eyes never left Jamal. He moved closer to the bed, cautiously, as if afraid of breaking something fragile.

Ian continued his explanation in a professional tone devoid of emotion. "We've successfully extracted the bullets and repaired his spleen and his shoulder the best we could, but there is some nerve damage. Regarding the spinal injury . . ." He hesitated, allowing the gravity of his

Chapter 16

words to sink in. "It's too early to determine the full extent. But we think he might be paralyzed."

"And his condition now?"

"We're keeping a close watch on him for any post-surgery complications, such as infection. He's not in the clear yet. More surgeries may be necessary. We need to schedule follow-ups immediately. The first forty-eight hours post-op are critical." Ian's lips curved. Not quite a smile, but something close enough to spark unease. He moved, closing the space between them just enough to make it noticeable. "And once he's discharged, he'll need continuous care . . . someone to be very attentive. Someone . . . hands-on."

Christian nodded. "Being attentive isn't an issue. I can manage that. What are the next steps?"

"Recovery can plateau if not handled properly. Edwards' condition leaves no room for error." Ian took another step closer—too close—and tilted his head a little, a faint smirk tugging at the corner of his mouth. "It's admirable, Christian, how committed you are. Not everyone is equipped for this kind of responsibility. It can be . . . exhausting," he remarked, his voice dropping to an almost intimate tone.

Jamal lay there, anger coursing through him, as he witnessed their exchange. He was unable to move a muscle, his body refusing him even the smallest motion. He strained to say something, anything. A word. A breath. But all that came was silence. His teeth clenched behind unmoving lips. Ian knew exactly what he was doing.

Christian, whether he was unaware or just choosing to ignore it, remained unfazed. "I'll manage," he replied curtly. But Ian wasn't done.

"That's wonderful. Because if we don't monitor his progress carefully, we risk permanent loss of function. And believe me . . ." His attention fixed on Christian's face now, as though Jamal wasn't even in the room. ". . . Edwards is not the kind of man who takes losing lightly. He deserves nothing but the best, wouldn't you agree?"

The words dripped like sweet poison. Jamal seethed at the implications. Ian might have started out talking about his recovery, but now it seemed this conversation had gone beyond medicine.

"Yes, I agree. So, how long before I can get the ball rolling?"

Ian swiped over the tablet's display before he looked up. "It could take months, maybe even years. It's a long road ahead. Recovery will be slow, and without constant monitoring, complications are almost guaranteed. Edwards will need a dedicated team to provide twenty-four-hour home health care. And someone by his side who isn't afraid to get their hands dirty. Though I suspect you're more than capable."

"I am. But if there's a way for me to get him out of here and home, I can—" Christian started, but Ian cut him off.

"No shortcuts. This isn't something you can rush. He's going to be here for a little while. In the meantime, work on getting a professional team to help you. If you want him to pull through, you'll follow my advice." His gaze lingered on Christian for a fraction too long, a glint of something unreadable flashing behind his eyes.

Jamal forced his eyes to Ian, willing every ounce of fury he could muster into his stare. For a split second, Ian glanced down, meeting it. It was a challenge exchanged in silence. Neither man blinked.

Dismissing Jamal entirely, Ian resumed his focus on Christian. "I'll have the nurses provide you with a list of available in-home nurses you can start interviewing." With a sudden change in demeanor, Ian's expression became almost predatory. He gave Christian a once over before dropping to a lower octave. "I'll personally oversee his progress and ensure he receives the best care possible."

"Thank you, Dr. Taylor. I'm grateful for all your assistance."

"Please, feel free to call me Ian. Of course, if you need anything—questions, extra support—you already know how to contact me." His offer was smooth and professional, but the underlying message was unmistakable. Ian's mouth curled into a confident smile, his intentions now clear.

Jamal desperately wanted to yank the tubes from his throat and scream at Ian to back off, to leave Christian alone. Jealousy mixed bitterly with his sense of helplessness. The memory of the gala night, with Ian laughing and openly flirting with Christian, was etched in his mind, a

Chapter 16

blatant reminder that his rival had the audacity to intrude on what belonged to him.

"Uh, could you excuse me? I need to step out and make some calls," Christian said rushed, clearly uncomfortable.

Christian then bent over the bed, his eyes searching Jamal's face with concern and tenderness. "I'll be right back. You're going to get through this, Jamie. I believe in you. We haven't come this far for it to end like this. Just keep fighting," he whispered, stroking his cheek before giving him a loving peck and slipping out of the room.

The silence between them stretched, but Ian didn't flinch under Jamal's weary stare. He offered a coy smile, sauntering closer to the bed with the ease of someone who always knew how to stir the pot just enough.

"Well, well, Edwards I've got to admit, you threw me for a loop. All this time, hiding that little rainbow flag behind the lab coats. Bold move," Ian's voice dripped in honey and mischief.

Jamal's eyes narrowed, but Ian held up his hands in mock surrender. "Relax, I'm not here to start anything. Just . . . observing." He leaned in slightly, lowering his voice. "Christian? Mmm. He's a handful, isn't he? All that fire in such a petite, pretty package. Honestly, I didn't see you as his type, but what do I know? Maybe opposites do attract." Ian straightened, letting his gaze linger just a moment longer on Jamal's face. "But if you don't make it through this little . . . setback, don't worry." He winked. "I'll be there to pick up the pieces. And Christian? He won't be lonely for long."

With a playful pat to the foot of the bed, Ian turned toward the door. "Rest up, Edwards. You've really got some competition now."

And with that, he pranced out, leaving the echo of his words hanging heavy in the room.

When the door opened, Jamal caught sight of Angela standing right outside. She wore a calm expression as her eyes quickly scanned the room before landing on him for a fleeting moment. It was just a brief glance, nothing more. She looked away and addressed Ian.

"You're Dr. Taylor, right?"

"Yes, how can I assist you?"

"May we talk about Dr. Edwards?" Her gaze slid past him, landing on Jamal again. This time, staying on him longer, though her face revealed nothing. She promptly turned back to Ian. "In private."

Ian hesitated, transferring his tablet from one hand to the other. He turned to look at Jamal, a faint smile playing on his lips. With a quick nod, he replied, "Certainly. Please, come with me," and the door slid closed behind them.

Angela didn't look back as they disappeared down the corridor. However, Jamal had seen it. That quick, elusive look. It wasn't pity or concern. It was something unfamiliar and indescribable, and it made his heart race.

Jamal knew that whatever was unfolding between Angela and Ian was merely the beginning, with repercussions that could unravel everything he had meticulously built.

Chapter 16

TRIGGER WARNING

For the next few chapters, this story describes violence against a medical patient and references assault, domestic abuse, drugging, physical and emotional abuse, murder, needles, poisoning, rape, sexual assault, torture and other topics that might be disturbing to some readers.

Please be mindful of these and other possible triggers.

17

IT'S REALLY ME, BOO

ANGELA SAT IN HER CAR WITH THE ENGINE OFF, HER GRIP tight on the steering wheel. It had been thirty days since Dr. Taylor sat across from her in his office. His words replayed in her mind: *"Angela, you and I both know caring for your former lover poses a conflict of interest. Others in my position might not agree with you handling this case. However, I don't see an issue. You once loved him, and now you wish for his full recovery from this senseless act of violence, don't you? I trust your intentions are genuine, Angela. Moreover, I expect that how you learned about this assignment will remain confidential. In the end, we both will get what we want."*

Jamal had done everything in his power to freeze her out—blocking her number, instructing his staff to reject her calls, and even alerting security to turn her away if she showed up unannounced. His goal was clear: to erase her from his world. But Angela had a trick up her sleeve.

She remembered Jamal's disdain for Dr. Taylor and the quiet turf war between ER and General Surgery that never quite simmered down. Banking on her hunch that Dr. Taylor would be the attending on Jamal's case, Angela reached out to a former colleague at Northside who owed her a favor. That friend slipped her onto the floor during a shift change, just long enough for Angela to catch Dr. Taylor between consults and in front of Jamal's door. It didn't take much convincing. Dr. Taylor, clearly an opportunist, saw the benefit immediately. And just like that, the locks Jamal tried to place on his recovery room had been picked, and by the one woman he thought he'd never see again.

A sudden knock on the passenger window startled her. Angela blinked, finding her coworker Sharon's grinning face peeking inside.

"Spacing out on us again?"

With a forced smile, she let go of the steering wheel as if it had scalded her palms. Angela picked up her bookbag and laptop, then stepped out into the cool afternoon air. She adjusted her coat, smoothing it over her light pink scrubs. Christian's corner condo stood at the end of a row of elegant homes, its sleek modern design softened by the lush greenery lining the walkway. Sharon and their other colleague, Izzy, were making their way up the stone path, joking about how "posh" the neighborhood was.

"Let's just get this over with," Angela grumbled under her breath while trailing behind them to the entrance.

Before she could ring the bell, the door swung open. Christian Hilcrest stood there with a welcoming smile. He wore a stylish sweater and slacks and exuded effortless charm on every level.

"Hello. You must be Angela. Dr. Taylor spoke very highly of you and your team. It means a lot to both me and Jamal that you're here. Please, come in." Christian stepped aside to let them enter. After closing the door, he extended a manicured hand.

Angela stiffened a bit but exchanged a firm shake. "Indeed, I am. I'm pleased to hear he had kind words about us." She nodded toward her colleagues and introduced them. "Mr. Hilcrest, this is Sharon and Izzy. Sharon specializes in mobility therapy, and Izzy is our respiratory expert. Together we're fully equipped to manage Dr. Edwards' care," she assured him with the practiced sweetness of a caregiver.

"Please, Christian. We'll be spending quite a bit of time together," he remarked while ushering them into a foyer decorated with modern West Indies art and African sculptures. Christian motioned toward the living

Chapter 17

room, where plush seating surrounded a glass coffee table. "Please, make yourselves comfortable. Can I get you anything to drink? Water, tea, or coffee?"

After they all declined, Angela unzipped her laptop case, extracting folders embossed with Northside Regional Hospital's logo. She placed them on the coffee table. "If it's alright with you, we'd like to review Dr. Edwards' care plan and begin setting up our nursing station today."

"Yes, absolutely." Christian sank into an armchair. His eyes bounced between them, stating, "His care is top priority. I know this recovery will be... challenging, but I trust your expertise completely."

Angela's stomach clenched, but her expression stayed neutral. She merely nodded, acknowledging his words without further comment. Sharon and Izzy murmured their reassurances, their voices empathetic and filled with real concern. Angela let them carry the emotional load. Being in the presence of Jamal's new partner was testing her patience, which was wearing thin already. But she couldn't afford to slip.

Not here.

Not now.

They spent the next hour going over all the details of Jamal's care, with Angela carefully outlining what Christian could expect from their medical team. When she finished, she opened the floor for further questions.

"No, I believe you've covered everything. We're really lucky to have you," Christian admitted, leaning in. "After the shooting, the media, the police reports. Dr. Taylor was right. It's all been so exhausting."

Izzy sighed sympathetically. "I can't imagine what you've gone through."

Angela nodded in agreement and offered reassurance. "It's entirely understandable, Christian. You both have been through a traumatic ordeal, but we're here to support you every step of the way. Shall we go see our patient now?"

"Yes, of course." Christian rose, his gaze drifting down the hall. "He's in the study. We converted it for..." He paused, swallowing hard, "... for convenience."

"Lead the way." Angela replied, standing up and adjusting the strap of her medical bag on her shoulder while keeping an unreadable expression.

The hallway extended before them, decorated with West Indian artwork, just like the rest of the house. A faint aroma of lavender mixed with wood polish lingered in the air. Christian led them to a door at the end of the hallway, pausing with his hand on the knob.

"Here we are," he announced, pushing it open.

Unlike the hall, the study carried the scent of disinfectant mixed with dread. Sunlight poured into the room through the large windows, their sheer curtains swaying in the breeze. The walls were a soothing shade of soft gray, accented by framed photographs. Bookshelves lined the space, holding leather-bound books and other decorative items. A hospital bed took up the center, its rails gleaming. Machines hummed: a ventilator, cardiac monitor, and an IV pole hung with clear bags.

And there he was.

Jamal lay motionless, his once-commanding presence reduced to stillness. His athletic frame seemed smaller now, diminished beneath the beige throw blanket draped over him.

Christian leaned over Jamal, pressing tender kisses on his forehead and whispering words of encouragement. Angela's hands shook, battling to hide the rage inside. She had no reason to be angry. Yet their open display of affection reopened old scars of love-starved moments, sparking a fierce anger that was hard for her to dismiss.

She loathed him, every inch of him. No amount of time could dull the fury simmering beneath her skin. Simeon's assurances about healing proved hollow against memories that remained raw. *Time won't erase what he did.*

But Angela held her tongue, biding her time. She would deal with the good doctor soon enough. Until then, she would play the part of the dutiful nurse, hiding her true intentions beneath a guise of professionalism. After all, revenge was a dish best served cold.

Christian reached out for Jamal's hand, grasping it. With a voice as soothing as honey, he caressed Jamal's cheek. "Hey, boo? Remember I told

Chapter 17

you we'd have a team to assist with your rehab? Well, they're here now. I want to introduce you to them."

Stepping forward, Sharon placed a hand over her heart. "Dr. Edwards, it's an absolute privilege to be here," she began, her tone reverent, almost giddy. "Your work in neurosurgery . . . it's revolutionary. We've all read about it. Assisting in your recovery is truly . . ." She paused, appearing to search for words. ". . . an honor."

"Absolutely," Izzy chimed in, her smile wide and earnest. "Everyone in our field knows your name. You've saved countless lives. Now it's our turn to help you." She looked back at Angela for support, her energy bubbling over.

"Yes, indeed. We're grateful to be involved in your recovery journey, Dr. Edwards," Angela stated, evenly. Her mask didn't crack. Her tone didn't waver.

Jamal slowly turned his head. Their gazes collided. His eyes bore into hers, pleading, questioning. Angela held his stare, allowing the reality to settle in. *No, you're not imagining things. It's really me, boo*, she mused silently, a subtle, knowing smile playing across her lips. She then shifted her focus to the equipment, speaking to Sharon and Izzy.

"Let's get started. Ensure all inventory is accounted for," Angela instructed authoritatively.

"We're on it," Sharon replied cheerfully, heading for the cabinets while Izzy began checking the machines.

Christian stayed nearby observing before he finally asked Angela, "He will fully recover, right? Dr. Taylor mentioned—"

"Recovery is unpredictable." Angela replied, smoothing Jamal's blanket with her thumb digging into the cotton near his hip. "But we'll prioritize keeping him comfortable."

A lie, wrapped in velvet.

Jamal's nostrils flared. He obviously understood.

"I appreciate whatever you can do to help his recovery move along smoother and I pray he'll be back on his feet soon enough," Christian said thoughtfully. He started to walk away but then stopped, raising his hand. "Oh, there is something else I wanted to discuss. I'm going away on a business trip soon. Could your team stay overnight? Dr. Taylor said Jamie requires round-the-clock care. I want to make sure he's never alone, especially in the evenings. The nights have been, well, quite challenging for him."

"Of course, we can arrange that." Angela grabbed her iPad, turning to her colleagues. After keying in the updates to their schedules, she confirmed, "I'll cover the afternoons into early evenings. Sharon and Izzy can alternate mornings and overnight shifts."

"That works perfectly for me," Sharon chimed in with a reassuring smile.

Izzy bobbed her head in agreement. "Yeah, it's fine for me too."

"Great. Glad we have that sorted out." Christian released a long sigh. He looked at Angela once more, expressing his gratitude. "Thank you again. It means a lot to know he'll be in good hands."

"Absolutely. That's why we're here," Angela responded, her tone neutral.

"Alright then, I'll let you get back to work. I need to get to the office. If you need anything, you know how to reach me. I'll see you this evening." Christian paused, his eyes briefly meeting Jamal's before adding, "Please, take good care of him."

"Oh, we most certainly will," Angela answered with a saccharin sweet smile.

As soon as Christian left, the energy in the room shifted, becoming lighter, freer, yet somehow heavier. A clock on the wall ticked louder than it should have. Angela sucked in a lungful of oxygen, heading over to their designated nursing area: a small corner of the room outfitted with cabinets, a counter, and sterile supplies. She began unpacking. Alcohol swabs lined up next to syringes. Gauze stacked in careful piles. Everything had its place and purpose.

Sharon called out to her. "Angela, do you need help with—"

"No. I've got it." Angela cut her off without looking up, her attention fixed on the supplies in front of her. She sensed Jamal watching her. She didn't even spare him a look. Instead, Angela continued opening packages, organizing tools, and wiping down surfaces.

Chapter 17

"Do you think this setup works for him?" Izzy's voice floated over from the other side of the room almost an hour later.

"It's more than fine. It's better than most home care arrangements I've seen," Sharon commented, glancing around.

"Meh, it's not that special," Angela mumbled under her breath. She adjusted the blood pressure cuff, ensuring it fit neatly in the drawer. With a quick peek over her shoulder, she noticed Jamal staring, drilling a hole into her back, but she remained focused on her work.

"Angela?" Sharon's voice cut through the low hum of activity.

Angela paused, setting a thermometer into its designated holder with care. She turned around, maintaining a composed expression, and replied in an even tone, "Yes?"

"We've finished everything here. Izzy and I are gonna head out now, but I'll be back later this evening for my shift. Call if anything comes up and you need me here sooner."

Angela gave a curt nod. "Okay, sounds like a plan. Thank you both."

"You're most welcome. I'll see you tomorrow," Izzy cheerily added before making her way to the door.

Angela stared at the room's entrance, listening until their voices and footsteps faded away and she heard the soft click of the front door closing. Taking a deep breath through her nose, she exhaled slowly while turning back toward the bed. Jamal's dark hollow eyes fixated on her with a disconcerting intensity.

She took a step forward, then another, and one more, until she was at the foot of the bed. Her hands curled into fists at her sides. For a beat, she said nothing. She stood there, staring back at him, letting the tension of unresolved anger and animosity hang between them like a tightened wire.

There was a time when looking at Jamal made her breath hitch. With that rich, dark brown skin, those deep-set eyes under long lashes, and those waves in his hair, sharp enough to make anyone seasick, left her captivated. His body, always sculpted from relentless hours in the gym, once felt like safety when wrapped around her. But that image was gone now. Burned to ash by lies and broken trust.

Now, all she saw was a stranger in a hospital bed. And far from the man she used to crave.

The man before her wasn't her lover, her protector, her future.

He was just the one who ruined it.

Finally, Angela snarled, her voice low and venomous. "Look at you. The illustrious surgeon, Jamal Edwards. Reduced to this." She gave his unmoving form a quick once-over, stopping on the sling holding up his legs, and the IV line inserted into his arm. "Helpless. Weak. Pathetic."

Jamal's eyes widened some in silent protest. A flicker of something passed through them, yet he didn't look away. She moved closer, bending until her face was level with his.

"I thought you'd be happier to see me. Say something!"

Jamal flinched. His breathing picked up, but he didn't move his mouth.

"I would ask if a cat got your tongue, but you're obviously not into that anymore. When were you gonna let me in on your filthy lil' secret, *Jamie*?"

He clenched his jaw and Angela snorted. That must've struck a nerve. Angela didn't have a problem with anyone being gay. She would've happily accepted her brother's decision to live out loud and proud. However, the lying and leading a double life, Angela was not about to overlook. Her former lover had played her, and for the whole world to witness. She straightened her posture and stepped away from the bed, strolling over to the nurses' station.

Angela moved methodically. Slipping on a pair of gloves, she drew the clear liquid from a vial into the syringe with a soft click-click-click as the plunger pulled back. The so-called truth serum drug that Mia had given her gleamed under the low light. With a tight, practiced smile, she turned back to Jamal's bedside and hovered over him.

Jamal's raspy voice cracked through the silence. "Wh-wh-what's that?"

"Ah, so now you wanna talk." Angela tilted her head. She held the syringe up between them, and announced, "Good. Because this? This right here is gonna make *you* talk."

She didn't wait for him to process it. The sharp point slid into the

Chapter 17

port on his arm, and she pushed the plunger down with steady pressure. The last drop vanished into his bloodstream. She glanced down at her watch.

Three minutes.

That's what Mia had said. They had three minutes until the truth spilled free. Angela peeled off her gloves and tossed them into the nearby bin with a snap. She paced once, twice, then stood still, dragging her fingers through her tangled curls. The silence pressed in, thick and heavy. She exhaled hard, grounding herself as the thud of her pulse thundered against her eardrums.

Turning back to the bed, she studied him closely. Jamal's eyelids began to flutter, his limbs settling, muscles slackening one by one. His breathing slowed, deeper now, heavier. The drug was working.

Almost time.

Now.

"Did you ever love me, Jamal?"

He blinked slowly, a fog descending over his gaze. "Yes, but not enough," he croaked.

Angela narrowed her eyes. "What the hell does that mean?"

"You were . . . it was a lot," he murmured, blinking harder like he was trying to stay present. "All of you. Rico . . . Desiree . . . the expectations."

Angela's stomach dropped, but she didn't interrupt. She let the silence press him. When he didn't say anything else, she continued.

"Why did you cheat on me, Jamal?"

His face twisted. "It was too much . . . too much to juggle. All of you . . . he was pressuring me."

"Who? Rico?"

Jamal nodded. "He knew. He always knew I wasn't keeping it real . . . said I needed to come clean, or he would."

Angela's breath caught. "What happened?"

Jamal's lips parted, his words sluggish but clear. "We argued. He said he was going to tell Desiree . . . said he was doing this for us."

Tears pricked Angela's eyes, but she refused to let them fall.

"What did you do?"

Jamal's eyes brimmed with something between guilt and numb detachment. Then he looked right past her and let out a low, bitter laugh. "You mean what I *didn't* do? I didn't save him."

Angela's throat tightened. Her voice dropped, sharp and deadly. "What did you do to him?"

Jamal's head lolled slightly to the side when he murmured, "It was finely crushed, mixed right into the strawberries, bananas and cream. He was drunk . . . so out of it, he didn't even think to ask about the nuts. Probably didn't notice the texture. Heh, didn't even question the taste."

Angela's pulse roared in her ears. She couldn't move.

A twisted smirk pulled at the corner of Jamal's mouth. His eyes locked on hers, glazed but lucid enough to deliver the truth. "I watched him swallow every bite . . . licked my fingers like I enjoyed it too. He never suspected a thing."

Angela's stomach turned, but she stayed rooted, her fists clenched at her sides.

Jamal continued, the words rolling out with cruel clarity. "He thought I was gonna fuck him that night. Even let me strap the ball gag in. Kept him quiet while it all set in. And when he started choking, panicking?" He paused, giving a shallow shrug. "I cleaned up . . . wiped everything down . . . made it look like I was never there."

He closed his eyes for a moment, but they snapped open, a sick sense of pride crept into his expression as he announced, "Told him, 'When they find you, they'll rule your death an accident.'"

A pregnant pause passed between them.

". . . and they did."

Angela's eyes burned. Not with tears, but with the kind of fury that couldn't be undone.

The man lying before her wasn't just a liar or a cheater.

He was a killer. And he had smiled through every second of it.

Angela snapped. In one swift motion, her hand came down, striking his cheek with a stinging blow. Jamal's head snapped violently to the side, causing him to let out an audible gasp.

SLAP!

Chapter 17

"How many times did you look me in the eye and lie, huh?" Angela asked. But didn't give him a chance to respond.

SLAP!

She struck him again, harder this time. The sting vibrated up her arm. Again and again, over and over, Angela's open palm connected with Jamal's face. Her breath came in ragged gasps. Her hand, red and raw, trembled.

"You really were gonna get away with this!" She paused, sucking in a lungful of oxygen, glaring down at him. Her expression remained stone-cold, betraying nothing of the burning sting on her hand. No tears. Not for him. "Recovery? Ha! You're gonna die here, *Jamie*," Angela hissed, venom dripping from every syllable.

Jamal's ducts brimmed with tears, but it garnered no sympathy from Angela. Looking down at Jamal lying defenseless on the bed, a sly, dangerous grin curled her lips. For a moment, she stood there, staring down at him, the tension between them thick and suffocating. A cold certainty washed over her. In this room, she wielded the power as healer and avenger.

"Remember, you brought this on yourself. But don't worry. I'll take care of you, exactly the way you deserve."

18

AWW, BABE DON'T CRY

Christian adjusted the cuff of his tailored blazer. "Emergency numbers are—"

"Taped to the fridge." Angela didn't look up from calibrating the feeding pump.

"I'll give you the store's direct line just in case." He scribbled something down on a sticky note from the desk and handed it to Angela.

She tucked the note into the pocket of her scrub top. "Jamal will be well taken care of. You don't need to worry."

"I'm not. I trust you and your team. This past month would've been totally different if I'd had to do this alone." Christian glanced over to the other side of the room where the flicker of a three-wick candle danced lazily, its scent of sandalwood and lavender wafting through the air. "Oh, one more thing," He turned back toward her. "Make sure you open the window in here during the day. Fresh air does wonders. Just don't forget to close it at night."

"Of course," Angela said with a nod. Her eyes followed the floating curtains, their sheerness curling in the draft.

Christian leaned over the railing to kiss Jamal's forehead softly, whispering something she couldn't quite catch. Then, he stood upright and spoke to her, "Alright, I'll call when I land."

"Safe travels," Angela murmured, her hands folded neatly in front of her.

She moved to stand by the window, listening to his footsteps recede down the hall until the front door clicked shut behind him. Angela watched Christian load his luggage into the car service and stayed there until they drove away.

And then the atmosphere changed.

"Time for your dose."

Angela turned to Jamal, whose eyes were shut, his breathing light and rhythmic. She approached his bedside holding a syringe, which she had filled with a potent cocktail to keep him weak. Tapping it twice with her finger, the faint tick-tick echoed in the silence. Her steady hands showed no signs of hesitation or remorse as she injected the medicine into Jamal's IV port. After administering the drug, Angela stepped back, placing the spent syringe onto the tray.

She peeled off her gloves with a sharp snap. Tossing them aside, she crossed the room, crouching next to the large duffel bag she'd brought earlier. Angela began rummaging through it, but before she could find what she was looking for, her phone rang. She rose to her full height and retrieved the device from her pants pocket. Once taking a glance at the display, she swiped to answer with the sweetest tone.

"Za, hola, bebé. What's up?"

"Not much, just checking in to see how your day is going."

Angela peeked back at Jamal, who was still asleep, and moved away from his bed toward the window. Noticing the three-wick candle dangerously close to the curtains, she slid the stand a few inches away to avoid any risk of fire. Leaning against the large windowpane, she responded, "It's going. The patient is getting some well-deserved rest."

"Angel, I'm really uneasy about this."

"I get it, but this is my job."

His long sigh didn't go unnoticed. The last thing Angela wanted to do was cause strife in their new relationship. Not after Simeon had done his

Chapter 18

due diligence checking into Jamal's background. Simeon initially told her he didn't have to, but after another nudge from her mother, he gave in and did a full background check. What he uncovered changed everything. Simeon learned that a few months ago Jamal and Christian had been arrested for indecent exposure and engaging in a lewd act. Even more disturbing, they'd been questioned in her brother's death. Though the police couldn't pin anything on them, and the medical examiner ruled the cause of death as anaphylactic shock, foul play had been suspected. Still, with no hard evidence, the case was closed.

But Simeon couldn't shake what he found, and neither could Angela. His discovery pushed her to reach out to Mia, who, with her underground connections, secured a vial of truth serum. Angela didn't just want clarity—she *needed* it. And if no one else was going to give her answers, she'd get them herself. Joining Jamal's rehab team wasn't about professionalism—it was strategy. The perfect cover. Working from the inside gave her access, proximity, and control. She wasn't there to heal him. She was there to dismantle the man who had shattered her trust, destroyed her peace, and, now she knew, taken her brother's life. Simeon, cautious but supportive, questioned Angela about being selected to lead Jamal's care team. Not wanting lies between them, she admitted she'd spoken to Dr. Taylor, who hadn't objected. She made it clear her motives weren't noble. They were personal. This wasn't about closure. It was about justice And though wary of the path she was taking, Simeon promised to stand by her, whatever she chose to do.

"What time will you be home?"

"I'm leaving here by six. I should be home within the hour."

"Be careful. And we're going to CTW today."

"But Za—"

"But Za my ass. You've been putting it off for the past couple of weeks. We're going."

Angela pouted but conceded. "Okay, fine. I'll go if you take me for ice cream after."

"You're going anyway. But I can make that happen too. See you soon. And for real, be safe."

"I will. See you in a few."

Angela hung up and stared outside. The seasons had shifted, and the heat of summer had given way to the briskness of fall. The city was now decorated with trees displaying vibrant hues of red, orange, yellow, and brown. A gentle breeze drifted through the open glass walls, carrying with it a slightly sweet, earthy scent. Angela still found it difficult to fathom how her relationship with Jamal had reached this point. She never imagined things would end this way between them. Her ex-boyfriend left her to be with another man. Everyone saw their scandalous affair aired out on a popular gossip show. He'd taken her for granted. Played in her face all the while she was going through the darkest period of her life—a darkness he caused when he murdered her brother. Simeon didn't understand. Jamal could not get away with it. Angela's fists clenched tightly at her sides.

She spun around, crossing the room in purposeful strides, heading for the duffel bag. Unzipping it, her hands moved quickly, rifling through its contents—tubes, gauze, vials, clamps—all carefully packed. The rustle of sheets behind her made her freeze mid-motion. Angela tilted her head slightly, listening. The soft hitch of breath confirmed it. He was waking up.

Angela's fingers tightened around the edge of the bag. Slowly, deliberately, she rose to her feet, turning toward the bed. Jamal's eyes were half-open now, glassy but locked on her. She could feel the heat of his stare, the silent question lingering between them.

"Why good evening, Dr. Edwards. Awake already?"

Jamal's head rolled to the side some. His gaze seemed unfocused, likely due to the stirring of consciousness battling against the haze of the drug. Angela stopped at the foot of the bed, her shadow falling over him like a dark cloud. He tried to speak, to protest, but only a low groan escaped his lips.

"You're not in control anymore, Jamal. That little cocktail I gave you. Let's just say you'll feel so much better . . . or worse. Either way, it's going to keep you nice and compliant."

Jamal's chest rose and fell faster, his pupils dilating.

Chapter 18

Panic.

Helplessness.

She watched it all unfold with a kind of morbid fascination.

"Relax, will you? I'm a professional. Remember?"

She put on a fresh pair of gloves and yanked the bedsheets away. The drone of the humidifier blended with the piercing sound of the alarms. The clear catheter tubing twisted into snake-like loops. Angela leaned over him, her face haloed by the surgical lamp.

Her fingers lightly grazed over the leg swing. It was a device meant to aid in Jamal's rehabilitation. Yet, Angela's imagination entertained darker uses for it. She grasped one of his legs, placing it carefully in the contraption. She did the same with the other one. Both of his limbs hung suspended, immobilized. The position forced his body into submission, exposing him to her twisted whims. With every click of the dial, she experienced a rush of satisfaction, a perverse enjoyment in her newfound dominance over him. Her hands moved to secure it properly to the frame of the bed.

"See? You can't even move. No options. Powerless. Just like my brother was. Does that scare you, Jamal?" Her face was now level with his, her breath ghosted against his ear, making him flinch.

His eyes flickered open fully now, fear swirling in their depths. His lips parted, but nothing came out except a strained exhale.

"It should," Angela warned, straightening. She stepped away from the bed, but not before tugging at the cords of the swing, testing its sturdiness.

With a predatory focus in her eyes, she went back to digging through the bag. Her heart raced with exhilaration. She finally pulled out a long, thick, black dildo, its silicone surface glistening under the lamplight. Angela turned around to face Jamal, a cruel smile playing on her lips.

"Look at what I have for you," she declared, brandishing and twirling it between her fingers like a weapon. "Isn't this exciting? I'm going to show you just how good it can feel."

Jamal's eyes widened, a flash of recognition sparking within the depths of his gaze. Angela relished the moment, that flicker of horror and defiance. He struggled against the restraints, but Angela tightened her grip on his leg, the swing locking him in place. Though he was growing stronger, at this moment his vulnerable body lay exposed. Completely confined, he couldn't do anything to stop her.

"No need to get all shy and nervous with me now. Since you enjoyed your lil' escapades with my brother and Christian so much, I figured I'd show *you* some pleasure. Let's see how you like it with me."

"Nooo," Jamal groaned, pleading with her, but Angela paid him no mind, running the tip of the dildo along his inner thigh.

Without warning, she grabbed his hips, pulling him closer to the edge of the bed. Angela positioned herself between his legs, but hesitated for a moment, wrestling with the last fragments of her humanity.

Images flashed behind her eyes: Tré gasping for oxygen. His last breaths while Jamal stood by and watched, unmoved. Her brother had begged for help. Begged. And Jamal had done nothing. Nothing.

A year and a half of deceit.

The constant deflection and empty promises to leave Desiree. Sneaking around with Christian, whispering false promises into her ear at night, telling her she was his future when he had already replaced her. That truth burned hotter than anything else.

The way he played both sides. Murdering her brother. The manipulation. The gaslighting. All the lies.

Her grip tightened. The last remnants of mercy crumbled inside her. Whatever humanity she had left—she buried it.

With a savage snarl, Angela plunged the dildo deep into his rectum. Jamal's eyes rolled back, and his mouth opened in a silent scream as the intrusion stretched him beyond endurance. Angela reveled in watching his face contort in disbelief, raw and unfiltered. Jamal bucked against her, but Angela's grip was like a vise.

"That's right! Take me fucking you over dry! No lube, you son of bitch! Do you even realize what you've done? What you took from me? You thought you could just walk out of my life, have this wonderful new relationship with Christian, and not pay for the heartache and embarrassment you caused me? I think the fuck not!" she seethed.

Chapter 18

The room filled with the obscene sounds of Angela's rage. The squelch of the toy violating Jamal's most intimate space, the harsh rasp of their combined breathing, the rhythmic creaking of the bed frame while she pounded into him with merciless abandon.

"I trusted you, Jamal! But you made me feel like it was my fault! This. Is. For. Every. Lie!"

He sobbed, his neck tendons straining as he writhed against the restraints. Angela slammed over and over into his ass with a ferocity she hadn't known she possessed. Each thrust into him was a testament to the depth of her anger. She wanted him to feel the full force of her wrath and the sting of his betrayal.

Angela watched as his pupils seemed to engulf his irises. "Oh, but I'm so proud of you. You're doing so good, Jamie. Look at how you're taking all this dick like a pro. Mia said you'd be able to handle the biggest one too. I didn't think so, but she was right."

Jamal's body convulsed, his eyes watery and filled with anguish. But his pleading gaze only fueled Angela's anger, pushing her to inflict more pain. His tortured gasps were music to her ears. She continued, relentless, each rough stroke carving out her revenge on him.

Suddenly, Jamal lost control, and his bowels emptied in a putrid rush. The stench of feces mingled with the antiseptic odor of the room. In disgust, Angela withdrew the artificial phallus, leaving Jamal whimpering. She stood above him, her chest heaving, her eyes blazing with feral intensity. Angela tore off her gloves and discarded them along with the toy into the biohazard bin.

"Code Brown," she muttered, moving over to the sink. She began cleaning herself up. Disinfectant burned her knuckles as she scrubbed her arms and hands furiously. "Don't worry, I'll just chart this as an accidental bowel expulsion."

When she finished, Angela turned to face him and their eyes locked, A wordless acknowledgment passed between them. Jamal's tears tracked toward the pillow. She moved over to the bed and leaned closer, her smile a veneer over the storm brewing within.

"Aww, babe don't cry. I bet you thought that was it, didn't you?

No . . . no . . . no." She rocked her head back and forth, swiping away the moisture from his face. Angela flashed a devious grin and declared, "This isn't over, Jamal. Not by a long shot. I'm going to make you suffer in ways you can't even imagine. And when I'm done, you'll beg me for mercy. But it'll be too late. You'll already be dead."

19

THIS WILL BE HIS DAY OF RECKONING

"You just missed him, Christian. He's taking his nap right now . . . Yes, of course. Sharon will be here, so you can video chat with him then. I'll let her know to expect your call. Oh, and I love the fit by the way. Real cute! . . . You're welcome . . . Alright, no problem. I'll chat with you tomorrow."

Jamal sensed her. A shift in the air, a presence that prickled his skin. He lay in bed, eyes flickering to the door, waiting. Although he'd regained the ability to speak, Angela kept him weak—just enough to suppress resistance, but not enough to raise alarm. The cocktail of muscle relaxers and sedatives she administered dulled his reflexes and drained his strength, reducing his voice to a hoarse rasp most days. He could manage short phrases, but sustained speech, especially anything loud or clear, was nearly impossible. When Christian called, Angela always made sure he was heavily medicated and asleep. And the few times he'd been awake, she stood over him, eyes sharp and daring, her presence alone warning him to stay silent. And Jamal knew better than to try to seek help from Sharon or Izzy. He couldn't predict how deep they were in Angela's pocket or what consequences might follow if he spoke up and no one believed him.

The squeak of Angela's sneakers echoed. She entered, her gaze locked on him instantly, and the room seemed to shrink. He attempted to speak, words forming at the tip of his tongue, but Angela cut him off before he could even draw a breath.

"Ugh! You stink! Inside and out, Jamal. You stink like rot," she spat, her upper lip curling in disgust.

It wasn't his fault he'd been unable to hold his bowels. The memories of three days of continuous sexual assault flooded his mind and replayed in his head like a brutal montage. She had stripped him of everything—control, dignity. She'd left him exposed, numb. He was a husk, hollowed out by her rage. Numbness was a refuge, but even that was slipping away. The room now reeked of feces, antiseptic, and something foul beneath it, the kind of smell that clung to walls and skin—the smell of death.

Angela's fingers curled around the sheet beneath him. He groaned. His body shifted lazily, like dead weight. Her jaw tightened as she yanked it, bunching the fabric in her fists.

"Get up," she hissed, planting her foot beside the bed for leverage, then gave another hard pull. He slid an inch, maybe two.

His mouth was dry, but he finally spoke. "Angela . . . puh-lease."

"Please shut up. Can't even move your mouth right. Just pathetic," she grunted through gritted teeth, digging her heels into the floor. The sheets tangled around him, but Angela kept pulling.

Jamal's fingers jerked slightly, dragging in a feeble attempt to grip the edge of the mattress. His hand scraped against the fabric, barely lifting. It was almost laughable. Almost. And with one final heave, Angela yanked Jamal off the bed with a force that took his breath away. His body hit the hardwood floor with a heavy thud, limbs spreading out awkwardly.

A pained groan rumbled in his throat. "Argh!"

"And stay down." Angela taunted, standing over him. Her chest heaved, strands of hair sticking to her damp forehead.

The exertion of pushing him seemed to invigorate her. Jamal watched her, helpless, while she reveled in his suffering, amplifying his defeat. He lay there, broken. She bent and began dragging him across the room. Her sneakers scuffed against the wood, and the bedsheets bit into his skin.

Chapter 19

Each jarring movement tore at his dignity, as Angela dragged him like a ragdoll toward the bathroom.

"St-st-stop." His voice rattled, barely audible.

She remained silent, except for the ragged breathing from the heavy lifting. His body protested, muscles strained against the shameful burden of being dragged, but he had little strength to fight back. After the truth serum, Angela had kept him sapped on muscle relaxers. The bathroom door loomed ahead, the faint scent of lavender soap mixing unpleasantly with his stench. She kicked the door open, the protector bumper preventing it from smacking against the wall. The tub sat waiting, water glinting under the muted fluorescent light.

"Bath time!"

He choked on his pleas, desperation rising. "D-D-Don't . . . do this."

"D-D-Don't tell me what to do."

Angela grunted, slipping her arms beneath his dead weight. Bit by bit, she hoisted him upright, dragging his limp body toward the edge. With one final heave and a sharp push, she sent him sprawling into the jacuzzi tub. The icy water was a shock to his senses. Jamal gasped when he hit the surface, the chill consuming him almost instantly. His limbs flailed instinctively as he fought to keep his head above water, sputtering and choking on the liquid that enveloped him.

Through his blurred vision, he caught a glimpse of Angela's face, devoid of any sympathy. She stood at the edge of the tub, arms crossed, watching him. Her expression was neutral, but her eyes glittered with something more, a twisted satisfaction at his struggle.

"But I thought you could swim?" she asked tauntingly, the disdain cutting through the air sharper than any knife.

Jamal's limbs grew heavier, and panic took hold. He fought against the water, the cold wrapping around him like chains, dragging him down. Desperately lifting his head above the surface, inhaling sharply, each breath was a precious commodity. Just as his body began to dip again, Angela reached in with one hand and yanked him up by the back of his shirt, just enough to keep his mouth above the waterline, just enough to keep him alive. Minutes ticked by while Angela just stood there, her expression unreadable to his suffering.

The shrill ring of Angela's phone cut through the tension, a needed intrusion into the oppressive silence. She answered, her voice lilting with joy. As he lay there, soaking in the chilling, numbing water, he could only watch, laughter ringing out in stark contrast to his desperation.

"Sí, bebé. You wouldn't believe the day I've had . . . nope, all bueno," she continued, her eyes flicking in Jamal's direction, amusement dancing on her features.

He was forced to be an audience to her happiness. Angela giggled, a sound he hadn't heard in weeks. It was sweet, playful, a cruel reminder of what he'd lost. The conversation was light, her words laced with affection. Jamal's chest tightened, the sound a knife twisting in his gut. How could she find joy when he was drowning? She glanced at him, her eyes cold despite the warmth in her voice.

"We discussed this, Za . . . He admitted it. So now I get closure, mi amor. Could you give me that? . . . No. And he won't take anything else. Not from me. Not from anyone else. This will be his day of reckoning."

When Angela hung up, the joyous mask slipped. Her icy demeanor snapped back into place. She redirected her attention to him in the tub. The muscle relaxer she'd given him earlier still had him in its grip. Jamal coughed and sputtered, bubbles dancing around him. He tried to form words that sank beneath the sound of the water splashing around him.

Angela crouched beside the tub, close enough for him to see the fire burning behind her piercing gaze. "You see, Jamal? Good men exist. And I should be thanking you."

His eyes darted to her, wide with confusion. *Get me out of this fucking water!* However, those words never left his mouth. Water dripped from his chin as he drew a ragged breath.

She continued, her lips curling into something that wasn't quite a smile. Her tone was mocking. "Because of you, I have Simeon now. He's somebody that recognized the treasure after you threw me away. He's a man who actually sees me. Who loves and affirms me. He makes me happy. So very happy. He's big too. In everything. Even bigger than that

Chapter 19

dildo you enjoy so much. Simeon's definitely a better man than you'll ever be."

Okay good! Jamal thought inwardly. He wanted her to be happy, to find someone who could give her everything he couldn't. To forget him. Now they both could move on. As if sensing his thoughts, Angela's expression shifted, her eyes narrowing with defiance.

"You think I'd let you have that? Happiness? Not a chance. Liars, cheaters, and murderers don't deserve happiness, Jamie," she seethed, the bitterness rolling off her tongue in waves.

"I-I, I just want you to be okay." Jamal's head drooped a little, his mouth opening as if to say something else, but all that came out was a broken rasp.

Angela tilted her head, mock pity flashing across her face. She leaned forward, her curls grazing his cheek as she studied him. "No! You can't have that either. You don't get to decide what's fair. You get nothing. Not after everything you've done to me."

In that instant, Jamal recognized the truth. It was not merely about him wishing for her to move on. It was about the life he'd stolen from her, the choices that had cast her into a dark space. Angela's hand gripped the rim of the tub as she rose to her feet, towering over him. Water rippled violently as he shifted weakly, trying to inch away from her glare. Angela stepped closer, her sneakers squeaking on the wet tile.

"You cheated on your wife, lied to her every time you walked through the door," she hissed icily. "And then you did the same to me, playing both sides while I sat there, believing you were different. You were living on the DL, playing in my face, while I tried to love you! You took the pieces of my heart and shattered them like they meant nothing."

With each accusation, Jamal's insides twisted. Each claim she made was true. He wanted to crawl into a corner, to escape the truth of what he'd done, but instead, he was here, forced to confront the wreckage he left behind. His breath came faster, his chest rising and falling as his eyes darted between her and the door. Angela stepped closer, blocking his view, forcing him to face her.

"But worse than what you did to me. You took Tré from us. *Do you even understand* what you stole from us? Tré wasn't just my brother. He was my best friend. He meant everything to me . . . to my mom . . . to my baby brother. He was our protector, our peace, our backbone when things got hard. You didn't just end his life, Jamal. You ripped a hole in our family that'll never heal." She paused, jaw clenched. Tears welled in her eyes, but they didn't fall. Her voice dropped to a raw whisper. "There were nights I thought about ending it. Sitting in the tub with a razor, and just . . . slipping under. Quietly. Joining him. 'Cause the grief was *that* deep. But I couldn't do it. I had to live for Mamá. For Junior. And for the people who still needed me here. While you . . . you just kept walking around like none of it mattered. Like we were all disposable. You destroyed us, Jamal. And now, you finally get to understand what that feels like."

Jamal made a feeble attempt to shake his head, his lips quivering as if forming some silent denial. His mind raced through the memories. All the moments he'd stolen from her. Regret coiled tightly in his chest. "I-I-I never meant to hurt you," he finally managed, his voice shaking.

Angela laughed again, harsher this time. "But you did hurt me. You hurt us. But not anymore. I see you for who you truly are—a fraud. A coward. A parasite feeding off everyone around you while you hide behind your perfect little act. Dr. Edwards, prominent surgeon of our community." She leaned down, her face inches from his. "Do you know what the irony of all this is? You actually believed you deserved happiness. You don't. Not after what you've taken from me. From all of us."

Jamal swallowed hard. The lump in his throat didn't move. His eyes glistened, his breaths shallow and uneven. Angela straightened, her expression hardening once more. Her tone was icy, detached as she continued.

"Fairness doesn't exist, does it? Not when men like you keep taking and taking without consequence. But tonight? Tonight, I'm taking something back."

The room stilled, save for the faint ripple of water as Jamal's body trembled beneath its surface. He needed her to understand—to feel just a sliver of compassion, a glimmer of the love that had once defined them.

Chapter 19

He locked eyes with her, hoping to find a spark of their past that might ignite some form of mercy within her.

"An-An-Angela . . ." His voice cracked like dry earth splitting under pressure. "P-P-Please. Just . . . just listen. Let's just . . . just talk, I can make it right."

"No!" she yelled back, her voice erupting like a crack of thunder. "There's nothing to talk about!"

Water sloshed against the tub's edges as Jamal struggled again, his muscles twitching helplessly against the lingering effects of the drug she'd slipped him. Jamal's body shook as he desperately sought a way out. What could he possibly say to change her mind? His thoughts spun, exploring the possibilities. Yet, every path led him back to his mistakes, leaving him feeling powerless against her unwavering anger. Still, he had to try.

"I-I loved you, Angela. I loved you!" He spoke louder. This time his words came out raw with fear. His gaze locked onto hers, wide and pleading. "I did. But, but I made mistakes, okay. I can fix thisss . . . g-g-give me a chance!"

She stepped closer, their faces mere inches apart, and he could see the fury raging behind her calm facade. Her lips curled into a sneer. "Give you a chance? To fix what? Like you 'fixed' your marriage? Like you fixed Tré? Like you 'fixed' us?" Her fingers dug into the edge of the porcelain tub, knuckles whitening. She took a step back, her eyes blazing with unshed tears, forcing Jamal to confront the full extent of his betrayals. "Finding out you were gay was one thing. But learning that you were cheating with Christian on *Baller Bizness*? That was a different level of embarrassment. How about fuck you!"

Jamal winced at the mention of his scandalous affair on the reality show. He wanted to argue, to justify himself against her storm of anger. But his guilt settled around him. Jamal knew the depth of his betrayals and the chaos he had caused—not just to Angela, but to the delicate fabric of their lives, already woven together by lies.

Angela paced the small room, frustration pouring out like water from a breached dam. "You think I didn't feel it? The distance? The way you looked at me like I was just some stand-in until something, or *someone* better came along? And all the while, you were sneaking around with Christian, lying to *both* of us. Playing house with me while building a whole other life with him." Her voice cracked, and the sight of her raw pain felt like a physical blow to him. "Maybe Tré didn't know what you were capable of, but now I do."

Her eyes narrowed, brimming with rage. "You took his life, Jamal. *You watched my brother die,* and then came back to me with blood on your hands and lies on your lips. You looked me in my face, held me when I cried, and the whole time you knew he was gone because of *you*. How do you even live with that? You destroyed my sense of safety. You turned my heart into a battlefield, and I let you. I *let* you in because I believed you were different."

Angela's voice dropped to a whisper, loaded with heartbreak and venom. "But you were worse . . . so much worse."

Her words hit him like a ton of bricks. The weight of her grief pierced straight through his defenses, cracking open the truth he'd buried beneath excuses. In that moment, it clicked—he hadn't just betrayed a lover. He'd taken the life of someone who once called him friend. Rico wasn't supposed to die, not like that. But he had. And the damage didn't stop there. Jamal recognized he'd left a trail of broken trust, a family in shambles, and a woman who now looked at him like a stranger. He wanted her to know that he hadn't meant for it to go this far.

"I-I-I—"

"I-I-I, save it," she snapped, turning away from him.

Jamal needed to keep her from doing something she would regret. He was scared. Was she going to kill him? It appeared this was the path Angela was taking, but he had to change her mind some way, somehow.

"Angela?"

She spun around to face him, fire blazing in her eyes. "Do you know how humiliating all of this was? To find out like *that*? To know you were smiling, yet lying to my face?"

"An—"

"Shut the fuck up!" Her voice ricocheted off the walls, silencing him once more. She stepped closer, bending down until her face was in front

Chapter 19

of his. Her voice was cold steel when she whispered, "I'm going to make sure you never hurt anyone else ever again."

It took over an hour for her to finish bathing him and getting him out of the bathroom. Angela maneuvered Jamal back into bed, her strength a constant surprise. Her touch was mechanical, efficient, as if handling an object rather than a person. Jamal lay there, helpless, feeling the cold inevitability of her plan closing in. He watched her, unable to look away.

The tense silence stretched between them while Angela moved around the room with unnerving calm. She collected the soiled bedsheets, a stark reminder of his humiliating loss of bowel control, and tossed them into the laundry basket with a nonchalant flick. She prepared the area for the next nurse's shift. Every scrub, every adjustment of the room's items seemed methodically planned, intensifying Jamal's sense of unease.

Eventually, Angela approached his bedside, a syringe glinting in her grasp. Jamal's heart pounded, terror mixing with disbelief. He couldn't look away. Each step she took was like a countdown to his demise.

"Angela, I'm sorry, okay! I'm sorry! Don't. Please, you don't have to do this," Jamal pleaded with her, desperation in every word.

Angela leaned in. Her free hand cupped his jaw roughly, forcing his face in her direction. "Oh, but I do. And you're not sorry, Jamal. You're just scared."

I am. I don't want to die. His lips quivered, but no more words came. His gaze darted about wildly, searching her face for something—mercy, forgiveness, anything. It wasn't there. Angela's quest for vengeance consumed her, her resolve unshakeable. And she had no one to stop her.

"This is Pavulon. The rate of metabolism is key. It can only be detected if the pathologist acts quickly. But by the time they do your autopsy, it'll all be gone. When they find you, they'll rule your death an accident."

Jamal's eyes bulged hearing the exact words he'd said to her brother. And with a swift flick of her thumb, she uncapped the vial. The faint chemical aroma hit his nose. Angela slipped the needle point into the IV port, quickly and precisely, her technique flawless.

"Angela, please," he begged, his voice breaking.

Unmoved, Angela pressed the plunger down, sending the lethal dose into his veins. Her tone was almost soothing. "Don't fight it, Jamal. Let it happen."

But he didn't want to. Not like this. Jamal fought with every ounce of strength, but the world began slipping through his fingers. The moments of clarity faded, replaced by the suffocating blackness closing in on him.

As his consciousness ebbed, he became aware of the drool pooling at the corners of his mouth, a sign of his waning battle. The whispers of regret echoed in his ears, yet the encroaching darkness was strangely inviting, an escape from the chaos of his existence.

In the abyss that enveloped him, Jamal floated amid a fog of recollections—familiar faces and events flickered like an old movie. Time seemed irrelevant, eluding his grasp as the consequences of his actions hit him hard. Brief moments of laughter and affection danced in and out of his mind, tormenting him with their transience.

Desiree's warm smile, radiant and full of life, slipped through his fingers like sand. The memory of meeting Angela for the first time, her infectious laugh spreading joy, seemed to vanish like a breeze. Christian's doe-like eyes swam into view, mirroring both the intensity of their shared passion and the painful truth of their relationship. His long-held secret tainted all his cherished memories.

Finally, Rico's swollen face appeared, a haunting reminder of his greatest betrayal. He had taken his friend's life, all because he couldn't admit the truth about himself. He was gay. If only he had been honest, maybe none of this would be happening.

"I'm so sorry," he whispered into the emptiness.

Every secret he had told was laid bare in those last moments. The echo of Angela's accusations resonated, amplifying the feelings of betrayal that coursed through him.

You don't deserve happiness.

Her words resounded. A desire for redemption that would never come. He wished to build a life with Christian, to embrace the beauty of their connection. Yet, now he lay there, slipping away, taken from a world

Chapter 19

he could never fully embrace. Jamal's body relaxed, his head tilting to the side as his eyes drifted closed.

A minute later Angela leaned in, waiting, watching.

No shudder. No last attempt at resistance. Just quiet surrender.

She placed two fingers against his throat, pressing into the skin.

No pulse.

No more pleading. No more lies. Only the sound of her own heartbeat, pounding loudly in her ears. The world seemed to narrow in on the still figure before her.

Angela snatched off the gloves and disposed of them. Her hands flexed at her sides, her nails biting into her palms. She thought she might cry. But no tears came. Instead, Angela released a long, shuddering breath that seemed to carry everything with it. The grief. The betrayal. She let it go, piece by piece until nothing remained. Then she stepped back and unclenched her palms. The finality of it thrummed through her, each second ticking forward without him. Without Jamal.

Now what? Her gaze shifted to the window. The city stretched beyond it, unaware of the justice served in this room. She watched the sheer curtains billow, their delicate folds resembling ghostly hands reaching inward, before her eyes landed on the three-wick candle. Its flames danced near the fabric, casting a flickering glow that mingled with the cool air and the scent of burnt wax.

Without a backward glance, Angela walked out of the room, ready to embrace life untainted by Jamal.

20

A NEW BEGINNING

Angela sat with Simeon and Bianca at the dining table, the room alive with the scent of saffron and seafood. A steaming dish of paella sat in the center. It was Bianca's pride and joy, its rich colors vibrant against the white tablecloth. Angela smiled, watching her mother fuss over the serving, ladling generous portions onto their plates.

Bianca wiped her hands on her apron. "Comer, comer! I didn't make all this for y'all to just look at."

Angela took a bite, savoring the familiar flavors. "Once again, you outdid yourself, Mamá."

They settled into a comfortable rhythm, the conversation drifting to Thanksgiving plans. Bianca was insistent on hosting, her enthusiasm infectious. Angela felt a warmth spread through her, grateful for the family she had, both by blood and by choice.

She observed Simeon and Bianca banter, her heart light. For now, everything felt perfect, the havoc of the past few months a distant memory. She allowed herself to bask in the moment, knowing how quickly it could all change.

Simeon tilted his chair back, balancing on two legs like he didn't have a care in the world. "You better get your skills up like Mamá if you wanna host Thanksgiving."

Angela shot him a look. "You've never had a problem eating anything of mine," she retorted, her tone playful but pointed.

Simeon chuckled, letting the chair fall forward with a thud. He leaned in as if sharing a secret. "I guess I'mma feen, cause now I can't get enough."

Bianca raised an eyebrow, her gaze bouncing between them. "You two are worse than my telenovelas. But I love to see it!"

The room filled with their laughter, a symphony of shared history and inside jokes. Angela felt the tension of the past weeks melt away, replaced by a sense of belonging. Simeon's presence was steady and familiar, a comfort she appreciated more than he could possibly know.

Angela took another bite of paella, savoring the flavors and the moment. She knew Bianca saw more than she let on, her maternal instincts always keen. But for now, Angela let herself enjoy the teasing, the warmth, and the feeling that she was exactly where she needed to be.

A sudden blast of somber music from the television mounted in the corner of the dining room shattered the light mood around the table. Angela jerked her head toward the screen just in time to see the red "Breaking News" graphic flash like a warning light. A knot tightened in her stomach before she even heard the reporter's first words.

"Welcome back to Atlanta News Now, I'm Rick Spanoli here with some breaking news. One person is dead, and seven others are injured after massive flames ripped through condominiums in an overnight fire in Fulton County. And we've just learned who the victim is. Atlanta News Now Kai'Lani Bryant has been on that scene all day today for us. Kai'Lani, what more can you tell us?"

"Good afternoon, Rick. This is such a tragic story. Behind me, you can see the area investigators have taped off. The first unit was completely gutted by the fire, and part of the structure has collapsed.

Neighbors say flames ripped through the homes on Chestnut Drive just after 8:30 p.m. Fulton County firefighters confirmed a family of three

Chapter 20

living in the second unit escaped safely. Tragically, the man living in the first unit was not as fortunate.

When crews arrived, they were informed someone was still inside. According to officials, a home health nurse, who had been caring for the victim, tried to reach him during the fire but was unable to get him out in time. She was treated for smoke inhalation at the scene and later released. Firefighters say the man was found unresponsive in a bedroom. Everyone else that got out on their own were taken to the hospital for minor injuries. Two of them were burned, and the other inhaled smoke. The fire also injured four firefighters, two of whom were treated for their injuries at a nearby hospital. And back out here live, the cause of the fire is still under investigation.

Rick, we've just received confirmation from the Fulton County Medical Examiner's Office, the victim has been identified as Dr. Jamal Devon Edwards, the third, a well-known, prominent surgeon at Northside Regional Hospital. You may recall, Dr. Edwards was among those injured in the shooting at the hospital just last month and had been recovering at home.

A heartbreaking end to this already tragic story.

Reporting live from northeast side Atlanta, Fulton County, I'm Kai'Lani Bryant for Atlanta News Now.*"*

Bianca's fork clattered onto her plate, her eyes wide. "¡Dios mío!"

The room fell eerily silent. Angela's heart pounded wildly, her thoughts a jumbled mess. Just hours earlier, her supervisor had called—waking her from a restless sleep with the urgent news that there'd been a fire overnight at Christian's condo. Now, hearing it confirmed on the broadcast made it real. She glanced at Simeon, their gazes colliding for a second. His expression remained neutral, but the tension in his posture was unmistakable. He knew. Angela reminded herself to stay composed, presenting a calm facade, concealing the chaos within.

Bianca murmured a prayer under her breath, her hands clasped tightly together. Her concern for Angela was evident. "Mija," she said softly, stretching her hand across the table with a soothing touch.

"I'm okay, Mamá," she assured, though inside, her reflections of the day before spun wild. The potential consequences were immense, exceeding what she had imagined. She should've closed that window.

Angela's phone rang, the sound slicing through the thick silence like a knife. She glanced at the screen, her coworkers' names flashing in tandem. Sharon and Izzy. She'd been waiting—anxiously checking her phone since her supervisor called earlier that morning. There had been no word from her colleagues. Until now.

"Hey, I need to take this," she rose from the table and made her way toward the living room. She took a breath, steadying herself before answering.

"Angela! I can't believe this is real." Sharon's voice cracked and came out in a frantic jumble of words. "Dr. Edwards, he, umm. Oh, my goodness, Angela he's dead! I really tried to get him out of there. But he was too heavy. And-and I couldn't get anybody to help me. Next thing I knew, their house was up in flames. I feel so bad."

Angela maintained a composed, yet sympathetic demeanor. "Oh, Sharon, try not to. From what I just watched it seems like there wasn't anything you could've done. I'm sorry you had to go through that, but I'm glad you're okay. This is such a tragedy," she replied, allowing a hint of disbelief to color her tone.

Izzy chimed in. "It really is. We were just talking to him yesterday. This really sucks. He was starting to show improvement too."

Angela took a moment to consider her response. "We really need to do whatever we can to support Christian. He loved Jamal so much. This is gonna be a great loss for him."

The line was silent for a couple of seconds, but Angela could almost hear their nods of agreement, trusting in her judgment.

"You're right," Sharon said finally, her tone resigned. "We'll rally around Christian. He'll need us."

"You can count on us," Izzy added. "Are you going to call him?"

Angela smiled, a small, secretive curve of her lips. "Yes, of course. I'll reach out to him," she promised, her deception flowing effortlessly.

After ending the call, Angela was left with a feeling of power. She

Chapter 20

knew she was the reason for Jamal's demise. The fire was an unexpected bonus. Guilt coiled in her chest, but it was tempered by victory. She tucked the phone back into her pocket, securing her secret. Safe.

Angela returned to the table. She sat down, her expression neutral, while her thoughts were far from settled.

Simeon broke the silence, his tone light. "Maybe this is a sign," he said, a knowing edge to his voice. "A new beginning. No more about the past."

Angela met his gaze, a flicker of understanding passing between them. His words were to reassure her, to let her know he was with her, no matter what.

She nodded, forcing a smile. "Vamos a comer. Mamá's paella is getting cold."

They finished their meal in a semblance of normalcy, the clinking of forks and quiet conversation masking the tension that simmered beneath the surface. Angela played her part well, her laughter light, her words carefully chosen. But inside, her thoughts were a whirlwind, a storm of guilt and relief.

They finished tidying up, her mother's house returning to its usual order. As Simeon and Angela prepared to leave, Angela caught Simeon's eye. A last look passed between them, the understanding clear and unspoken. The night had been a test, and she had passed. Her path was clear, her secret intact. For now.

EPILOGUE

Six months later...

"Someone's gonna come in here and catch us, Za."

"No, they're not. I told Roc to open up later."

"What? But how?"

"As part owner, I think I have some pull."

"So arrogant."

"So horny. You think I'mma wait until after our session to get in this sweet pussy? Nah, I need her wrapped around my dick now."

"Well, I wanna wrap my lips around him first," Angela flirted, her sights lowering to the tent growing in the front of his sweatpants.

She maintained eye contact with Simeon, dropping to her knees. Her hands ghosted over the flat plane of his stomach before reaching lower to tug at his pants. In a single, swift move, she stripped him of his joggers and underwear, revealing his bulging erection to open air. She took it in her hand, marveling at its length and girth. So big. It twitched in response to her touch. Her mouth watered at the thought of tasting him. She teased the rim, eliciting a groan from deep within his throat. Her tongue darted out to trace the vein on the underside of his shaft while her hand wrapped around the base. Angela used her serpent-like muscle to swirl around the blooming tip of his pulsing member, while her free hand slipped down to fondle his balls.

Gazing up at him with hooded eyes, Angela licked her lips before engulfing him in one smooth motion. Her lips tightened around him, sucking hard. Simeon let out a low grunt as she bobbed her head up and down. His hands found their way to her hair, drawing her closer. She ran hers up his muscled thighs, the taut skin straining beneath her fingertips. Her cheeks hollowed while she worked his shaft, suctioning hard enough to evoke a guttural moan from Simeon.

"Fuuuck, angel! That pretty lil' mouth is so talented."

She pulled off his dick with a wet pop and peered up at him with eyes glazed over with lust. "¿Te gusta eso?"

"Me encanta. Keep going." Simeon struggled to pant out.

With renewed vigor, Angela went back to work on him. Closing her eyes, she focused on the sensation of his flesh sliding to the back of her tonsils. Each time she took him deeper, she sensed his hot cum pooling at the tip of her tongue. It was driving her wild. Simeon's fingers dug into her shoulders, bucking his hips forward roughly.

"You're so fucking good at this. I can't wait to feel you coming on my dick."

Angela smiled around the thick mushroom tip before pulling off. "I wanna feel you inside me . . . now."

With urgency, Simeon helped her from the floor. He stripped himself of his shirt and Angela's clothing within seconds. Angela squealed when Simeon roughly threw her against the wall covered in climbing holds. The impact sent a thrill through her core, a muffled cry escaping her lips at the unexpected pleasure. He grasped at her hips and hoisted her up, aligning their bodies perfectly. The warmth of his skin on hers made Angela shiver with delight, and she opened her legs wider to allow him access. His hips snapped forward, and the head of his dick breached her entrance, making her gasp and squirm in anticipation. Simeon seemed to hesitate for just a moment before slowly pushing inside, and then filling her completely.

He growled against her neck. "That's it. You can handle it. Take every fucking inch."

"¡Oh dios, sí!" Angela cried, throwing her head back in abandon.

While Simeon moved within her, their mouths met in a fiery kiss that sent sparks flying between them. Their tongues danced together, teasing and exploring every nook and cranny of each other's hot caverns. Angela wrapped her legs tightly around his hips, arching her back to meet his every stroke, lost in the ecstasy of their union. The friction between them was exquisite, sending waves of pleasure rippling through their bodies like lightning striking over and over again.

The smell of sweat and sex filled the air as they moved together faster

Epilogue

and faster, moans echoing off the walls around them. The obscene sounds of their copulation and flesh slapping came together in a primal rhythm that was almost hypnotizing. Angela moaned, the sound ragged and desperate.

"More. I need more, Za. Fuck me harder."

"Keep eggin' me on, angel and you gon' need crutches when I'm done fucking you," Simeon groaned against her lips.

His hips pumped harder, pushing deeper into her wet heat with each thrust. Angela's legs shook. The familiar heat began building inside her, the sensation only intensified by the way Simeon was pounding into her. The friction between them was exquisite, each movement becoming more urgent. Simeon let out another low grunt, his body moving faster with each stroke. His hands left her hips, tracing up her sides before reaching up to her breasts. He pinched her nipples hard, making her squeal from the pain and pleasure.

With a sudden, powerful thrust, he plunged deep inside Angela, hitting her G-spot with force. She cried out, her body convulsing in pleasure as waves of intense warmth washed over her. Her muscles clenched tight around him, holding him deep inside as they both climaxed. Simeon let loose a primal roar that shook the very foundations of the room while he emptied himself into Angela's womb.

As they collapsed onto their pile of clothes on the landing mat, Simeon let out a throaty laugh. "Damn, girl," he said between gasps for air. "You make me lose control every time."

As she caught her breath, Angela grinned mischievously. "Well, what can I say? I'm glad I have that effect on you." She ran her fingers through his hairy chin, feeling satisfied.

Simeon smirked, his eyes dancing with desire as he pulled her closer. "You're a little minx, aren't you? Always pushing my limits."

"I can't help it if you can't resist me." She nuzzled into his neck, breathing in his scent.

He leaned in to kiss her, his lips trailing down her neck. Shivers went down her spine as Simeon whispered, "And who said I wanted to resist?"

They sat there in comfortable silence for a while, basking in the afterglow of their passion. Simeon broke the quiet as he traced circles on her back with his fingers. "You know, angel, I never knew I could feel this way about someone until you."

It had been six months since their lives changed forever. Jamal had died. There had been a fire. As discussed with her team, Angela contacted Christian to deliver the devastating news. He had some questions, but after she explained Sharon's futile attempt to rescue Jamal, Christian thanked her for trying to save the love of his life. Approximately two months later, the medical examiner determined Jamal's death resulted from natural causes. He most likely succumbed to an infection stemming from his injuries. Identifying the cause was challenging, as he had been burned beyond recognition. Since the fire occurred after his death, there was no evidence of smoke inhalation. Ultimately, as Angela had predicted, the drug she'd given Jamal was no longer traceable. She'd killed him and gotten away with it.

Angela turned to look at him. "You always know just what to say."

Instead of responding, Simeon reached into his joggers and produced a small, black velvet box, opening it to reveal a sparkling four-carat diamond ring.

Angela's eyes widened, tears glistening at the corners. "Simeon . . ."

"I mean it, Angela. I promise to cherish you, to support you, and to stand by your side through all the highs and lows that life may bring. Together, we can conquer anything. You've brought so much light into my life. I can't imagine it without you by my side. Will you do me the honor of being my wife? Will you marry me?"

Angela's heart swelled with emotion as she whispered, "I love you, Simeon. More than any words can express. Yes! Yes, I will marry you!"

Simeon gathered her into a tight embrace, murmuring into her hair. "And I love you more than anything in this world, my angel. You are my everything."

And in that moment, Angela knew their love was a force to be reckoned with, strong enough to weather any storm that came their way. With the diamond ring sparkling on her finger, Angela recognized how far she

Epilogue

had come—from the ashes of a shattered past with Jamal to this bright, life-affirming promise. Every challenge and every tear had brought her to this moment, to a future brimming with hope and a love that heals and transforms.

THE END

THANK YOU

Thank you so much for reading! I ask whether you enjoyed this story or not, to please consider leaving a review wherever you purchased this book and/or mark it as read on Goodreads. I also hate errors, but they do happen. If you catch any, please send them to the publisher directly at info@flamesentertain.com with **ERRORS** as the subject.

AFTERWORD

Whew! So, it is done. We've finally gotten Jamal's sorry ass up out the MoVerse. Listen, there were a few times where I wanted to pull a Sheila Carter on y'all. Only my Y&R fans know what I'm talking about. I done told y'all, my mama raised me on them soaps. That's why I live for the drama and chaos around relationships. I could've brought Rico/Tré back, but I wasn't able to come up with a believable return. Sure, he could've road off into the sunset with Christian. But what about Angela and all the grief that she went through? She almost overdosed and ended up in a psych ward when he died. Then there was coming up a believable explanation of how Rico/Tré pulled off this elaborate act of faking his own death. Nah...this was absolutely poetic. I had to give Angela *this* justice. Wouldn't you agree?

And, if you didn't peep the dedication, let me tell you here. Crystal Luckey aka Krysta Luxe, my fave book reviewer and author buddy, thank you!! I love you fren! It's because of you that we even had a budding love story between Angela and Simeon. Y'all this woman almost cussed me out about the original ending I wrote for Angela. I had Angela unaliving Jamal and getting away with it by reasons of insanity, only to be in another psych ward talking to her brother Tré, which would've been a figment of her imagination. Yeah, I know, after everything Jamal did to Angela, she deserved a big boy. Ahem, a big dog as her mother Bianca said. And she got that!

So, can we talk about Simeon? He was an absolute joy to pen. I needed visual inspiration and my readers in Mo's Corner chose him. Shout out to Shannon, Andrea, and Vee McLove—thank you for helping me name him Simeon Zaire Ingram. I wanted him to be everything that he was and more for his earth angel. This man was ever present, attentive and Angela's rock of Gibraltar. His childhood crush became his fianceé, now soon to be forever.

I hope y'all enjoyed this twisted ride through love, lies, and lethal consequences. Jamal broke hearts, took a life, and thought he could

Afterword

outrun the wreckage he left behind. He played God with a scalpel and secrets—but Angela? She played judge, jury, and executioner.

To my editor, Krystal, as always, I appreciate your patience on this journey through my authorship. We've finally gotten through all the major players of the Enough series!! As much as you were down for your boy Jamal, I know I made you loathe him with this. At least you knew it was coming. I'm just happy to know you loved every minute of it. Thank you for the guidance, wisdom and mentoring that you provide on every single project, especially this one. I cannot thank you enough for the care that you take on ensuring my stories convey everything what I want, and that's to have an immersive experience each time they open my books. Once again, I'm so grateful to have you in my corner and on my team.

To my betas and proofreader, P. Bancy I cannot thank y'all enough for your feedback in ensuring the readers received a thoroughly read story free of boring parts, useless scenes, and plot holes. Because of you and with your help, this story is presented in a professional way for readers to enjoy error-free!

Lisa, thank you so much for having my back and making sure those missed editorial items didn't fall through the cracks. I truly appreciate your constant support—for me and my stories. You always show up, and it doesn't go unnoticed.

To the love of my life, Gregory aka Mr. Flames, thank you for being *my* rock of Gibraltar while I pen these stories. I can count on you to sit out on the deck with me for hours, listening to me ramble on about people who live in my head. And never once have you given me the side eye. If anything, you've given our readers some witty anecdotes and bomb ass love scenes. Get ready, 'cause we're about to do it all over again!

Lastly, to my readers who show up for me every single time, THANK YOU SO MUCH! There are never enough words to express how much it means to me you're a part of my world. Just know that I appreciate each and every one of you. My Flames, keep burning bright. I see you!

Stay tuned, there's so much more to come in the MoVerse!!!

ALSO BY MO FLAMES

SERIES

Enough

One Ain't Enough

One Still Ain't Enough

One Is Enough

Infinity

Make You Mine

Love in Minor

Love in A Minor

～

STANDALONES

Reckless Desire

Christmas with the Carters

Falling for Jordyn

Love on the Sidelines

～

NON-FICTION

Girl, He Don't Want Your Ass,
The 10 Signs He's Not Interested

CONNECT WITH MO

Let's stay connected on social media.

Patreon – https://www.patreon.com/c/moflames

Mo's Corner – https://bit.ly/MoFlamesCorner

Facebook – https://www.facebook.com/mo.flames

Instagram – https://www.instagram.com/moflames_author

TikTok – https://www.tiktok.com/@moflames_author

Threads – https://www.threads.net/@moflames_author

ABOUT THE AUTHOR

Mo Flames is an avid reader, writer, wine lover and a super fan of The Office. She pens contemporary romance stories with complex characters, controversial topics, and unpredictable plot twists. Mo's experiences and creativity fuel her written words. She's never been bashful about racy relationship topics. She's unashamed and unapologetically real. It echoes with her tagline, 'leaving that fire between the sheets . . . literally.'

When she's not writing, she enjoys playing the Sims, reading romance and suspense, binge watching The Office, Snapped, Criminal Minds or any crime television shows. She resides in Atlanta, GA with her husband and daughter.

Make sure you connect with Mo!

https://linktr.ee/moflames